Paul Doherty is one of the most prolific, and lauded, authors of historical mysteries in the world today. His expertise in all areas of history is illustrated in the many series that he writes about, from the Mathilde of Westminster series, set at the court of Edward II, to the Amerotke series, set in Ancient Egypt. Amongst his most memorable creations are Hugh Corbett, Brother Athelstan and Roger Shallot. Paul Doherty's newest series is set around the mysterious order of the Templars.

Paul Doherty was born in Middlesbrough. He studied history at Liverpool and Oxford Universities and obtained a doctorate at Oxford for his thesis on Edward II and Queen Isabella now headmaster of a school in north-east London and l his wife and family near Epping Forest.

Praise for Paul Doherty:

'Teems with colour, energy and spills' *Time Out*

'Paul Doherty has a lively sense of history . . . lyrical descriptions' *New Statesman*

'Extensive and penetrating research coupled with a strong plot and bold characterisation. Loads of adventure and a dazzling evocation of the past' *Herald Sun*, Melbourne

'An opulent banquet to satisfy the most murderous appetite'
Northern Echo

'As well as penning an exciting plot with vivid characters, Doherty excels at bringing the medieval period to life, with his detailed descriptions giving the reader a strong sense of place and time'
South Wales Argus

By Paul Doherty and available from Headline

The Rose Demon
The Soul Slayer
The Haunting
Domina
The Plague Lord
The Templar

Mathilde of Westminster mysteries
The Cup of Ghosts
The Poison Maiden

Ancient Roman mysteries
Murder Imperial
The Song of the Gladiator
The Queen of the Night
Murder's Immortal Mask

Ancient Egyptian mysteries
The Mask of Ra
The Horus Killings
The Anubis Slayings
The Slayers of Seth
The Assassins of Isis
The Poisoner of Ptah
The Spies of Sobeck

Hugh Corbett medieval mysteries
Satan in St Mary's
Crown in Darkness
Spy in Chancery
The Angel of Death
The Prince of Darkness
Murder Wears a Cowl
The Assassin in the Greenwood
The Song of a Dark Angel
Satan's Fire
The Devil's Hunt
The Demon Archer
The Treason of the Ghosts
Corpse Candle
The Magician's Death
The Waxman Murders
Nightshade

The Sorrowful Mysteries of Brother Athelstan
The Nightingale Gallery
The House of the Red Slayer
Murder Most Holy
The Anger of God
By Murder's Bright Light
The House of Crows
The Assassin's Riddle
The Devil's Domain
The Field of Blood
The House of Shadows

Egyptian Pharaoh trilogy
An Evil Spirit Out of the West
The Season of the Hyaena
The Year of the Cobra

The Canterbury Tales of murder and mystery
An Ancient Evil
A Tapestry of Murders
A Tournament of Murders
Ghostly Murders
The Hangman's Hymn
A Haunt of Murder

PAUL
DOHERTY

NIGHTSHADE

headline

First published in Great Britain in 2008 by
HEADLINE PUBLISHING GROUP

First published in paperback in Great Britain in 2008 by
HEADLINE PUBLISHING GROUP

2

Cataloguing in Publication Data is available from the British Library

ISBN 978 0 7553 3841 2 (B-format)
ISBN 978 0 7553 4679 0 (A-format)

Typeset in Perpetua by Palimpsest Book Production Limited,
Grangemouth, Stirlingshire

Printed in the UK by
CPI Mackays, Chatham ME5 8TD

Headline's policy is to use papers that are natural, renewable and recyclable products and made from wood grown in sustainable forests. The logging and manufacturing processes are expected to conform to the environmental regulations of the country of origin.

HEADLINE PUBLISHING GROUP
An Hachette Livre UK Company
338 Euston Road
London NW1 3BH

www.headline.co.uk
www.hachettelivre.co.uk

To Robert Potter of Derby, an avid reader and keen medieval sleuth

Prologue

Certain malefactors and disturbers of our peace have, by force of arms, broken into our treasury within the Abbey at Westminster.

Letter of Edward I, 6 June 1303

'The well-fed body and delicate complexion are a tunic for the worms and hell fire!' Brother Gratian, a Dominican of the Order of Preachers, shook one bony hand free from the sleeve of his black and white gown. A finger, thin and pointed as a bodkin, jabbed up at the lowering grey skies as if the threatening snow clouds would break to reveal Christ, seated in glory and surrounded by angels wielding swords of fire, coming to judge the people of Mistleham in the King's shire of Essex. Some of that market town's citizens would sagely agree that such a Day of Doom was just. For had not Mistleham become a haven of murder and mayhem? The Dominican's powerful voice rang out, cutting like a hiss of steel across the marketplace crowded in by town houses, the guildhall and the brooding mass of St Alphege's, the parish church, with its four-square crenellated tower, grey brick and grimacing gargoyles. The dirt-strewn, slippery cobbles echoed to the usual sounds of carts rumbling and horses clattering, their sharpened hooves sparking the stone. Peasants trod wearily as they moved from one stall to the next, looking to barter or to purchase. Now all fell eerily silent under the preacher's eloquent voice: even the bailiffs gathered around the stocks, waiting to imprison a huddle of malefactors, paused in their shouting and cursing. Raucous laughter at an adulterer forced to carry a prostitute on his shoulders to the stocks, her skirt pulled up, bare legs swinging, faded abruptly away. The Dominican's voice rang as clear as the sacristy bell that announced the elevation of the host during mass, the ice-cold morning air serving as God's silver trumpet for this preacher, Lord Scrope's personal chaplain and confessor.

'The body is vile,' Brother Gratian proclaimed, 'stinking and withered. The pleasure of the flesh is, by its very nature, poisoned and corrupt. It brings down upon you a shoal of God's curses.' The Dominican's ever-growing congregation nodded and murmured amongst themselves. They realised Brother Gratian was referring obliquely to the Free Brethren of the Holy Spirit, those wandering beggar-preachers who had swept into Mistleham and taken over the haunted, derelict village of Mordern deep in the nearby forest. The Free Brethren had preached how the flesh was sweet and its pleasures wholesome. Indeed, it was rumoured, if the men amongst the Free Brethren made love to a woman, they, like Adam did for Eve in Paradise, could restore her virginity. Lord Scrope, who'd recently gone riding by on a charger draped in a mantle, dressed in a costly diapered tunic woven in Constantinople, silken breeches pushed into pure leather boots, gold spurs winking in the sunlight, had brought a savage end to such nonsense.

'Satan,' Brother Gratian's voice grew even stronger, 'roams our roads with his demonic packhorses! On each are millions of souls, bound and fettered, all destined for hell. Satan's head is larger than that of a horse or any other animal. He has bushy hair, and a sweeping forehead more than two hands broad. He has large soft ears like those of a baboon, enormous brows, owlish eyes in a fat face and a cat's nose. A cleft lip closes over fangs like those of a ravenous wolf, sharp and red.' Brother Gratian's voice was now so carrying it could even be heard inside St Alphege's with its graceful pillars, arches and columns, delicate stone tracery and windows glazed with jewel-like studded glass.

In a darkened corner of that church, near the mercy seat close to the lady chapel, Lady Hawisa Scrope and

Domina Marguerite, abbess of the nearby convent of St Frideswide, paused in their conversation. They had been discussing a fresh approach to Lord Scrope about those corpses still hanging deep in the forest around the village of Mordern. Now they drew apart. Lady Hawisa's face, white as hawthorn blossom, puckered in concern. She rubbed her eyes, glanced at Abbess Marguerite, then raised her eyes heavenwards. She was about to continue her conversation when a more sinister, threatening sound echoed like the crack of doom, low but powerful: the drawn-out braying of a hunting horn. Lady Hawisa sprang to her feet and hastened towards the coffin door, the side entrance to the church. She threw this open and ran outside. Again the hunting horn sounded, promising violence and sudden death. The people of Mistleham were already scattering, fleeing for refuge; some even brushed by her, flinging themselves into the church. Across the square, archers and men-at-arms wearing the russet-green livery of her husband, Lord Scrope, came spilling out of the Honeycomb tavern, bows strung, arrows notched. Others were drawing swords and daggers. Traders deserted their stalls; women clutched children to shelter in doorways. Again that dreadful horn brayed, but from where? Lady Hawisa gazed wildly around. More people were running towards the church, screaming, 'Sagittarius, Sagittarius!

The Bowman, the Bowman!' Brother Gratian came hastening across. For a man who preached so often about death, he now seemed particularly frightened at the prospect. He paused before Lady Hawisa, opened his mouth to speak, then thrust by her to join the others flocking into the church.

'Come on, hasten!' someone behind Lady Hawisa shouted from the safety of the porch.

She turned and gazed back across the square. Eadburga, daughter of Oswin, ostler at the Honeycomb, was hurrying towards her clutching the hand of Wilfred, her beloved. They were shouting and screaming as they raced across. Lady Hawisa heard, or thought she did, the ominous twang of a longbow. Someone grabbed at her arm, trying to drag her into the church, but all she could do was stare at the fleeing lovers. Eadburga abruptly staggered, turning sideways even as the long barbed shaft that had pierced her back broke through her chest in a flurry of blood. The young woman crumpled to the ground as Wilfred, still clasping her hand, turned to help. A second arrow lanced his neck, straight through flesh and bone, cutting off breath and life. Wilfred collapsed to his knees, hands fluttering, blood bubbling between his lips as his eyes glazed over in death.

I

Who are the malefactors? Who knew about the robbery? Who offered and gave the robbers help, counsel and assistance?

Letter of Edward I, 6 June 1303

Sir Hugh Corbett, Keeper of the Secret Seal, personal emissary of Edward I of England and a member of the King's Privy Council, embraced Lady Maeve, his wife, and heartily wished he was back in bed with her at Leighton Manor in Essex. He held her close, her blond hair tickling his cheek, her soft lips brushing his skin, he hugged her once more, savouring her delicate perfume, then stood back. Maeve smiled even as her lustrous blue eyes brimmed with tears, and brought up the fur-rimmed hood of her dark green cloak. Corbett thought it made her look even more beautiful, but those tears! To curb his own sadness he glanced over his shoulder at his two companions waiting on their horses. Ranulf-atte-Newgate, Principal Clerk in the Chancery of the Green Wax, red hair tied tightly behind his head, green eyes watchful in his pale face, nose slightly pinched by the cold, caught his gaze and turned away as if distracted by the clamour around the palace gate. Beside Ranulf, Chanson, Clerk of the Stables, tousle-headed and garbed in grey, was doing his best to control the sumpter pony carrying their bags and chests. Corbett glanced back at Maeve. She had now hidden her distress at her husband's imminent departure by bringing forward their two children, Edward and Eleanor. Corbett crouched to hug both, rose, kissed Maeve passionately on the lips, then turned, gathered the reins of his horse and swung himself up into the saddle. He pretended to busy himself with his war belt as well as adjusting the black woollen cloak about him. Then he glanced back at Maeve, mouthed a message of love and, turning his horse's head, led his companions out of the palace gate along the trackway to London Bridge.

Corbett, like Ranulf, kept his hood pushed back to give him a better view of this crowded thoroughfare, guiding his horse prudently along its icy rutted surface. He slouched low in the saddle, blinking away the tears, staring fixedly ahead of him. Ranulf rode just behind him to his right, Chanson to his left. The Clerk of the Stables had now hoisted the lance bearing the stiffened pennant displaying the royal arms emblazoned in glorious scarlet, blue and gold, the rampant leopards proclaiming to all and sundry how these were king's men, not to be interfered with or impeded in any way. Even a vexillation of royal knight-bannerets pulled aside for these clerks, whom they immediately recognised and saluted. Corbett nodded courteously. Ranulf raised a hand, aware of how these royal bully-boys were studying them closely. Corbett's departure from Westminster certainly caused a stir. Heads turned, eyes narrowed against the bitter cold. People watched these two important clerks garbed in black leather jerkins, their dark green hose pushed into red boots of Cordova leather, one gauntleted hand grasping the reins, the other beneath their cloaks ready to draw sword or a dagger. Those who did business at Westminster recognised that the Keeper of the Secret Seal was off on the King's affairs. The presence of Corbett in the royal palace always provoked a sea of murmuring and whispering, speculation about what might be happening. After all, these were dangerous times. The war across the Scottish march was not progressing as well as the old king would have wished, whilst the powerful London merchants, with gangs of rifflers at their beck and call, were growing increasingly resentful at the King's constant demand for money to finance his struggle against Wallace in Scotland as well as to equip his war cogs patrolling the Narrow Seas against the privateers of Philip of France. Royal business, however, was secret. Corbett was the last man to discuss the reason for his departure with anyone. Instead he settled himself comfortably in his saddle, lost in his own thoughts about Maeve. Christmas and the twelve holy days had certainly passed like a dream, a heart-warming, grace-filling, soul-enriching period. Corbett had never felt so happy in his life. Once again he murmured a prayer of thanks.

'*Ego tibi Domine gratias et laudem* – I give you thanks and praise, oh Lord.'

Oh yes, the turn of the year had proved good. Epiphany had come and gone like a watch in the night, then a royal courier had arrived at Leighton with a scroll sealed by Edward himself, a writ summoning Corbett *cum festinacione magna* – with great haste – down to the King's palace at Westminster. Corbett had ignored the great haste, insisting that Maeve and the children also join him at his lodgings in the old palace. Edward, of course, had proved to be a generous, hearty host, praising Maeve's beauty whilst merrily fussing the children. However, when all the courtesies were done, the King, iron-grey hair falling down to his shoulders, had grabbed Corbett's arm and led him out across the frost-laced palace gardens, through the south door of the great abbey and into the cloisters. Corbett sensed where they were going. The King was now silent and morose, no longer the jovial lord but muttering to himself, clawing at his silvery moustache and beard. He pushed his way through the knight-bannerets gathered round the door and started down the steep steps broken off halfway, the gap spanned by a long wooden plank, and into the cavernous circular crypt of the abbey with its eight ground-level windows and huge central pillar. Corbett detached himself from the King and put his hand in the gap, then stared around at the empty coffers, caskets and leather treasury sacks that littered the floor. Edward sat down on a coffer, glaring round, face all fierce as he muttered his favourite oaths, 'By God's hand' and 'By God's thigh', followed by a litany of filthy imprecations against those who'd dared to dig their way through one of those windows to rob the royal treasury of gold, silver, jewels and precious goods. The riflers had even removed the stones from the *arca*, the stronghold built into the centre of the massive pillar.

'They'll all hang, Corbett!'

'Yes, your grace.'

'Listen,' the King hissed, 'how silent it is.'

Corbett walked back to the fortified door leading to the crypt steps. He was aware of the cold and the darkness, how the many candles and cresset torches flickered and flared in vain to drive back the gloom.

'Silent, your grace,' he agreed. 'The good brothers are still lodged in the Tower?'

'Over a hundred of the good brothers will rot there,' the King snarled, 'until I discover the truth and get all my treasure back. You know that, Corbett!'

The Keeper of the Secret Seal certainly did. He had been party to the ruthless investigation into the great conspiracy to rob the royal treasury in the crypt of Westminster. The King's own hoard allegedly safe in this hallowed place, the mausoleum of his family. It should never have happened. The crypt was protected by eighteen-foot-thick walls, narrow windows, fortified doors and stairs with the steps removed halfway down to create a gap that only a specially made plank could span. Yet the outrage had still occurred. The sheer effrontery of it had shocked even the cynical officials of the Chancery and Exchequer, who dealt every day with a legion of rogues and vagabonds. The robbery had been the fruit of an unholy alliance between London's underworld, led by Richard Puddlicott, a former clerk, and some of the leading monks of the abbey. Puddlicott had seduced the good brothers, supposedly followers of the rule of St Benedict, by bringing into the abbey musicians, courtesans, food and wine for midnight revelry, whilst other conspirators, under the cloak of night, had weakened one window in the crypt, working secretly in the cemetery beyond to create a gap. At last they had forced an entry on the eve of St Mark and the vast treasure hoard had been taken. The leading monks had been fully aware of the conspiracy and co-operated eagerly. So much treasure had been taken that precious items had been found at Tothill, in the fields around the abbey and even fished from the Thames. The rest of the haul had abruptly appeared on the London market, the greedy goldsmiths looking the other way as they bought and sold what was clearly not theirs. Edward had been absent in Scotland, but his fury had known no bounds. He had dispatched commissioners, Corbett included, into London and the entire community of the abbey had been committed to the Tower. Courts of oyer and terminer moved through every ward of the city, names were mentioned, suspects were arrested, even dragged out of sanctuary in clear violation of ecclesiastical law. The King demanded, time and again, that the treasure be recovered whilst anyone involved in its disappearance was to be arrested and taken to the Tower.

'I'll grind such arrogance to dust.' The King bit on the quick of his thumb and spat out a piece of skin. 'Corbett,' he gestured at a nearby chair, 'sit down. I need to talk to you.'

Edward scratched the corner of his mouth as he studied this enigmatic clerk, olive-skinned, cleanly shaven, his long face hard and resolute except for the laughter lines around the firm mouth and deep-set eyes. He glimpsed the grey amongst Corbett's raven-black hair, now pulled back and tied in a queue to rest on the nape of his neck.

'We are getting older, Corbett,' the King grated. He stretched out and gently tapped the clerk on the cheek, 'but you are still my soul companion, Hugh, my faithful servant.' His words echoed round that cavernous chamber. 'I trust you as I do my own sword arm.' Edward's right eye drooped, almost closing, a common gesture whenever the King's humours were disturbed. 'That is why I have brought you down here to talk in the silence.'

Corbett steeled himself. He respected Edward of England, a man of iron who, despite his many faults, imposed order on a chaos that, if unchecked, would sweep away Corbett's world of logic, reason, evidence, the rule of law and all the trappings that kept the *utlegati* – the wolf men – lurking beyond the light. Nevertheless, Corbett was wary of princes, and none more so than Edward, especially when he acted maudlin.

'Your grace,' he gestured round, 'the light in here is poor, it's freezing cold, my wife and children . . .'

'Hugh, Hugh . . .'

'Is it this, your grace? I thought the conspiracy had been broken.'

'This is not just my treasure hoard,' Edward declared, beating his chest. 'It is part of me.' He edged closer, hitching up the neck of his sack-like tunic then plucking at his coarsely woven breeches tucked into cowhide boots.

Corbett hid his smile. Edward of England liked nothing better than to play the role of the peasant farmer when it suited him.

'I brought you here because something about which I must tell you belongs here. I'll not keep you long. I must go to the royal mews,' Edward murmured. 'One of our beloved falcons is ill. Whilst you, Corbett, must be off to Mistleham in Essex, to question Oliver Scrope, lord of the manor.'

'Your grace,' Corbett protested, 'you promised me rest until well after Hilary.'

'I know, I know.' The King waved a hand. 'But I need you in Essex, and I'll tell you why.' He breathed in deeply. 'Early last year a wandering group of Beguines, male and female, who called themselves the Free Brethren of the Holy Spirit, landed at Dover. They journeyed into Essex on to the manor lands of Lord Oliver Scrope. You've heard of him?'

Corbett shrugged.

'He owns vast estates, a man certainly blessed by fortune if not by God,' Edward added cynically. 'Oliver is an old comrade-in-arms. He and I have fought shoulder to shoulder in Wales and along the Scottish march. You do recall him?'

Corbett pulled a face, then shook his head.

'Yes you do!' Edward teased. 'You said he had the face of a bat: balding head, with protuberant eyes, puffed cheeks and ears that stuck out.'

'True. I remember,' Corbett conceded. 'A small, thick-set man, hot-tempered and violent. Your grace, comrade or not, Scrope has a nasty soul, a man of blood. He took to killing like a bat to flitting. He butchered some Welsh prisoners outside Conwy, didn't he?'

'Yes, yes.' Edward grimaced. 'Oliver is a fighter. He is also a hero, Corbett, a Crusader who escaped Acre when it fell thirteen years ago to the Saracens. Fought his way through, brought back a king's ransom in precious goods. I converted a great deal of it into land for him and married him off to a rich heiress fifteen years his junior, Lady Hawisa Talbot. However, one thing he did not hand over to me,' Edward narrowed his eyes, 'was the Sanguis Christi.'

'The Blood of Christ?'

'An exquisite cross of thick pure gold,' the King's eyes gleamed, 'studded with five huge rubies allegedly containing blood from Christ's precious wounds. According to legend, the rubies were embedded in the True Cross found by the Empress Helena a thousand years ago. The Sanguis Christi, along with other wealth, was seized by Scrope when he fled Acre. On his return to England, he solemnly promised me, after I had given him so much help and favour, that the Sanguis Christi would be mine, either when he died or after twelve years had elapsed. It is now January 1304.' Edward smiled. 'The twelve years have elapsed. The Sanguis Christi should be mine.'

'Then summon him to Westminster!' Corbett declared crossly.

'Ah, that's just the beginning.' The King smiled. 'Scrope is a wily man. He was with the Templars in Acre. The Sanguis Christi and all the treasures he seized once belonged to that order. They have demanded everything back, particularly the Sanguis Christi. Scrope has utterly rejected their plea. I support him in this.' He grinned. 'Naturally. The Temple, according to rumour, have sworn vengeance. They've sent formal envoys to Lord Scrope demanding the return of their property. Scrope has refused, so the Templars, in a secret consistory, have passed sentence of death on him. Now,' the King sighed, 'I do not know whether this is the work of the General Chapter or just extremists, but so far they have made little progress.'

'Couldn't the Pope intervene?'

'The Pope sprawls in Avignon, firmly in the power of France, who, as you know, has no great love for the Order of the Temple. Anyway, His Holiness claims that Scrope's treasures are the just plunders of war, whilst our archbishop, old Robert Winchelsea, when he is not in exile, fully agrees.'

'But you are concerned that the Temple may seize the Sanguis Christi?'

'As is Lord Scrope. He has received mysterious messages.' Edward closed his eyes. '"The Mills of the Temple of God grind exceedingly slow but they do grind exceedingly small."'

'How were these messages delivered?' Corbett now forgot the freezing gloom, deeply intrigued by what the King was saying.

'Oh, writs and letters, anonymously and mysteriously delivered at Scrope's great manor hall.'

'So you need me to collect the Sanguis Christi before the Temple do?'

'Precisely!'

'But the Temple will object to you having it.'

Edward clicked his tongue. 'They can object until the Second Coming, Corbett. I'll simply say I am holding it in trust until the matter is decided, which will be never! Moreover, Scrope has demanded my help before he hands it over. There is more to the story than a beautiful gold cross and five precious rubies.'

'You mentioned the Free Brethren of the Holy Spirit?'

'Yes, yes.' The King breathed out noisily. 'You know what is happening, Sir Hugh. The Pope wallows in luxury at Avignon, bishops, priests and clerics live lives alien to their calling. Europe is plagued by wandering groups attacking such decadence; fraternities, companies and sisterhoods all claiming a special revelation from God. The Free Brethren of the Holy Spirit were one of these. Like the Beguines, the Columbini, the Pastoreux, they believed that true religion should be free of all structures, strictures and hierarchy. Men and women, they argued, should live in their natural state and not feel guilty over sexual matters or any other burdens of sin. Property should be held in common, as should all wealth and income. The sacraments are not necessary, particularly marriage.' Edward fluttered his fingers. 'You know how the hymn goes. Anyway, this company of Free Brethren, male and female, under their leaders, who rejoiced in the names of Adam and Eve, moved into Mistleham. At first Lord Oliver tolerated them . . .'

'Why?'

'He had other problems. Not only was he being menaced by the Temple, but new threats were emerging like prostitutes from some filthy runnel. Again warnings were anonymously delivered, following the same lines as the earlier though slightly different. Yes, that's how it goes.' Edward scratched his head. '"The Mills of the Temple may grind exceedingly slow and exceedingly small, but so do the Mills of God's anger."'

'And their origin?'

Edward pulled a face. 'Scrope visited me on the last Sunday of Advent and confessed all this, but he didn't know who was threatening him and why this new menace had emerged.' The King opened and shut the battered lid of a looted coffer next to him. 'However, by then, one problem had been resolved, the Free Brethren of the Holy Spirit had ceased to exist.'

'Your grace?' Corbett leaned forward. In December he'd been busy in Canterbury, but on his return he'd heard chilling tales from Essex.

'Lord Scrope,' Edward refused to meet Corbett's gaze, 'is most orthodox. He prides himself on having fought in Outremer, on being a Crusader, a knight with personal loyalty to the Holy Father. Little wonder,' the King laughed drily, 'that he won protection from that quarter. You see, Corbett, the Free Brethren had moved to Mistleham and lodged in the nearby deserted village of Mordern, which in itself has a sinister history. Once settled, they merged with the local people. At first they were more of a curiosity than a threat . . .' Edward paused. 'Until Lord Scrope abruptly decided otherwise. He accused them of robbery, poaching, lechery and, most importantly, heresy.'

'Heresy?'

'Heresy,' Edward agreed. 'Lord Scrope is a strict believer. He was encouraged in this by his personal chaplain, a Dominican, Brother Gratian.'

Corbett sat back, allowing himself to relax. Although he didn't like it, he realised why he had been summoned here. The Dominicans worked as papal inquisitors, constantly vigilant against heresy.

'Lord Scrope turned on the Free Brethren. He summoned up his levies and attacked them as they sheltered in the derelict church of Mordern. Those who survived,' Edward sighed, 'Lord Scrope summarily hanged from the oak trees around the church.'

Corbett stared hard at the King as he recalled stories of a heinous massacre in Essex that had seeped into the Chancery offices at Westminster.

'Lord Scrope maintains they were outlaws, heretics,' Edward continued. 'He was supported by Brother Gratian with letters and scripts from his minister general as well as the curial offices of the Pope at Avignon. He claims he has God's own mandate to root out heresy whenever he sees it.'

'This Gratian, how long has he been with Lord Scrope?'

'God knows!' Edward retorted. 'He certainly does not act on my authority.'

'So the Free Brethren of the Holy Spirit are all dead?'

'Yes, but to make matters worse, Scrope refuses to have their corpses buried. They still lie out at Mordern or dangle from the trees. Scrope says they should rot where they died as a warning to others.'

'You could send in commissioners.'

'Oh no.' Edward smiled. 'Lord Scrope is supported by Holy Mother Church whilst both Lords and Commons are hot against such wandering groups.'

'And the good people of Mistleham?'

'Encouraged by their newly elected mayor, Henry Claypole, they were only too willing to support Lord Scrope in his assault on the Free Brethren. You know how it is,' the King added bitterly. 'A shire town, a community hostile to strangers. If a bucket went missing, the Free Brethren were responsible. If a woman was seduced, the Free Brethren were to blame, especially with their singular views on the sins of the flesh.'

'And there was some truth in these accusations?'

'Of course! The Free Brethren were what they claimed to be, expounders of free love, professional beggars living on their wits as well as the charity of others.' Edward rubbed his hands together. 'Look, Corbett, Scrope acted *sine auctoritate* – without authority. I want to warn him that that must never happen again, and under my authority, we must have those corpses buried, secretly but properly.'

'And the others?' Corbett asked. 'Anyone of note?'

'Henry Claypole, the mayor. A true firebrand. Some say he's Scrope's illegitimate son, a by-blow, the result of his dalliance with a certain Mistress Alice de Tuddenham. Claypole believes he is the legitimate heir to Scrope, whom he served as a squire in Outremer. A bustling, fiery man, Claypole is used to the cut and thrust of politics, though I think he's an empty vessel that makes a great deal of sound. The parish priest is Father Thomas. He served with us in Wales as chaplain. I promoted him to many benefices but then he converted and took true religion, claiming he wanted to serve God's poor. He resigned all his benefices and sinecures. His family hails from Mistleham, so I appointed him to the church there, or at least,' Edward grinned, 'Scrope and I persuaded the bishop to do so. Then there's Lady Hawisa. I suspect she has no real love for her husband, but she is faithful enough, vivacious, intelligent and comely, though a little tart of tongue. Finally, there's Scrope's sister Marguerite.' Edward stretched and smiled.

'Marguerite Scrope,' he repeated. 'Fourteen years ago, Corbett – though perhaps you don't remember her – she was one of the leading beauties of the court: a singular sort of beauty, different from the type of woman who sits in her window bower and makes calf's eyes at any knight who passes by. No, Marguerite loved life, dancing, hunting and hawking. I often teased her that she should have been born a man. She thanked me courteously then roundly informed me she was happy with the way she was. By the time her brother came home from Outremer, something had happened to Marguerite; she became withdrawn and reflective. She entered the Benedictine order as a nun, her qualities were soon noted and, with a little help from friends at home and court, she was appointed Abbess of St Frideswide, which lies in its own grounds just outside Mistleham. I doubt if she has really changed. I had a letter recently signed by both her and Father Thomas, protesting at her brother's destruction of the Free Brethren and demanding that I exercise my authority to ensure their honourable burial. Never mind them, Corbett! Essex is vital, a shire that straddles all the great roads to and from London and the eastern ports. I don't want any disturbance there. I want this settled. I'll be visiting Colchester soon. I want Scrope brought to book before the Sagittarius or Bowman does it for me.'

'Sagittarius?'

'The Bowman,' Edward explained. 'A mysterious killer who appeared in Mistleham without warning just after the New Year, as if that town didn't have enough problems. An archer, a skilled one, armed with a longbow, the type we brought from Wales. He announces his coming only by the blast of a hunting horn. Some people claim he's Satan, or a ghost or one of the Free Brethren come back to haunt them. When the horn blows, somewhere in Mistleham, or on the roads outside, a person always dies: a well-placed arrow to the throat, face or chest. So far five or six people have been killed in this way. Most of them young, cut down like running deer.'

'Attempts have been made to capture him?'

'Of course.' Edward laughed drily. 'Hugh, you've served in Wales; think of the power of those long-bows. Yew staffs, the ash arrow whistling through the air. A master bowman, a skilled archer, can be a silent, deadly killer. Shafts can be loosed in a matter of heart-beats, then he disappears into the forest or an alleyway with no sight or sound.'

'You mentioned the Free Brethren of the Holy Spirit. Could any of them have survived the massacre and be exacting vengeance?'

'I doubt it,' Edward replied, chewing the corner of his lip. 'The Free Brethren apparently carried no arms, though there are rumours to the contrary. Even if they did, such people are not skilled in the arts of war.'

'And this is not directed against Lord Scrope but the townspeople of Mistleham?'

'Well it could be.' Edward paused. 'Hugh, Lord Scrope committed murder. If the Free Brethren had perpetrated a felony, they should have appeared before the justices of oyer and terminer or even been summoned before the assizes, but to be brutally cut down, massacred? Now I can't appear to be protecting a group of wandering rogues against a manor lord, definitely not one as powerful as Scrope, but if this bowman continues his attacks, sooner or later people will look for a scapegoat. I don't want some uprising in Essex. I want the matter brought to an end, and you're the best man to do that.'

'And you are sure, none of the Free Brethren survived?'

'I doubt it. Father Thomas reports there were fourteen in number, and there were fourteen corpses, each carrying the brand of their guild upon them. A cross,' Edward patted his chest just beneath his throat, 'here. Father Thomas tried to reason with Scrope, but that ruthless bastard is adamant. The corpses still remain unburied. No one escaped.' The King sucked on his lips, then gestured round. 'You must be wondering why I brought you here. This is my treasure house, Corbett – evilly looted. I kept my precious goods here, gifts from old friends and Eleanor . . .' He blinked away the tears that always came when he mentioned his beloved first wife, Eleanor of Castile, now buried beneath her marble mausoleum in the abbey above them. 'You know the story, Corbett? I was in Outremer when my father died. Eleanor was with me. A secret sect of assassins who lived with their master, the Old Man of the Mountains, in their rocky eyrie in the Syrian desert, had marked me down for death. They struck, the assassin stealing into my tent with a poisoned dagger. I killed him but he still wounded me. Eleanor, God love her, sucked the poison from the gash and saved me.' Edward sighed noisily. 'I dedicated the dagger to St Edward the Confessor and placed it here in the crypt. Those whoresons stole it! One of the gang, John Le Riche, tried to sell it in Mistleham, but he was trapped by Scrope and his minion Claypole. They hanged Le Riche out of hand and now hold the dagger. Scrope, to impress me, is acting the hero-saviour, but I don't believe his tale. I want that dagger back and the truth behind Le Riche's abrupt capture and even swifter execution. Do what you have to.' Edward searched in his wallet, pulled out a small scroll and handed this to Corbett, who unrolled it. The writing was in the King's hand, the writ sealed with his privy seal: 'To all officers of the Crown, sheriffs, bailiffs and mayors. What the bearer of this letter has done, or is doing, is in the King's name and for the benefit of both Crown and Realm . . .'

'Sir Hugh, master!' Hugh broke from his reverie and glanced quickly to his right. Ranulf, who had been studying him closely ever since they left Westminster, gestured ahead. 'We are approaching London Bridge, master.' He smiled. 'It's best if we are vigilant.'

Corbett gazed around. This was a part of the city where one's wits and sword must be sharp and ready. A bank of mist was rolling in from the Thames. The roar of the river as it poured through the arches of London Bridge, breaking around the protective starlings, sounded like a roll of drums, not quite drowning the clamour of people surging along the busy thoroughfare overlooking the river bank. The cries and yells of watermen, bargemasters and weary rowers mingled with the shouts of traders and their apprentices offering a variety of goods from hot pies to leather bottles. A group of enterprising hawkers had set up stalls to sell wineskins, purses, leather laces, deerskin bags, belts and all sorts of medicinal herbs to those making their way down to Westminster, up on to the bridge or further north to the gloomy mass of the

Tower. Another line of suspicious-looking marketeers offered fur from 'monstrous, mysterious beasts in the East with fair heads, bodies as black as mulberry, with crimson backs and multicoloured tails'. These itinerant traders were now being carefully questioned by market beadles over their licence to sell in the area.

Corbett surveyed the crowd, watchful against any violence or protest at the royal standard Chanson had displayed, yet apart from a yell deep in the crowd about how the King's testicles should be enshrined in a hog's turd, there was no open resentment. Business certainly looked brisk, as was royal justice. The stocks and thews were full of street-walkers, ribalds and drunkards, not to mention the sky-farmers, counterfeit men caught red-handed in their trickery. A butcher guilty of selling foul meat had been singled out for special treatment; he was forced to stand in a cart beneath the gallows with the rotting entrails of a pig wound around his throat and the lower part of his face to rest just beneath his nose. A man who'd pulled the hair of an archdeacon in a brawl was now having his own plucked out. The screaming victim was being stridently lectured how, when punishment was finished, he must walk barefoot across the bridge three times with scourgers following behind. A little further on a wandering preacher pointed to an execution cart, its wicker baskets full of the remains of Scottish rebels, beheaded, quartered and pickled, to be displayed on London Bridge. He openly warned: 'Man born of a woman lives only for an hour. His days are bound in wretchedness and woe! He bursts forth like blossom only to fall quickly to the ground, to pass away like a shadow, nowhere to be found.'

Closer to the entrance to London Bridge, great beacon fires blazed in empty pitch casks. Around these gathered the poor, the infirm, drooling beggars and the dribbling insane. Franciscans dressed in coarse brown robes moved amongst these offering bread and strips of boiled meat. The sick and their ministers rubbed shoulders with the serjeants-at-law moving up and down to the courts of Westminster, all adorned in their splendid scarlet robes and pure white silk coifs. Along the river's edge ranged a line of scaffolds decorated with stiffened frozen cadavers on whose shoulders kites, ravens and crows settled to pick and pluck at brain or eye whilst women squatting beneath the gibbets offered scraps of clothing from the hanged as talismans against ill luck.

Corbett took in all these scenes, the tawdry, the macabre, the swirl of evil and good. He pulled up his cowl and stared at a group of Flagellantes, garbed only in linen shifts from waist to ankle, their backs laid bare. These shuffled in a line, intoning the verse of a psalm as they hit each other with whips tied into thongs and pierced with needles; the blood cascaded down their bodies to soak their linen shifts and stain their feet. Corbett muttered a prayer to himself. He must leave the soft warmth of Maeve's world. He was about to enter the Meadows of Murder, go through the Valley of the Deadly Shadow. Behind him, Ranulf noticed his master's agitation and breathed a sigh of relief. Master Long Face, as he secretly called Corbett, was breaking free of his Christmas dream.

Ranulf, if the truth be known, had been bored during the holy days, more concerned about his own career prospects and very wary of the sharp-eyed, keen-witted Lady Maeve. Now, he clicked his tongue, the game had begun again. He recalled with relish his own secret meeting with the King after the Jesus Mass earlier that day. Corbett and Lady Maeve had followed the King out of St Stephen's Chapel, then moved to greet the Chief Justices, Hengham and Staunton. The King had plucked Ranulf by the sleeve and shepherded him into a window embrasure overlooking the old palace yard. Edward had pulled him close, eyes gleaming like those of a hunting cat.

'You'll be off to Mistleham in Essex, Master Ranulf.'

'Yes, your grace.'

'Take care of Brother Corbett.'

'Yes, your grace.'

'You're ambitious, Master Ranulf, keen as a limner.

I can do much for you.' The King was so close Ranulf smelt the fragrance of the sweet altar wine he had drank at the Eucharist. 'Keep a sharp eye on Lord Scrope, a bustling, evil man with a vile temper and murderous moods.'

'Yes, your grace.'

'Yes, your grace,' Edward echoed. 'Yet I tell you this, Master Ranulf, if Scrope threatens Corbett, if he is a danger with that foul temper of his . . .' He glanced away.

'Your grace?'

'Kill him, Master Ranulf, kill Scrope! Show no mercy to that rebel who has taken the law into his own hands!'

'By what right, your grace?'

'By my right, Master Ranulf. Keep this close, for you and you only.' Edward pushed a sealed scroll into Ranulf's hand and left.

The Principal Clerk in the Chancery of the Green Wax had opened the scroll and read the message: 'Edward the King to all officials of the Crown, sheriffs, bailiffs and mayor, know this, what the bearer of this letter has done he has done for the good of the King and the safety of the realm.'

2

On that day the justices began their deliberations.

Annals of London, 1304

Father Thomas knelt beneath the rood screen in the freezing darkness of his parish church. On trestles before him, draped in purple and surrounded by ghostly glowing funeral candles, lay the corpses of Wilfred and Eadburga, faces white as wax, their horrid wounds now dried, nothing more than purple stains, their limbs all washed and anointed. Tomorrow Father Thomas would sing their requiem mass and take the coffins out through the corpse door into God's Acre for burial. He moved, trying to ease the cramp in his legs and thighs. How many had been killed now? Seven? Yes, seven. These two unfortunates, and then there was Edith and Hilda, slain while leaving their cottage, and Elwood the blacksmith's son, cut down as he trotted out a horse for his father to inspect, Gwatkin the carter and Theobald the fuller. Father

Thomas was distracted by the glittering sanctuary lamp. He stared into the darkness, glanced up at the tortured face of Christ on the cross then back at the pyx hanging on its thick silver chain above the high altar. Was all this the truth? he wondered. Did Christ die and rise again? Did the appearance of bread house the resurrected body of Christ? He adjusted the purple stole around his neck and shifted his bony knees on the hard, cold paving stones. He gazed fearfully around. Blackness! Silence, except for the scurry of mice in shadowy corners. A freezing cold night! Father Thomas thought of his warm cot bed and the diced stewed meat bubbling in that heavy cauldron above the hearth fire, hot and spicy. He shook his head, grasped the Ave beads wrapped round his fingers more tightly and intoned a verse from the psalm:

> One thing I asked of the Lord, for this I long.
> To dwell in the house of the Lord, all the days of
> my life.
> To savour the sweetness of the Lord and behold
> his holy temple.

This was followed by the De Profundis: 'Out of the depths have I cried to you, oh Lord . . .'

Father Thomas stopped and moved restlessly. He was distracted. Did the ghosts of Eadburga and Wilfred hover here? Did the departed souls of the other murder victims congregate around him beseeching God's vengeance? Yet on whom? The Sagittarius, the Bowman? Who could it be? This mysterious, silent assassin had appeared in the New Year. Father Thomas glanced towards the lady altar to his left and the comforting light of candles glowing there. He would have to walk. He rose to his feet and, taking a cresset torch from a sconce in the wall, slowly paced out of the nave under the rood screen into the sanctuary and then back down the transepts, thinking all the time. The killer must be a master bowman, a skilled archer like himself. Was the Sagittarius imitating him, a parish priest who had also indulged in murderous thoughts towards Lord Scrope? Who had played the role of God's avenger? Who had, in the past, seriously contemplated a violent end for that evil manor lord who had led Father Thomas' beloved brother to his death? Best not to think about that! He must concentrate on the present danger. Was the Sagittarius' abrupt and brutal appearance linked to the deaths of those unfortunates at Mordern? Father Thomas paused and closed his eyes. He'd gone out there. The corpses still lay sprawled, covered in their shrouds of snow and ice. Bodies still dangled from the trees, necks twisted, heads askew. To kill was one thing, but to refuse to bury the dead . . . Was the Sagittarius a member of that company who had survived? Yet the priest had inspected each of those corpses, counted them carefully. There'd been fourteen members of the Free Brethren and fourteen had died. Yes, he was sure of that!

He walked on towards the north door of the church, now bolted and locked, and paused. He was tempted to open this as he did whenever he baptised a child, so that any demons could leave and cluster in that part of God's Acre reserved for them. Ah well! He walked on absent-mindedly reciting his Aves and Paternosters, feeling the hard dried beads thread through his fingers. He tried to sooth the turmoil of his soul, to distract himself from the rage seething inside. Lord Scrope had a great deal to answer for! Now and again he glanced up the transept, eyes drawn by the candle burning before the Pity, a large statue of the Virgin Mary with the dead Christ resting in her lap. He paused near the baptismal font and stared at the painting of St Christopher, a huge figure bearing the infant Christ done in vivid hues, around it drawings of phoenixes, pelicans and mermaids. Father Thomas made the usual prayer whilst staring at the image of that saint, reciting a verse from the psalms that the Christ-bearer would save him from violent and sudden death that night.

Father Thomas continued on. He knew where he

was going. He walked around up the other transept and paused before the painting that took up a great section of the wall from the floor to just above his head. Father Thomas closed his eyes. He recalled the day Adam and Eve, the leaders of the Free Brethren, had presented themselves at the door of his church. He could still recall the distinct image of two beautiful human beings. At the time he had wondered if in Eden the real Adam and Eve had looked like that: lovely faces framed by golden hair, blue eyes sparkling, full of laughter and innocent merriment. Father Thomas considered himself a hard man. He had fought in the King's levies in Wales. He had wandered battlefields stinking with rotting corpses. He had examined his own conscience and found himself full of ancient sins and fresh lusts whilst working hard as a pastor to free others from Satan's iron grip. He was not soft or sentimental, given to tearful emotions. He prided himself on not being . . . what was that French phrase? *Faux et semblant* – false and dissembling! Nonetheless, those two leaders of the Free Brethren had touched his heart with their winsome ways and merry smiles. They had arrived at St Alphege's carrying heavy leather panniers, explaining how they were also itinerant painters and artists, skilled in wall frescoes and paintings as well as depictions on stretched canvas. They offered to render a similar service to St Alphege's in return for food and other purveyance. When Father Thomas demurred, they promised heartily that if their work was not to his satisfaction they'd whitewash it over. Eventually he had agreed. The nave of the church was not in the gift of the manor lord but in his, and he had letters from the bishop confirming this.

Accordingly, on the Feast of St Mary Magdalene past, Adam and Eve, with two assistants from the Free Brethren, had moved into St Alphege's, working in the clear light of day though helped by the occasional candle and lantern. At first Father Thomas had been a reluctant bystander, often wandering down to inspect their work after he'd celebrated the Jesus Mass or rung the Gabriel Bell reminding the townspeople to honour the Virgin. Some parishioners had objected to the work but many had been interested to see the grey walls of their parish church bloom with colour. Adam and Eve chose as their theme the Fall of Babylon from the Book of Revelation and other sources. Once the walls had been dressed and primed, they had brought the scene to vivid life with their brushwork in an eye-catching array of red, green, blue, gold, yellow and black against a white marbled background. Now the priest moved the cresset torch closer to study this scene once again, ignoring the dancing shadows and the strange eerie sounds from around the church.

'Babylon has truly fallen,' he whispered. In the painting the soaring towers and gateways of the City of the Great Whore were being consumed by a swirling storm of fire that swept backwards and forwards above a bubbling sea of boiling blood. Black rain pelted down. Flames belched from windows and doorways. Defenders stood along the crenellated battlements, stark against the blue-red sky dominated by a fire-breathing dragon with scaly green wings, black claws and a brilliant red tail. The malignant beast, that horror of hell, was now swallowing the souls of those who'd served the Great Whore, digesting them and excreting them as dung. Figures in swirling white cloaks, apparently angels, sent up a rain of arrows against the defenders of Babylon dressed in russet and green. In one of the castle chambers a man lay on a bed, a cup in his hand. The next scene, set in a large banqueting chamber, showed Judas, his neck adorned with the noose he'd used to hang himself, feasting with other sinners at a great banquet of toads, snails and reptiles cooked in burning sulphur, whilst drinking fiery liquid from flame-encrusted goblets. In the final picture Judas and his minions were fleeing up a Valley of the Dead, staring fearfully backwards, unaware that the path at the far end of the valley was blocked by a soaring cross bearing the crucified Christ, his wounds gleaming like beacon lights.

The entire tableau was decorated around the edges with strange symbols and leafy plants; it was about three yards long and stretched from just below the floor to the sill of the transept window. Father Thomas had been deeply impressed and so were members of his parish council. Visitors to the town flocked into the church to view the new painting. The entire company of the Free Brethren, with their strange biblical names – Seth, Cain, Abel, Joshua, Aaron, Esther and Miriam – also arrived to dance with joy. Dame Marguerite, Lady Abbess of St Frideswide, accompanied by her ambitious chaplain Benedict Le Sanglier, came to admire, as did Scrope with his escort of henchmen. The manor lord had studied the painting closely, then grunted his approval.

Father Thomas sighed. He replaced the sconce torch in its holder beneath the memorial plaque to the memory of Gaston de Bearn, then read the pious inscription to this kinsman of Scrope and Dame Marguerite's killed at Acre. He glanced at Gaston's coat of arms, a kneeling stag, its antlers crowned, carved above the year of the Frenchman's death, Anno Domini 1291. The priest whispered the requiem and walked back to kneel in front of the Pity, staring up at the serene face of the Virgin. He prayed an Ave, still distracted about the bloody events of the past. He had hoped the painting would make the Free

Brethren more acceptable. True, they entertained strange fancies about the Church's teaching, and their views on marriage and the love act were bawdy and lecherous, but the flesh was always weak. Father Thomas beat his own breast, murmuring, '*Mea culpa, mea culpa* – through my own fault, through my own fault.' Had he not entertained strange fancies about Lady Hawisa, with her beautiful white face, full breasts and slim waist? And what about parishioners like Mayor Henry Claypole, who processed so solemnly into church on Sunday and holy days, faces all devout, hands clasped in prayer? Father Thomas smiled to himself. He had sat with all of them in the shriving pew and heard their litany of sorry sins, about the brothels and bawdy baskets they frequented when they journeyed to Chelmsford, Orwell or even Cheapside in London. Their wives were no better, hot and lecherous as sparrows at a smile from some young man. Ah, Father Thomas reflected, that was where the present tempest had been sown. Stories of dalliance between townsmen and female members of the Free Brethren and, even worse, the attention some of the young men amongst the Free Brethren had shown towards wives and sweethearts in Mistleham. Tales of pretty trysts in the autumn woods; even whispers of a village wench conceiving a love-child. Other allegations had floated about like dirt through clear water, of livestock being poached and property stolen.

A sound down near the corpse door made the priest whirl round. He peered fearfully through the poor light. Nothing! He'd left the door off the latch in case the parents of Wilfred and Eadburga wished to come and pray. Guilty at his desertion of the dead, he walked back to the coffin trestles and pulled back the funeral cloths. He stared at the waxen faces, the absolution of all their sins pinned to the white cotton shifts. He blessed both corpses and sniffed the smoke from the funeral candles, but even their fragrance could not hide the mustiness of the air. Father Thomas breathed in deeply. Lord Scrope, perhaps to win him over after the massacre, had promised to renovate the entire church. The priest took some comfort from that. After all, a few of the stone flags were sinking, the walls were mildewed, whilst the wood in the chancel screen was beginning to rot. Again that sound. Father Thomas turned slowly. There was someone hiding in the church, deep in the shadows. He was sure of that. The creak of the corpse door, that cold blast of air. He walked towards it, swallowing hard, trying to control his own fear.

'No further, priest, stand still.'

Father Thomas obeyed. 'Who are you?' he called out.

'I am Nightshade,' the voice replied.

Father Thomas strained his hearing. The voice was cultured, melodious and soft; he couldn't recognise it. 'Why do you call yourself that at the dead of night?'

No answer.

'Why come sneaking into our parish church and hide in the shadows? Why not step into God's light? Why give yourself such a name?'

'Do you know what nightshade is, priest?'

'A poisonous plant, deadly in its potion, deadly in its effect. Is that you?'

'I am the other meaning of nightshade. Don't you know it, priest? It is that time of the night when the darkness grows a little deeper and the demons lurk.'

'Are you a demon?'

A soft laugh answered the priest's question. 'I am God's judgement, priest.'

'On whose authority?'

'My own! Blood cries out. Vengeance is to be exacted. Retribution imposed.'

'Are you the Sagittarius, the Bowman?'

'Are you?' came the mocking reply.

Father Thomas wiped the sweat on his hands along his gown.

'Why not move into God's light?'

'I am in God's light.'

'So why are you here?' the priest insisted. 'Why

come in the dead of night to threaten a priest keeping vigil over two dead innocents?'

'No one is innocent, priest, you know that. You must deliver a message, a warning to Lord Scrope. Tell him that before the Feast of the Conversion of St Paul, he must stand beneath the market cross of Mistleham and make a full confession of his sins.'

'He'll never do that.'

'At least he'll be warned.'

'Or what?'

'Retribution for all his sins,' hissed the reply.

'Why not warn him yourself?'

'Oh, don't worry, priest, I will and I shall, but remember what I've said: all his sins.'

A few hours later, on the eve of the Feast of St Hilary, just as the night turned a dull grey, Lord Oliver Scrope knelt at his own prie-dieu in the reclusorium that he had built on the Island of Swans at the heart of his manor demesne. His lips moved soundlessly as he stared at the diptych of Christ's Passion and reflected fearfully on judgement and retribution.

'*Jesu miserere*,' he whispered. '*Jesu miserere* – Jesus have mercy on me.' He closed his eyes, then shook his head. His morning devotions were ended. He hitched the ermine-lined bed-robe of dark blue damask closer about him, crossed himself and rose.

He stared round and drew practical comfort from this, his own hermitage and retreat. He had always been drawn to the Island of Swans, even as a child when he, Marguerite and cousin Gaston used to cross the water and play amongst the ruins. On his return from Acre, he had extended his estate and immediately built this retreat, round in shape, similar to a dovecote, fashioned out of heavy grey stone with a sloping roof of dark slate. In many ways it was reminiscent of the peel towers he had seen when fighting along the Scottish march or outside the Pale in Dublin. The interior, however, was much different from those grim strongholds. Lord Scrope had insisted on every luxury: polished wooden floors, an elevated recess for the bed with its goose-feather bolster and mattress, soft linen sheets and heavy gold-fringed hangings. In the far corner was a narrow ease chamber with a latrine, lavarium, and spice and soap stall. The gleaming floor of the retreat was covered in precious furs specially imported from Norway, whilst brilliantly embroidered Flemish tapestries decorated the walls. Sacred pictures and medallions hung between these, their gilt gleaming in the light from pure beeswax candles and shuttered lantern horns. Copper braziers, their caps perforated, added warmth and sweetness, as did the mantled hearth built into the wall with its own stack or flue for the smoke to escape. A phrase around the base of one of the pictures caught Scrope's eye; though executed in bright gold lettering, it now seemed like a summons of doom: 'What profit a man if he gain the whole world but suffers the loss of his eternal soul . . .'

Lord Scrope shivered and moved to the hearth to warm himself. He stared at the carved face of the woodwose at the centre of the mantle shelf; painted black with red eyes and gleaming white teeth, the entire head was crowned by a halo of forest greenery. On reflection Scrope did not like that face with its slightly sneering expression, and he vowed to have it changed as soon as he could. He picked up his finely carved wooden goblet of wine, leaned against the mantle shelf and stared down at the flames licking the dried bracken. Outside, a fresh fall of snow covered the ground. The lake had not yet frozen, though when he'd been rowed across the previous evening, the water had been bitingly cold, flecks and splashes stinging his face. Scrope sipped the mulled wine; of course it was warm in here. The six window openings were firmly shuttered and protected by leather hangings and thick blue woollen drapes.

Scrope had tried to sleep but been unable to. His soul was agitated by memories of the past, his heart rattled about recent worries. He absent-mindedly muttered a prayer. He reflected on the words of the psalm, how unabsolved sins from the past stretched out like a trap to seize the guilty. His night had been racked by the usual nightmares: the screaming and whirling missiles over Acre; Gaston, face all bloodied, staggering along that path; the furious hand-to-hand fighting across the courtyards where the fountains turned crimson with blood; the heart-stopping terror as they struggled to reach the donjon. And afterwards? The Temple treasure-hold, that serjeant arguing with him . . . Lord Scrope scratched his head and hid his own guilt beneath a seething rage. The arrogant impunity of those Free Brethren! How dare they display such mockery! How could they know his dark secret? Some survivor from Acre, but who? It did not matter. They had provoked their own downfall! Now Edward the King was interfering, reminding Scrope of his promise about the Sanguis Christi, how the attack on the Free Brethren had not been according to statutory law or ordinance of the council. Scrope's powerful friends in church and state at Westminster had protected him; they had also dispatched messages that the King was sending no less a person than Sir Hugh Corbett, Keeper of the Secret Seal, into the shire with full power to investigate what was happening at Mistleham. Corbett! Scrope knew him, lean of face, dark-eyed and sharp-witted, a clerk who could not be threatened or bribed.

Scrope gripped the goblet more tightly, listening to sounds from outside. He promised himself that he would go and check on Romulus and Remus, the great mastiffs who protected the edges of the lake. He eased himself down into the chair and stretched one hand out towards the fire. So much danger! The Sagittarius, an assassin sent by the Temple? Or a survivor of the massacre at Mordern? Yet surely they had all been killed? Brother Gratian had assured him of that, whilst the Dominican had also affirmed that Scrope had only done God's will, so why be afraid? He must deal with all his problems. Father Thomas could be persuaded. Marguerite would, as always, be the loving, supportive sister. He must escape from all these troubles and spend more time enjoying the delicious body of his wife. Of course the Sanguis Christi and the assassin's dagger would have to be returned.

Scrope put down the goblet, took the silver chain from round his neck and moved to the great chest at the foot of the bed. He knelt down, undid the intricate locks on the chest, pushed back the lid and drew out the black coffer with its silver bands and three more locks, each with its own special key. He opened this and stared greedily at the treasures within. The Sanguis Christi, pure gold, those great red rubies glinting even in the dim light of the reclusorium; beside it other precious items looted from the Temple's treasure hoard in Acre. They'd never get those back! The Sanguis Christi he'd hand to the King as a gift, a bribe, a reminder of how loyal Lord Scrope was. He'd also send the King a letter recalling those great days when they'd served shoulder to shoulder in Ireland, Wales or pursuing Scottish rebels through the mist and heather north of the border. He'd entertain Corbett. He'd use Brother Gratian to explain how the Free Brethren were a menace, a threat to the King's peace as well as the teaching of the Church.

Lord Scrope delved deep into the chest, took out a velvet bag, undid the cord and shook out the assassin's dagger. He held it up, the curved steel blade with its wicked point, the bronze handle carved to give a firm grip, the red ribbon of the assassins, the personal emblem of the Old Man of the Mountains, faded and worn, still tied around it. The precious dagger looted from the King's treasury in the crypt of Westminster Abbey! Scrope had read the writ dispatched under close seal by the Chancery office, detailing the items stolen as well as a list of those involved. He'd openly alerted his own henchmen, including Master Claypole the mayor, to keep a watching eye on strangers who entered Mistleham to barter or sell precious goods. Claypole, a goldsmith, had done well in the secret negotiations over such precious items. One of Puddlicott's lieutenants had appeared and boldly approached the good mayor with this dagger and the offer of other valuable items: the robber, John Le Riche, had been seized and easily silenced. The dagger, of course, could not be concealed. Scrope and Claypole had searched for the rest of the treasure but – Scrope ground his teeth – had not found it. Another example of malicious meddling by the Free Brethren! He'd duly informed the King about the dagger. Edward had been so grateful; he should remember that! As for Le Riche, a leading member of Puddlicott's gang, Scrope had decided the dead did not gossip. He'd summarily tried the thief and hanged him on the gibbet at the crossroads leading into Mistleham.

Scrope put the items back, securing the locks of both coffer and chest. He felt better. He walked to the great heavy oaken door, pulled back the grille and peered out. The grey light was now brightening. It was time he returned. He undid the lock, drew back the bolts at top and bottom, opened the door and stood at the top of the steps, bracing himself against the piercing breeze. He stared down at the small jetty where his boat was moored, the approaches to it lit by fires still burning merrily in their great pitch casks. The fresh snow that now carpeted everything had not extinguished them. He stared across the lake, searching for Romulus and Remus. He peered at the cluster of great oaks; the fire built to warm the dogs had burnt low. He glimpsed the dark shapes lying against the whiteness. Something was wrong! His heart skipped a beat; he whistled, but there was no sound, nothing but the cries of rooks and crows. He glanced across the lake: those two poles on the far bank should not be there. Forgetting even to close the door behind him, Scrope hastened down the steps; his slippered feet made this precarious, so he kicked them off, hastening along the jetty and almost threw himself into the boat. Cursing loudly, he pushed away, powerful arms pulling at the oars as he glanced fearfully over his shoulder.

Scrope reached the small mooring place, clambered out and stared in horror at the severed heads of his mastiffs, their snarling faces now frozen masks, necks still bright with blood, one impaled on each side of the jetty, nothing more than hunks of meat. Despite the snow freezing his feet, Scrope was only aware of the fear that sent his heart racing, his stomach churning. He clambered up the hill towards the fire where the dogs should have sheltered: their cadavers now lay next to it, the snow around drenched dark with blood. Scrope crouched down and stared at the long shafts that pierced their carcasses, two in each, death-dealing blows. He clambered to his feet and staggered back, and it was then that he heard it, cutting through the chilling air: the braying sound of a hunting horn.

3

Touching the purchase from a stranger who, recently, after the breaking of the treasury at Westminster . . .

Calendar of Patent Rolls, 1303–1307

Corbett sat back in his chair and listened to the sweet voices of the choir from the minstrel loft of the great hall in Mistleham Manor. He slipped his hand beneath his cloak and touched the silver amulet Lady Maeve had given him at Christmas inscribed with the words from Luke's Gospel: 'Jesus however, passing through the midst of them, went on his way.' He smiled to himself. Lady Maeve had assured him that wearing such an amulet, with the words describing Jesus' miraculous escape from a hostile crowd intent on murder, would always keep him safe. Corbett was certainly glad that his journey to Mistleham had proved safe despite the long, hard riding. They had spent a night at a wayside tavern, cold and dingy, though the food had been good. One of the horses had shed a shoe, so they'd paused at a blacksmith, but eventually they'd reached Mistleham safe and sound.

As soon as they entered the town, Corbett sensed a swirl of violence and fear. A cold, hard day. They'd ridden across the cobbles past the market cross. The stalls were still open. People milled about. Bailiffs clustered around the stocks. Children played. Dogs ran loose. The usual turmoil and clamour of a market day. They'd passed the church; Corbett glimpsed Father Thomas on the steps and the priest had raised a hand in blessing. It seemed as if everybody knew the King's men had arrived. People drew aside giving sharp glances from behind hoods and veils. A few of the young ladies flirted with Ranulf as they made their way through the town. A wealthy, prosperous place. The busy market square was fronted by sturdy timber houses, their wood painted pink, white or black, some of the gables gilded, a few of the lower windows full of gleaming glass. The stalls offered a wide range of goods from skinners, goldsmiths, furriers, butchers, clothiers; their customers appeared well dressed in their long heavy gowns, dresses, tunics and cloaks of brown, green, red and blue. Bailiffs and beadles went about their business. The court of pie-powder sat under the lychgate leading into the parish enclosure. To all appearances Mistleham was a noisy, bustling place but Corbett had sensed the lurking fear and tension of a town under siege. This brooding sense of unease was brought sharply to his attention when a madcap, a moon-fairy in fluttering rags, came dancing out of a runnel to block their way. He had a sharp, dirty face, frenetic eyes, a nose hooked like a bird's and a tongue too big for his mouth. He wore a dirty red hood adorned with shells; in one hand he carried a willow wand, in the other a used pomander which he'd sniff then glare around. He did a jig in front of their horses. Ranulf made to ride forward and drive him away, but Corbett held up his hand.

'*Pax tecum*, brother.' He took off his gauntlet, plucked a coin from his belt purse and spun it towards the fool, who caught it neatly.

'You're not as foolish as you appear.'

'Never has been for old Jackanapes.' The fool sniffed at the pomander and glanced slyly up. 'Old Jackanapes knows you King's man. Come to judge the wicked, have you?' He smiled, upper lip slightly curled to reveal rotting teeth. 'Judgement day not too soon! How long will the wicked prosper, eh, King's man?' Then he was dancing away, calling at them to pass on.

Mistleham Manor proclaimed the same wealth and power as the town. Corbett's party approached the house along a snow-covered path which wound its way through an avenue of oak, beech and elm bordering snow-covered paddocks. The manor, built square on a slight rise, was of gleaming honey-coloured stone especially imported from the Cotswolds. It boasted a black-tiled sloping roof, chimney stacks and spacious windows, some filled with stretched horn, others with mullioned or even painted glass in their gleaming black frames. The magnificent front door was approached by sweeping steps. The main house had been built as a long hall with an upper storey, wings having been added at either end; a fourth side completed the square, which was pierced by an imposing gateway in the middle. This led into a great cobbled yard or bailey where kitchens, stables, outhouses, smithies, kennels and servants' quarters were situated. Retainers wearing Scrope's livery of russet and green came bustling out to take their horses, whilst others escorted them into the house to meet Brother Gratian. The Dominican whispered how there had been 'an unfortunate and very unpleasant incident earlier in the day', but declared that, God willing, Lord Scrope and Lady Hawisa would meet them later at a special dinner arranged in their honour.

Corbett was given his own chamber along the Jerusalem Gallery in the east wing of the house. Ranulf and Chanson were to share the Damascus Room, the name given to a chamber above the great gatehouse. Scrope, Corbett quickly learnt, lived in luxury: tiled floors on the ground level, gleaming floorboards on the upper storeys. The walls of the manor were half covered in shiny oaken linen panels, the plaster above painted a light restful green and adorned with coloured cloths, small tapestries, diptychs, paintings and exquisitely carved crosses. The furnishings were equally splendid, finely cut and carved out of gleaming wood, clearly the work of skilled craftsmen from London or Norwich. Corbett's chamber was the one always given to any guest of honour. Brother Gratian whispered how the King himself had stayed there around Michaelmas three years ago and thoroughly enjoyed himself. Corbett cordially agreed. The room was dominated by a great four-poster bed adorned with red and gold hangings and silver tassels. On each side of the bed stood small oaken tables with six-branch candelabra; the candles were long, tapering and pure white. A chest with its own locks and clasps rested at the foot of the bed for Corbett's possessions, and against the far wall was an aumbry with hooks and racks for clothes. The window embrasure, its small panes all glass-filled, had cushioned seats. Beneath the small oriel window stood a writing table with a high-backed leather-quilted chair. In the centre of the table a silver crucifix stretched above a tray of sharpened quills and an array of ink pots, sander, pumice stone and parchment knives. The room was warmed by small wheeled braziers, capped and glowing, easily moved around to give off their herb-scented heat. A huge lavarium stood in one corner, bearing a great bowl; its other tray held a wicker basket full of rare soap, and the rods jutting out from the main stem were draped with napkins and towels. Brother Gratian explained how servants would bring up hot water as well as a wooden tub for bathing. He added that an ease chamber stood close by on the gallery outside whilst – he pointed to the table just inside the door – wine, water and ale would always be available.

Corbett half listened as Chanson stored away his Chancery panniers and coffers. He was more interested in studying the Dominican. He had met members of this order before; a few he'd liked, others seemed totally absorbed with some special task given to them by God. Brother Gratian belonged to the latter. Garbed in his black and white robes, a cord tied tightly around his waist, feet in their heavy sandals, he was a true inquisitor. He had a narrow face, hard black eyes and a slightly twisted nose above prim, bloodless lips: a hunter, Corbett concluded. Gratian's speech was clear, his movements sharp and precise, long bony fingers constantly enforcing his words. A man, Corbett reasoned, more concerned with justice than compassion, and one who apparently regarded Lord Scrope as a true pillar of Holy Mother Church. At first the Dominican was rather nervous of the royal clerks, but eventually Corbett's watchful silence was taken as approval and he led them on a tour of the mansion, Ranulf and Chanson trailing behind. The Principal Clerk in the Chancery of the Green Wax glared at the back of the Dominican's balding head and recalled that fateful day in Newgate years ago when he'd been led out to be hanged for a litany of petty felonies. A Dominican had shrived him as he waited for the execution cart, assuring him that his stay in purgatory would be long: little comfort, Ranulf reflected, after his neck had been stretched at the Elms. A short while later Corbett had appeared, Master Long Face staring at him with that strange amused gaze, and Ranulf's life had been transformed. Ranulf clicked his tongue. Eventually he caught Chanson's attention and began to cleverly mimic the Dominican's mannerisms as he showed them the great hall, the solar, the perfect jewel of the private chapel, the kitchens and sculleries full of steam and savoury smells as cooks busily prepared the evening banquet.

Corbett was keen to investigate the tension he sensed in the manor. He had already glimpsed the cadavers of the two great hunting dogs, legs peeping out from beneath the rough sacking thrown over them in the manor bailey. Moreover Brother Gratian proved strangely reluctant to take them out through the gateway at the back of the manor. Corbett gently insisted, so the Dominican escorted them along the path to the brow of the hill which swept down to the Island of Swans and its impressive reclusorium. Corbett was immediately taken with the ring of shimmering water, the jetties facing each other, the steep steps leading up to the heavy door of the reclusorium. Then his attention was diverted by the great reddish-brown stains near the edge of the lake as well as similar ones further up the hill, near the remains of a fire built close to a copse of trees.

'What happened?' Ranulf asked watching servants and retainers, garbed in Lord Scrope's livery, scurrying about amongst the trees. In the far distance mounted figures could be glimpsed: undoubtedly Lord Scrope and his henchmen searching for something. 'What happened?' he repeated.

'The Sagittarius,' Brother Gratian replied reluctantly. 'A mysterious bowman who is terrorising Mistleham. He has already slain a number of innocents. Apparently last night,' he continued hastily, 'or early this morning, the Sagittarius entered the manor lands. Lord Scrope had withdrawn to the reclusorium.' Brother Gratian pointed to the island.

'Why?'

'To pray, to reflect, to meditate.'

'Why?' Ranulf repeated.

Brother Gratian's cold, pinched face broke into a

wintry smile. 'You had best ask Lord Scrope that.' He hurried on. 'The Sagittarius committed trespass. He killed the mastiffs, severed their heads and stuck these on poles down near the jetty. Lord Scrope was furious.' The Dominican was gabbling now. 'That's why he was unable to meet you, whilst Lady Hawisa has withdrawn to her own chambers.'

'Why kill the mastiffs?' Ranulf persisted. 'Were they used during the massacre at Mordern?'

'It was not a massacre,' Gratian retorted, 'but the extirpation of a nest of heretics, lecherous fornicators and thieves, and yes,' he faced Ranulf squarely, 'the mastiffs were used in the attack on that lawless rabble at Mordern.'

The conversation had definitely chilled the Dominican's mood. Corbett tactfully declared that he was cold, so Gratian led them back to the kitchens for goblets of mulled wine spiced with nutmeg, and a platter of manchet loaves, soft cheese and butter. Afterwards Corbett withdrew to his own room. Ranulf and Chanson, at their master's secret direction, were to wander the manor listening to conversations, the rumours and gossip in the hall, kitchen and stable. Corbett checked certain items in his own chamber then went to the small chapel. He lit a taper before the black-stone carving of the Virgin and knelt on the quilted prie-dieu. He prayed for Maeve, his children and the King. To lighten his mood he softly sang his favourite hymn to the Virgin: 'Alma Virgo Dei'. He blessed himself and returned to his own chamber, where he stripped, wrapped a cloak about himself and slept until Ranulf roused him. He rose, shaved, washed and changed into his best; a long murrey-coloured jerkin over a white cambric shirt and black hose pushed into a soft pair of leather boots. He put his chain of office around his neck and the large signet ring bearing the royal arms on the middle finger of his left hand.

Corbett, now sitting in the great banqueting hall of the manor, secretly hoped he would not have to exercise the power that ring gave him. He broke from his reflections, sat back in his chair and continued to listen to the sweet songs from the minstrel gallery, followed by the soft melodies of the viol, rebec and lyre. He tapped his fingers on the ivory-coloured tablecloth in appreciation of the music whilst admiring the wealth of the hall: the great fire roaring merrily in the carved mantled hearth, the polished wood posts and furnishings, the jewelled silverware on the high table and the exquisite salt cellar fashioned out of costly jasper. Catherine wheels, their rims studded with gleaming lamps, had been lowered to strengthen the light from the silver-chased candlesticks as well as the cresset torches blazing along the walls.

Corbett also used the musical interlude and the silence it demanded in the hall, on the dais as well as among those sitting below the salt, to quietly study his host and other guests. Lord Scrope, dressed in a costly red robe, his fingers, arms and neck adorned with glittering rings, bracelets, brooches and clasps, looked the powerful seigneur. Corbett had met him years ago and the passage of time had not improved his estimation of the King's old warrior comrade. Lord Oliver was a choleric man, his ugly face indeed like that of a bat, his narrow, darting eyes full of his own importance and pride. A dangerous man, Corbett concluded, quick-tempered and cruel, who could carry out a massacre like that at Mordern without any scruple or regret. Lady Hawisa, sitting on her husband's left, was totally different, with her comely ivory face, serene grey eyes and laughing mouth. She was garbed in a light blue dress tied high around the neck, a filigreed chain around her waist, a cream-coloured veil covering her rich black hair. She had a merry laugh and a welcoming, courteous voice. Before they had taken their seats, she had asked the clerks about their journey then quietly insisted that they must find everything at Mistleham Manor to their liking.

Corbett leaned forward and glanced down the table. Ranulf was sitting on Lady Hawisa's left. The

Principal Clerk in the Chancery of the Green Wax had immediately shown a deep liking for her. Corbett silently prayed that Scrope did not take offence at Ranulf's open admiration and consequent flirtation with his wife. He caught the eye of Father Thomas, smiled and nodded. He had met the priest during the King's campaign in Wales. Father Thomas had a hard, lined face under thinning grey hair, a frugal man dressed in a simple brown robe, his bleak austerity offset by gentle eyes. During their meeting before the banquet, Corbett had noticed how the priest barely sipped at his wine, being more concerned with threading the Ave beads around his bony knuckles. Next to him was a bird of different character: Master Claypole the mayor, lean and tense like a ferret, with close-set eyes, a nose sharp as a quill, his lower lip jutting out as if ready for any argument. Corbett felt his elbow brushed and turned to a smiling Dame Marguerite, Lady Abbess of St Frideswide, small, petite and pretty-faced. He found it almost impossible to believe that this elegant abbess, her face framed by a snow-white wimple under a black veil, was Lord Scrope's blood sister. She played with the gold ring on one of her fingers, emblazoned with what looked like a deer, whilst beating gently on the tablecloth, thoroughly enjoying the music.

'But I am hungry,' she leaned forward grinning

impishly, 'whilst my chaplain is ready to eat his own knuckles.'

Corbett leaned forward and nodded at Master Benedict, who, throughout the music, had been staring at Corbett, eyes all anxious, fingers to his lips. Corbett glanced away to hide his own annoyance. Benedict Le Sanglier was an ambitious priest, a Gascon bearing letters from the Archbishop of Bordeaux. He had, during their meeting before dinner, attempted to show Corbett these as well as declare how desirous he was of securing a benefice at court.

'I mean,' he pleaded, pulling a pious expression, 'I want to give good service, I am most skilled as a clerk.' Westminster, Corbett ruefully conceded, was full of such men clamouring for promotion. Benedict Le Sanglier was from the English-held province of Gascony; now in England, he was determined to secure advancement through the royal service into a host of benefices. Corbett had eventually been rescued by Ranulf, who whispered how the abbess' chaplain, with his clear eyes, smooth shaved face and mop of neatly cut blond hair, was truly a sheep in wolf's clothing.

Corbett sipped the sweet wine, then hastily put his goblet down as the music ended. Brother Gratian abruptly rose to sing grace in a high nasal tone. After the benediction, the trumpeters in the minstrel gallery blew long, sharp blasts as the cooks processed in carrying the main dishes, venison, pork, quail and fish all served in piquant sauces, whilst servants hurried along the dais with jugs of the richest claret. A true feast. Corbett ate well but drank sparingly, appreciating that the real business would begin once the banquet ended. He became involved in courteous but bland conversation with Scrope and Dame Marguerite about the doings of the court, the politics of Westminster, the Scottish threat, the weather and the urgent need for the King to implement his Statute of Highways. Frumentaries and pastries were served. Tumblers, acrobats, jesters and buffoons did their whirling jigs. Scrope's troubadour, who rejoiced in the name of Shilling, led the ale minstrels and gleemen in singing an old Crusader hymn, which Corbett thoroughly enjoyed.

The meal then ended. Those dining beneath the salt around tables ranged along the hall, Chanson included, were left to their feasting whilst Lord Scrope and his guests on the dais adjourned to the solar on the floor above. This was a comfortable timber-rafted room, the area around the great hearth partitioned off by screens decorated with scenes from the life of King Arthur. Chairs and stools had been placed before the roaring fire; tables in between these bore goblets and jugs of wine and ale. Scrope and Lady Hawisa took the central chairs, gesturing at the others to take the same seating arrangement as at the banquet. At first Corbett was surprised that all had been invited, but then concluded that Lord Oliver must view his other guests as allies and supporters. Once the servants had withdrawn, Scrope, his sweaty face wreathed in a false smile, gestured at Corbett.

'Sir Hugh, you are most welcome. I understand his grace has sent you to deal with certain matters.' He played with the ring on the little finger of his left hand.

'The Sanguis Christi.' Corbett decided the time for courtesy was over.

'It will be handed over as promised.'

'And the assassin's dagger?'

'That too!'

'To me?' Corbett demanded.

'The assassin's dagger is truly the King's,' Scrope agreed.

'Stolen by felons.'

'Apprehended by Lord Oliver,' Master Claypole intervened 'as well as by the vigilance of the King's loyal subjects in Mistleham.'

'Yes, yes,' Corbett soothed. 'The felon Le Riche tried to sell the item to a goldsmith?'

'Namely me.' Claypole smirked. 'I too am a member of that guild. I lured the thief to the guildhall, where Lord Oliver's men were waiting to arrest him.'

'And the dagger is of rolled gold?' Ranulf asked innocently. He and Corbett had rehearsed these questions on their journey here.

'Ah, no.' Claypole looked confused.

'So why sell it to a goldsmith?' Corbett intervened. 'I mean, he had no other items taken from the crypt?'

'Of course not!' Scrope snapped. 'Corbett, what are you saying? Le Riche attempted to sell a dagger as something precious. He was seized, tried and hanged. I understand that other members of the gang did similar business in different parts of the kingdom.'

'I was there,' Brother Gratian broke in.

'Were you really?' Ranulf asked.

'I shrived the prisoner,' the Dominican replied.

'So,' Corbett leaned back in his chair, 'Le Riche was apprehended in the guildhall, he was disarmed and searched, the dagger was found upon him and he was detained?'

'In the dungeons beneath the guildhall,' Claypole snapped.

'On the morrow he was tried before me and Master Claypole,' Lord Scrope declared. He gestured at Benedict Le Sanglier.

'I was a witness. It was all done according to the law,' the chaplain spluttered. 'An evil man, Sir Hugh! Le Riche had been caught red-handed, a traitor . . .'

'I do have the power of noose and tumbril in these

parts,' Lord Oliver trumpeted. 'You know that, Sir Hugh! Le Riche was a self-confessed traitor, a felon caught red-handed, publicly proscribed by the Crown, which had dispatched letters to me and the sheriff at Colchester. In accordance with those instructions I seized Le Riche, tried him, then hanged him.'

'You could have held him over for further questioning.'

Scrope made a dismissive gesture. 'A petty felon,' he declared, 'who fled with an item stolen from the royal treasury. He could say nothing else, provide no information, except plead for mercy. I showed him that mercy. Brother Gratian shrived him, I gave him wine and food, a comfortable cell.' Scrope shrugged. 'And then I hanged him.'

'That is true,' Dame Marguerite intervened, her face all smiling. 'Master Benedict here was an official witness at the execution.'

'And?' Corbett turned to the abbess' chaplain.

'He seemed wandering in his wits,' Master Benedict declared. 'He sprawled in the execution cart, isn't that true, Brother Gratian? Father Thomas, you too were there.'

'A poor unfortunate,' the parish priest replied, 'long-haired and bearded, poorly clothed. He could hardly stand to climb the ladder. The town's hangman had to hold him.'

'And all he carried when arrested was the assassin's dagger stolen from Westminster?' Corbett insisted.

'Sir Hugh,' Lady Hawisa intervened, her pretty face all concerned, 'what are you alleging? I was in Mistleham with my husband when Mayor Claypole sent a scurrier with the news that Le Riche was detained.'

'Are you,' the mayor declared, 'implying that Le Riche carried more than a dagger? If he did, we certainly did not see it!'

'When was Le Riche caught and hanged?'

'In November, around the Feast of St Cecilia.'

'Yet the robbery at the abbey took place last April. Didn't you ask the felon where he'd been for the last seven months?'

'Yes, in hiding.'

Corbett nodded as if this satisfied him, though in truth it certainly did not. Suspicions pricked his mind, but he thought it would be best to leave the matter for a while. He sensed the mood was changing, but there again, it always did once the pleasantries and courtesies were over, the outer skin of the onion, as Ranulf once described it, peeled off. Now they were to probe what lay beneath.

'So the Sanguis Christi, you will hand it over?'

'I have said I will . . .'

'To me, the King's envoy?'

'Sir Hugh,' Scrope crossed his legs and smiled, his lips belying the anger blazing in his eyes, 'I am no rebel, traitor or thief suing for terms. I shall give the King, as I solemnly promised him, the precious relic. I shall do so very soon. Brother Gratian here will return to Westminster. He will hand over the Sanguis Christi. He will be my envoy.'

Corbett ignored Ranulf's hiss of disapproval and stared into the fire. He recalled what he and Maeve had discussed in their solar at the Manor of Leighton, how an individual being was more than flesh and blood, but spirit, the invisible contained within the visible. So it was here: bland stories and easy lies concealed devilish trickery.

'And the Free Brethren of the Holy Spirit?' Corbett glimpsed the abrupt shift in Scrope's eyes and sensed he was walking into a trap. 'Fourteen people,' he continued remorselessly, 'butchered. I believe they were unarmed and not accused of any crime; no law or authority was invoked.' He let his voice trail off. He sensed he was only helping Scrope, who now sat clearly enjoying himself, chewing the corner of his mouth. Gratian also sat up, preening like a cat. Corbett became acutely aware that the more he said, the deeper the trap would become. Scrope had prepared carefully for this confrontation.

'Do continue, please.' The manor lord smiled. 'What

is it, Sir Hugh? Do you want me to go to Westminster and plead before Staunton and Hengham at King's Bench?'

'That could be arranged,' Corbett replied quietly. 'I could swear out the writ now; Ranulf would draft it for sealing.'

Scrope turned and shouted at the door. The captain of his guard tumbled through, a tough-looking soldier with balding head and popping blue eyes in a wine-flushed face.

'Bring out the arrow chest, Robert, the one taken from Mordern.'

The fellow bowed and hurried away.

'Now,' Scrope turned and pointed a finger at Corbett, 'listen, Sir Hugh. The Free Brethren of the Holy Spirit were French, one of those many groups who wander the face of God's earth preaching the freedom of religion. Their name is legion. They accept what they like of Holy Mother Church's teaching, then peddle their own theories. Some are harmless enough, others are highly dangerous, a real threat to the soul, emissaries of the Lord Satan.'

Corbett held his peace.

'The Free Brethren arrived here at the beginning of Lent last year. Fourteen in all, they gave themselves biblical names. Their leaders, Adam and Eve, were presentable enough but took to lying like a bird to flying; golden-haired and golden-mouthed, they were most persuasive. I allowed them to settle in the village of Mordern. They offered labour in return for food.'

'They executed a fine painting in my church, Sir Hugh, finished around the Feast of St Augustine. Vividly beautiful, isn't it?'

A murmur of approval greeted Father Thomas' words; this faded at a knock on the door. The two retainers brought in a battered arrow chest. They placed this in front of Lord Scrope, bowed and withdrew. The manor lord, with a flourish of triumph, kicked back the jutting lid with the toe of his boot. Corbett nodded at Ranulf, who crouched down and began to lift out the contents: two longbows, the yew still gleaming; two quivers of long ash arrows, iron-tipped, with grey goose feathers; two Brabantine crossbows; the same number of battle axes; daggers and Welsh stabbing swords, short and squat with wicked-looking points and serrated edges. Corbett picked up a bow about a man's height in length. It was fashioned completely out of yew with a firm cord grip and stringed with powerful twine. He twanged this, pulling it back slightly as he repressed his own nightmares about the bloody havoc these longbows had wreaked during the King's campaign in Wales: men pierced through by arrows from such powerful weapons, deadly enough to bring down a mailed warhorse and its armoured rider. A master bowman could loose ten shafts in the space of a few heartbeats. He put the weapon down and, with his foot, sifted amongst the others.

'They're new,' he murmured, 'but according to all the evidence, they were penniless. Moreover, they landed at Dover . . .'

'Precisely.' Scrope's tone was almost a jeer. 'They carried letters from the cardinals at Avignon, sealed and dated over a year old.' He turned and snapped his fingers. Brother Gratian handed over a leather pouch; Scrope emptied the contents and handed the tattered scrolls to Corbett. The clerk unrolled these and studied them closely. They were yellowing and fingered with age, though they still carried the purple seal of the curial offices at Avignon. Issued under the name of Cardinal Caetani, they were the usual licences granted to such wandering groups, asking that the Free Brethren of the Holy Spirit be allowed safe passage.

'The port reeves of the Keeper of Dover,' Corbett murmured, 'would see these. They'd search their baggage, find no weapons or contraband and allow them through the gates.' He paused. 'As far as their religion was concerned,' he added drily, 'I am sure the good fathers at Avignon were not fully appraised of the Free Brethren's attitude to the Church's teaching on certain sensitive matters. So,' he concluded, 'how did they buy these weapons? How did they obtain the silver needed?'

'Or did someone else supply them?' Ranulf asked.

'And for what?' Corbett mused. 'But,' he pointed at Scrope, 'you only found these weapons after your attack on the Free Brethren?'

'No, no, no.' Scrope smiled, shaking his head. 'Brother Gratian, tell them what happened.'

'By late autumn,' Brother Gratian leaned forward as if he was a preacher in his pulpit lecturing his congregation, 'rumours were rife about the activities of the Free Brethren. Horrid allegations were levelled about their lechery, their lack of honesty, their deceit. Moreover, they were openly preaching doctrines rejected by our Church. Anyway, I went into the forest of Mordern, to the village there, to reason with the Brethren, to ask them to restrain themselves, even to clear the accusations laid against them.'

'And did they respond?' Corbett asked.

'No.' Gratian shook his head. 'More's the pity, Sir Hugh! They just mocked and ridiculed me. Their mood had changed. I didn't like it. They were not hospitable. True, they offered no violence, but they refused to obey. Now, outside the deserted church there's a headstone, long battered by the rain and weather. As I left the meeting, I noticed how it had been recently used as soldiers do to sharpen their blades. When I came back, I informed Lord Scrope.'

'I immediately became suspicious.' The manor lord took up the story. 'Sir Hugh, stories were rife of deer being poached, of quail and pheasant being brought down. One of my verderers found an arrow embedded in a tree trunk. So I decided to investigate further. I sent my huntsmen into the forest with strict instructions to watch and observe the Free Brethren. Now for most of the day they went about their usual mischief, wandering into Mistleham or the farms around. Occasionally they'd congregate in Father Thomas' church. They were, to all appearances, harmless enough except for those stories, but I maintained a strict watch. Eventually one of my verderers reported that he'd espied them practising archery deep in the forest, and from what he reported, they were skilled at loosing and often hitting their mark. One suspicion begets another. I had them more closely watched. Towards the end of October, Adam, their leader, left the community and journeyed towards the coast. He visited Orwell, where he frequented a tavern, the Lantern Horn, being closeted with the captain of a small cog, Robert Picard.'

Corbett glanced up. 'I've heard that name.'

'He is a well-known smuggler, contraband as well as people who wish to leave or enter the kingdom without licence. When this was reported back to me I was intrigued. Here was a group of men and women sheltering on my lands, causing disruption, and the subject of foul allegations. They were not what they pretended to be. They were well armed, possibly preparing to attack this manor then flee to seek passage at an Essex port and go beyond the seas. Why? They had been in England for over six months and spent most of their time in Mordern, close to here. I reasoned they'd discovered my wealth, perhaps even heard stories about the Sanguis Christi. They plotted to attack Mistleham Manor, Corbett. I have a right to defend what is mine. Moreover, I am responsible for the King's peace in the area. The Free Brethren were thieves, lechers and heretics.'

'Rumours,' Father Thomas interjected. 'There are always rumours about this or that.'

'But sometimes true!' Claypole snapped. 'My daughter Beatrice, my only daughter, she was much taken by one of the group, a young man called Seth. I did not like him. She would seize any opportunity to escape from the house and meet him, either in town or on its outskirts, even in the forest itself. What did he have to offer, what did he want except to slake his own lust?'

Corbett sensed the hatred and anger in the mayor's face and voice, a man deeply insulted by the Free Brethren.

'Why didn't you just disarm them?' Ranulf asked. 'Take them by surprise, holding them prisoner for questioning?'

'But I did,' Scrope murmured, rubbing the corner of his mouth. 'I did, Master Ranulf! I sent Brother Gratian here with a formal summons that they present themselves either here or in the guildhall.'

'And their response?'

'They mocked me,' Brother Gratian replied. 'They said they would beat me like a dog and go about their business. They did not have to answer to any summons or to any lord.'

Corbett nodded understandingly. Scrope was preparing a defence that would be accepted before King's Bench or any court in the land. He was lord of the manor. He had well-founded suspicions that a coven posed a real danger to the King's peace. He had sent them a formal summons to appear in his court to answer the charges. They had not only refused but mocked his messenger.

'Early in the morning on the Feast of St Ambrose I summoned my own men,' Scrope declared, 'and levies from the town, about a hundred and fifty men in all. We entered the forest carefully. I took my mastiffs Romulus and Remus with me. We would use them to make sure that none escaped . . .'

'Did they have guards, sentries?' Corbett asked.

'Oh yes. He was killed, offering resistance, and the alarm was raised. Once again I sent Brother Gratian forward, carrying a cross. He pleaded with them to surrender. They replied with,' Scrope pointed to an arbalest, 'a crossbow bolt. My men attacked. The Free Brethren resisted where they could but they hadn't time to arm themselves properly. We forced the church. It was all over very swiftly. Eight were killed outright; the other six were seriously wounded. Eve was killed. Adam received a blow here.' Scrope pointed to the side of his neck. 'I asked him to confess, and he just cursed me. My blood was up; the heat of battle still thrilled me. I ordered him and the rest to be hanged on the nearest trees. By the time the Jesus bell tolled it was all finished.'

'Then what happened?'

'We searched the village, especially the church,' Scrope declared. He paused for effect, lifted his hand and snapped his fingers. 'We found these . . .'

4

Who knowingly received the said treasure?
Letter of Edward, I, 6 June 1303

Brother Gratian picked up two pieces of parchment and handed them to Corbett. The first was a skilfully and very neatly drawn map of Mistleham Manor, particularly its walls, gardens and grounds, the Island of Swans and the reclusorium. The parchment was of good quality, the ink a deep black. The second was a coarser parchment but easy to read, short and terse, an indenture in which Robert Picard, master of the cog *Mortmain*, promised to take, sometime before the eve of the Nativity, the Free Brethren of the Holy Spirit to a port of their choosing in Hainault, Zealand or Flanders, the choice being made once they boarded his ship. The price fixed was half a mark per person, the date on the indenture December 1303. Corbett smiled to himself. Picard was a well-known rogue, notorious for smuggling, closely watched by the sheriffs of East Anglia: a character the clerks of the

Exchequer would love to interrogate. He was, however, as wily as a snake. He must have heard about the massacre and would disappear for months.

'See, Corbett?' Lord Scrope could hardly contain his glee. 'I was justified in my attack. This coven was causing mayhem on my lands, concealing weapons, pretending to be what they were not. They had a map of my manor and an indenture to take sudden flight. Tell that to his grace the King.'

Corbett ignored the implied insult.

'Did you discover anything else?'

'No.'

'Why did you leave the corpses? Why not bury them?'

'A warning to everyone else, especially the people of Mistleham.' Scrope leaned forward. 'Don't forget, Sir Hugh, as Master Claypole remarked, the Free Brethren did have their admirers and supporters amongst the townspeople. I wanted this matter to be brought to an abrupt end.'

'Are you sure they all died; no one fled?'

'No one,' Scrope declared. 'I took the two mastiffs, Romulus and Remus. They searched but they could detect no trail, no sign of any fugitive. Moreover, I inspected all the corpses, as did Brother Gratian and Father Thomas; they knew their faces, they could account for each and every one of the Free Brethren.'

'Too true,' the parish priest murmured sadly, 'all dead. May God rest them. My lord,' he turned to Corbett, 'vengeance has been carried out; they must be given honourable requiem, the corpses disposed of somehow. Yet now,' he added wistfully, 'the ground has grown very hard.'

'I will come to that,' Corbett intervened. 'So,' he turned back to Scrope, 'the Free Brethren are all dead?'

'Yes.'

'When you searched the church, you discovered the weapons and those two documents?'

'Yes.'

'Anything else?'

'No.'

'And yet,' Corbett continued remorselessly, 'it's not finished. This Bowman, this Sagittarius, has emerged to exact vengeance. He has already killed five—'

'Seven!' Scrope retorted. 'Most of the killings take place on lonely paths, someone coming out of a door, but the last two, Eadburga and Wilfred, were slain in God's own daylight in our marketplace.'

'So this Sagittarius must be a master bowman,' Corbett declared, 'someone very skilled, moving fast.'

'I would say so.'

'And the victims are chosen at random?'

'So it seems,' Lady Hawisa interjected, 'but all were

young people, Sir Hugh, full of life and love.' She smiled at Ranulf.

'Revenge, then,' Corbett declared, 'for the killings at Mordern? So there must have been a fifteenth member?'

'We know of no such person.' Scrope scratched his head. 'I have questioned Brother Gratian and Father Thomas on this. Master Claypole also has done his searches. There was no fifteenth member.'

'Or someone deeply devoted to the Free Brethren?'

'But who?' Lady Hawisa asked. 'Sir Hugh, you've heard my husband. The Free Brethren had friends amongst the young of the town, but a skilled bowman, someone prepared to kill and kill again?'

'True,' Dame Marguerite intervened. 'Wilfred and Eadburga were killed just outside St Alphege's, where I was sheltering. Master Benedict was guarding the side door. I'd come to meet Lady Hawisa; we were talking. Sir Hugh, it was so sudden, that horrid horn sounding.'

'Horn?' Ranulf asked.

'Always, before the Sagittarius strikes,' Scrope murmured. 'Three blasts of a hunting horn.'

'Then death comes showering down,' Benedict whispered.

'And now he has struck at you.' Corbett gestured at Lord Scrope. 'Your two mastiffs were killed last night. How could that be done?'

Scrope just shrugged. Corbett decided not to pursue

the matter any further. He would have to reflect. Both he and Scrope knew that in Wales, enemy bowmen had crept into the King's camp and loosed their deadly shafts at anyone they chose. He could imagine that something similar had happened last night at the manor. The Sagittarius scaling the curtain wall, probably dressed in a white cloak, moving swiftly. The dogs, dozing by the fire, would be aroused, dark shapes against the snow and glowing flames, an easy enough target for a skilled archer.

'So, to answer my earlier question.' Ranulf half smiled. 'The mastiffs were slain because they were at Mordern?'

'Or as a warning,' Brother Gratian declared.

'But there is more, isn't there, my lord?' Father Thomas leaned forward, hands fluttering.

'Two nights ago,' Lord Scrope had lost some of his arrogance, 'the same day Wilfred and Eadburga's corpses were laid out in the church, Father Thomas received a visitor. He didn't call himself the Sagittarius but Nightshade. God knows why he took such a repellent title; however, he threatened that unless I make full confession of all my sins at the market cross, more vengeance would follow.'

'What sins, Lord Scrope?' Ranulf asked sardonically.

The manor lord didn't even glance at him, let alone reply.

'My lord,' Corbett was eager to break the tension, wary of Scrope's violent temper, 'the Free Brethren came here to the manor?'

Scrope nodded.

'And Father Thomas, they visited your church?'

'Of course,' the priest murmured.

'And they must have gone to St Frideswide to beg, to seek help?'

'Yes, they did.' Dame Marguerite smiled. 'Sir Hugh, I found them harmless enough. The young men, well, they were lean, fit as greyhounds. They certainly caused a flutter amongst the novices, yet in my dealings with them I found them fairly innocent, a little stupid, naive, living as if they were flowers under the summer sun. But we were all young once, we all had our dreams. I felt for them. They teased me about my vows of chastity and the rule of St Benedict. Still,' she smiled, 'I found them honest. I gave them work on our land, gardening, clearing away rubbish, pruning a herb, cutting a hedge, clearing outhouses and latrines. They always worked hard, I always paid them.'

'And you, Master Benedict?'

The chaplain blushed and shuffled his feet. 'I was taken by some of the young ladies. They were fair and gracious. They would tease me about my celibacy and asked why I didn't imitate the poverty of Christ. I admit, Sir Hugh, I could find no answer to that. They were not of my calling but they meant well. I am sorry they are dead.'

'You are sure of that?' Corbett asked. 'That they were all killed?'

'Yes,' Dame Marguerite intervened. 'When I heard about the attack, I couldn't believe all had been slain. I asked Brother Benedict here to go to Mordern. He knew all of the members by face if not by name. He came back to report that all were dead. I disagree with my brother: perhaps they did deserve execution, perhaps they were a threat to the King's peace, but now they are dead, they must be buried.'

'And so they will be.' Corbett straightened up. 'I carry the King's warrant in this matter. Tomorrow morning, Lord Scrope, I, and some of your retainers, will go out to Mordern. We will collect the corpses. If the ground is too hard, which I suspect it is, they will be burnt. Father Thomas, Master Benedict, you are most welcome to come. I would like the corpses blessed, given the rites, some prayers. God's work and that of the King shall be done.' Both priests agreed. Lord Scrope pulled a face and looked away. 'One final matter.' Corbett lifted his hand. 'Lord Scrope, you returned from Acre about twelve years ago, yet the events we have just described occurred only in the last twelve months.' He paused. 'So, let me get the sequence of events clear in my own mind. The

Free Brethren arrived last year at the beginning of Lent, early March 1303?' Everyone nodded in agreement. 'They moved into the forest of Mordern and settled in the deserted village there. At first they were accepted. You, my lord, disliked some of their teachings but they seemed innocent enough.' Again a murmur of agreement. 'They worked in the parish church,' Corbett continued, 'rendering a vivid painting. Then, during November last, Lord Scrope, your suspicions were aroused that the Free Brethren were not what they pretended to be: the sharpening of weapons, the practice of archery in the forest, the journey to Orwell. You decided to strike, and by the end of Advent, the Free Brethren were all dead. In the New Year the Sagittarius appeared, inflicting vengeance wherever he could. Now all this occurred in the last year. So what has changed? You, Master Benedict, have been in England for how long?'

The chaplain blew his cheeks out. 'Oh, about fifteen months. As I told you, Sir Hugh, I did good service in Bordeaux and I was given letters of accreditation to the Lady Abbess here.'

'Yes, yes, and you, Brother Gratian?'

'I have been Lord Scrope's confessor for about a year. He wrote to our house at Blackfriars and asked them to choose a man. They selected me, and I was happy to come.'

Corbett was about to continue when the lowing of a hunting horn brayed through the night. Not even the thickness of the manor walls or the shutters across the windows could dull the threatening sound. Corbett thought he had been mistaken, but then the note came again, braying long and mournful.

'Where is he?' Lord Scrope whispered. 'He must be here.'

It was as if some evil wraith had swirled into the solar. A deathly silence, followed by clamour as people sprang to their feet. Corbett was more interested in the horn-blowing and wondered how close the Sagittarius was to the manor. Scrope, however, was hurrying towards the solar door, the sound of servants running echoing along the gallery outside. Everyone followed the manor lord out, but Corbett gestured at Ranulf to stay.

'Are we under attack?' Ranulf whispered. He had changed for the banquet, dressed similarly to Corbett, though he'd also brought his war belt. He went to pick this up from the floor but caught Corbett's quick shake of the head and stopped even as the third horn blast echoed from the darkness outside.

'What do you think, master?'

'Murder!' Corbett whispered. 'The demon that slumbers like bread in an oven. A person can appear witless as a pigeon yet be as swift as the wynkin.

Appearances do not matter here. Murder nestles like a fledging bird in its nest, growing in strength then, one day, taking sudden flight. This is what is happening, Ranulf. Ancient sins bursting to ripeness, spitting out their poison.' He paused as Dame Marguerite, followed by her chaplain, slipped back into the solar, closing the door behind them. Corbett could hear Lady Hawisa calling for more lights and lanterns as her husband organised others into searching the demesne. 'Madam.' Corbett made to rise, but Dame Marguerite gestured otherwise as she sat in Scrope's chair, indicating that Master Benedict sit next to her.

'Sir Hugh, I do not know what is happening,' she declared breathlessly, 'but I am sure there is no real danger to us now. I must tell you this.' She shook one hand free from her voluminous sleeve and leaned closer. Corbett caught the fragrance of her light perfume. 'My brother is truly a man of blood,' she whispered hoarsely. 'The Free Brethren may have been heretics, thieves, lechers, whatever he may accuse them of, but to cut them down so ruthlessly, to assume the role of God's avenging angel . . .' She shook her head. 'I will be swift as a hawk in its swoop, Sir Hugh: one man did survive the massacre at Mordern. In truth, an idiot, a jack of the woods, a madcap; he saw what happened.'

'Who?' Ranulf interrupted.

'Jackanapes, an orphan, weak in wits but blunt in tongue,' Dame Marguerite whispered, glancing fearfully at the door. 'He dresses like a buffoon and lives off the charity of the manor and the likes of St Frideswide. You must meet him.'

Corbett recalled the jerking, ragged-haired beggar man who had greeted them as they passed through Mistleham.

'He saw what happened?'

'Yes. He'd gone there early in the morning before the attack was launched to beg for food.'

'How did he escape?' Ranulf asked. 'Hounds were used.'

Dame Marguerite turned to Master Benedict.

'Jackanapes is fey and witless,' the chaplain declared. 'He comes down to St Frideswide to beg, that is how I found out what happened. He gabbles and babbles. Jackanapes does not like to sleep in any enclosed space but out beneath a bush or under a tree. He calls such places his windswept castles of the greenwood. He was there when the Free Brethren were massacred. He was nestling high in a tree.'

'Which is why he escaped the dogs?'

'I would say so,' the chaplain replied. 'He told me little except that the felon, John Le Riche, stayed in Mordern for a while, sheltered by the Free Brethren.'

'Are you sure?' Corbett asked.

'As God created Sundays,' the chaplain replied, 'that is what Jackanapes told me. And something else: Le Riche was hanged on a Friday in November just after dawn and left dangling there; within the hour, so we understand, his corpse had vanished and has never been seen since.'

Corbett glanced at Dame Marguerite, who shrugged.

'Did he truly die?' Ranulf asked. 'It has been known in London for a condemned man to bribe the hangman.' He gestured with his fingers. 'A leather collar around the neck and throat, the knot placed differently, painful, but the condemned doesn't choke. You were there, sir, when Le Riche was hanged?'

'Of course.' Master Benedict closed his eyes. 'He was wearing a long tattered gown, but yes, a high collar. However, he was listless and quiet. He was hoisted up the ladder and quickly turned off. He jerked for a while and then hung soundly, just swinging. The light was grey, morning was breaking. It was bitingly cold. Demons of ice battered our fingers and noses. We all turned and went our ways. I remember the execution cart crashing and slithering on the ice behind us.'

'Why are you telling us this?' Corbett asked.

'The truth,' Marguerite declared, her face no longer smiling. 'I simply cannot sit and listen to my brother spin his web of conceit and lies.' She blinked, her lips a thin bloodless line, staring at the screen behind Corbett as if fascinated by the exploits of Arthur and Guinevere. 'He grows more ruthless by the month.'

'Is there anything else?' Corbett asked.

She shook her head.

'And these warnings?' Corbett asked. 'I did not raise the matter with Lord Scrope. Do you know of them? Warnings delivered to your brother?'

'Warnings?' Dame Marguerite's face softened. 'What warnings?' She paused as Lady Hawisa, accompanied by Father Thomas, opened the door and swept into the chamber. Ranulf, concerned at Hawisa's agitation, went across and clasped her hand. Father Thomas sat down on a stool, face in his hands; he rubbed his cheeks and glanced up at Corbett.

'Lord Scrope is organising a search of the demesne, but I doubt if he'll find anything.'

Lady Hawisa retook her seat, glancing prettily at Ranulf.

'Sir Hugh.' She shifted towards Corbett, her smile fading.

Corbett walked across. 'You know your husband has received warnings?'

'I know,' she murmured.

Corbett sat on the small footstool near her chair. 'You've seen these?'

'Once or twice,' she replied, rubbing her brow. 'My husband . . .'

Corbett glanced up. Lord Scrope, the door off its latch, had slipped quietly into the room, Brother Gratian like a shadow behind him.

'Her husband,' Lord Scrope slammed the door shut, 'will answer any of your questions here in his own house. There is no need to ask others.'

'And the hunting horn?' Corbett ignored the manor lord's hot temper.

'Master Claypole will see to that.' Scrope went across to the fire, turning his back to warm himself.

'Master Claypole is so useful for so many things,' Lady Hawisa murmured.

'What do you mean by that?' her husband declared. 'I have known him years.'

'Yes, you have,' his wife replied sweetly. 'He was with you at Acre, was he not? A squire?'

Corbett caught the drift of her question.

'What are you implying?' Her husband walked across.

Corbett rose to his feet.

'Nothing!' she said wearily. 'Husband, you hold the Sanguis Christi, you are being threatened about that. You receive warnings about confessing your sins at the market cross.'

'Tell me,' Corbett intervened, 'who actually went to Acre?'

'Myself, cousin Gaston and other men from Mistleham. We'd heard how the Saracens intended to drive the Templars and all Christian forces from Outremer. We were full of idealism. Gaston and I were young knights. We wished to seek adventure rather than chase the Welsh up their valleys or hunt for Scottish rebels amongst the drenching heather. A party of us took the cross in St Alphege's church and journeyed east to join the garrison at Acre. Soon afterwards the city was invested by the Saracens. You know the story. Acre fell, we escaped, others didn't. We lost good men, Corbett, and a great deal of silver and wealth. When Acre was about to fall I hastened to the Templar treasury. I took what I could. I rescued it from the hands of the infidels and brought it back to England. God was rewarding me and others for our good work.'

'And yet you now have warnings; the Templars and others threaten you.'

'They have . . .'

'May I see these warnings?'

Scrope pulled a face, then clicked his fingers. Brother Gratian hurried off. Corbett stood staring at the floor. The rest of the company had fallen silent, each busy with their own thoughts. He glanced quickly at Ranulf. The Principal Clerk in the Chancery of the Green Wax was thoroughly enjoying himself, but that was Ranulf. He liked to see Corbett enter a room like a cat stealing into a parliament of mice. Corbett winked at him and went back to his thoughts, listening to the burning twigs snapping in the hearth. Old sins, he thought, dried and hard, now brought to burning: that was what was happening here.

'Sir Hugh, Sir Hugh.'

Corbett broke from his reverie. Brother Gratian had returned with a small chancery pouch. Corbett took it and shook out the contents. The scrolls were small and thin, the warnings very similar. The vellum was of high quality, the script neat, fully formed and easy to read. One set in red ink, the other in black, but apart from this, there was no indication of their source. Corbett studied the carefully formed writing sifting the contents into two, though the message was always the same. The first, 'The Mills of the Temple of God grind exceedingly slow but they do grind exceedingly small', and the second, 'The Mills of the Temple may grind exceedingly slow and exceedingly small, but so do the Mills of God's anger.'

'And how were these delivered?'

'Sir Hugh,' Scrope replied, 'traders and merchants are common visitors here. They bring supplies as well as letters or petitions from the markets, the town and the surrounding villages. A scroll pushed into the hand. They cannot remember who, how and when for every scrap of parchment they are given.'

Corbett handed them back.

'My lord, whatever you say, these warnings are not linked to what is happening here at Mistleham but to events many years ago.' Corbett paused. 'Are you sure there is nothing you wish to tell me?'

'Sir Hugh,' Scrope replied, sitting down in his chair and rubbing his knees, 'if I have to confess, then I would do so to Brother Gratian, but for the rest, this is nothing but villainy. I sent out search parties to look for the source of that horn but I am sure nothing will be found.' He gestured at the parchments. 'The same for those. You've seen the warnings, but there again, Corbett, like you I have lived with danger all my life. Whatever comes, I shall face.' He glared at his wife. 'And in future,' he glanced back at Corbett, 'if you have questions about my doings, then ask me.' He rose to his feet, clapping his hands softly. 'I am sorry the banquet ended like this, but I am only the victim, not the cause. Sir Hugh, you look as if you have something more to say.'

Corbett walked forward. He stood before the manor lord and stared down at him. 'I do, Sir Oliver. Your mastiffs Romulus and Remus were slain?'

'Yes.'

'Then I give you a fresh warning,' Corbett whispered,

'and I do so most solemnly. If I were you, Lord Scrope, I would reflect very carefully on my circumstances and make sure I was well guarded both day and night. True, warnings have been delivered but they've yet to be fulfilled. However, time presses on, the hour grows late and we must all retire.' Corbett turned away, determined that Lord Scrope would not have the last word. 'Tomorrow morning, before the Jesus Mass, Master Ranulf and I will go out to Mordern, seek out the corpses of the Free Brethren and give them honourable burial. Father Thomas, Master Benedict, I would be grateful for your presence, and you, Brother Gratian. The Office of the Dead must be recited, the law of Holy Mother Church observed.' He raised a hand. 'I bid you good night . . .'

Master Henry Claypole stood in the embrasure of the great bow window of the guildhall in Mistleham overlooking the marketplace and stared down at the ice-covered cobbles. A fresh dusting of snow had fallen. Master Claypole likened that to God's grace sprinkled out to cover the dirt and foulness of the deeds of men. The mayor of Mistleham had slept poorly. He'd organised the main search of the manor lands but found no indication of where the Sagittarius had been. Some of those who had accompanied them even claimed the horn had been blown from behind the walls. He'd returned to the manor to find Lord Oliver in a foul mood. Corbett was determined to go to Mordern, and Claypole and a company of town soldiers were to accompany him. Corbett was to be watched! The arrival of the King's men had deeply disturbed Claypole. Corbett was dark and brooding like some falcon on a branch, coldly surveying both the present and the past, whilst the other one, Ranulf, with his bright red hair, neatly combed and pulled tight into a queue at the back of his neck, long white fingers constantly caressing the hilt of his dagger, green eyes darting, taking in everything, lips twisted in a half-cynical smile . . . Claypole had met such men before, who were fully aware of their power. Yet Ranulf was different. He was eager to exercise it whatever the consequences. He and Corbett were two justices come to probe hearts and minds. Claypole quietly cursed Lord Scrope. He was the root and cause of all this. He simply did not know when to call an end, to walk away, to say he had had enough and wanted no more.

Claypole stared at the mist trailing about. It was still dark; even the busiest of traders had yet to stir, so all was quiet. He glared down at the empty market-place. He recalled massing there so many years ago, ready to enter St Alphege's to prostrate himself and take the cross. So long ago, so innocent, so free of sin, and now what? He always tried to forget Acre: the raging fires, the horrid roll of the enemy kettle-drums, their green banners flapping in the dry wind, the shrieking battle cries, the terrible news of how the walls had been breached and they must fall back. Scrope shouting at them where to go. Gaston lying wounded in the infirmary. Claypole's dreams were disturbed by the chaos that had ensued. The final days as the sky above Acre became lighted by the fiery missiles of the Saracens, their white-robed dervishes, scimitars and daggers rising and falling like the blades of reapers. Scrope's desperate gamble to flee the impending nightmare. Yet they had escaped! They'd returned to England to be hailed as Christ's warriors, Crusaders, men of faith who'd shown themselves true to their vows. They'd also, Claypole reflected, returned very wealthy, the result of Lord Scrope's plundering of the Templar treasury. For a while all had been quiet, peaceful, and very enjoyable. Master Claypole had settled down and married the daughter of a goldsmith, using his marriage to climb even further up the ladder of preferment. A happy marriage, he reflected, a simple-minded girl, merry in bed, who had produced a daughter, Beatrice, whom Claypole loved above all things. A happy, quiet time living on the fat of the land, until those Free Brethren had arrived.

At first Claypole had been dismissive, yet even he had been taken by them, especially young Eve with her oval face, beautiful eyes, and long blond hair falling down to her shoulders. He recalled the guilty pleasure during the festivities at the cherry fair. A balmy Sunday evening; Vespers had been sung. Claypole had found himself alone with her, distant from the rest, deep in the cherry orchard. He'd drunk deeply of claret; he'd stroked and caressed her breasts, ripe and full, loosened from her bodice, whilst she had pressed her lips against his face and whispered all sorts of sweet things as they lay together like lovers. Afterwards Claypole had tried to pay her, but Eve had just laughed mockingly, saying his coins weren't worth what she had given him. How sauce for the goose was good for the gosling. He didn't know what she meant until he heard the whispers after the morning mass or at meetings here at the guildhall: how his Beatrice was much taken by young Seth. He'd watched his innocent daughter like a cat would a mousehole. He found to his horror how she would slip from the house early in the evening, saying she was going to meet this person or that, but he learnt the truth. Beatrice was meeting her lover in the orchard. Rumours milled about. Then Lord Scrope, that dark shadow across his life, had summoned him to the manor to show him the warnings, to whisper about the danger the Free Brethren posed . . .

Claypole, agitated, rubbed his mouth. He dared not cross Scrope – if the manor lord died without heir, Claypole intended to press his suit. Scrope had never told him the truth but kept it dangling like a lure on a string. Had Alice de Tuddenham been validly married to him? If so, Claypole was his legitimate heir. Yet how could he prove that? The blood registers covering the time of his birth had gone missing from the parish chest. Was that Scrope's work? Or Father Thomas, who claimed he'd never seen them? Or Dame Marguerite, who'd always resented his claims? Why didn't Scrope tell the truth, or was that how he wanted it? To lure his so-called illegitimate son into nefarious schemes such as dealing with the likes of Le Riche? Despite the warmth, Claypole shivered. Now that was dangerous. Scrope's greed might still trap them in a charge of treason.

'Sir?'

Claypole, startled, looked over his shoulder. The captain of the town guard stood waiting, dressed in half-armour. He said the men were assembled in the courtyard below, horses harnessed and ready.

'Sir, we should leave now!'

Claypole sighed, picked up his cloak and put it about his shoulders, snapping the clasp shut, easing the war belt around his waist. Only the dead waited for them at Mordern, yet he had to be careful! He glanced through the window. A horseman had ridden into the square and was now dismounting. Master Benedict had arrived. It was time to be gone. Claypole went down to the guildhall yard, nodded at the captain of the guard and stood on a stone plinth.

'We are to go out to Mordern this morning. We have unfinished business,' he declared. 'You know the King's men are here. The corpses of the felons we killed must be given honourable burial or burnt; either way they will disappear.' His words were greeted with silence. He noted the sombre looks and whispers as he grasped the reins of his horse and mounted. This was a highly unpopular task. He'd warned Scrope about it from the start. They should have buried the corpses and forgotten about them. Now they had to return in cold blood to where hot blood had been spilt, lives extinguished like the wick of a lamp. He gathered the reins and dug in his spurs, urging the horse forward. The gates of the guildhall yard swung open. Claypole and the others cantered out, the clatter of their horse's hooves reassuring him with a sense of power. They crossed the market-place. Jackanapes, in his tawdry refinery, was, as usual, sitting near the horse trough close to the church. The beggar man jumped up as Claypole approached, running towards him, leaping about, hands extended.

'Master Mayor, Master Mayor,' he cried. 'I have news!'

Claypole reined in and stared at this frantic figure, face all wan with cold, eyes dancing with madness, mouth gaping to show half-chewed food.

'The Sagittarius has come again,' Jackanapes shouted. 'I know he is here. I wait for my reward.' He'd hardly finished when the shrill blast of a hunting horn shattered the silence of the marketplace. Even those beggars sleeping in the dark nooks and crannies shook themselves awake and crawled deeper into the shadows. Again the blast of the horn. By now Claypole's men were stirring, turning their horses, swords half drawn, seeking out the danger. A third blast. Claypole dismounted hurriedly, trying to keep the horse between himself and any possible assassin. He heard the twang like the strings of a harp being plucked, followed by the whistle of the darting shaft. A scream startled his horse. Claypole stared in horror at Jackanapes, who was now staggering back, an arrow shaft embedded deep in his chest. The madman tried to keep his balance, hands flapping, face jittering, mouth opening and shutting even as the blood spurted out. Another arrow sliced the air, followed by the gargle of a man choking on his own blood. The mayor moved his horse. Jackanapes had been the sole target. The poor fool had slumped to his knees, a shaft through the side of his throat completing the work of the other deep in his chest. Jackanapes stared dully at Claypole, lips parted, mouth dribbling blood, then he pitched forward on his face, twisting in his death throes on to his back.

5

They stayed there two nights . . . before advancing with arms towards Westminster.
Palgrave, *Kalendars of the Exchequer*

Claypole gave vent to his fury and fear, yelling at his men to scatter and search even as Corbett, Ranulf and others from the manor galloped into the square. Claypole stared at the leading riders. It was like a dream. For a moment, just a brief while, those two royal clerks on their great destriers, cloaks fluttering about them, cowls up, their horses moving slightly sideways in an aura of misty sweat and hot breath, seemed like the Angels of Death entering Mistleham. Claypole shook himself from such a doom-laden dream and gazed around. Already, despite the early hour, the commotion had aroused the many households in the warren of chambers, rooms, garrets and attics fronting the square. Shutters were flung back, candles and lanterns glowed at windows, doors creaked open, dogs were barking. Father Thomas, a stole about his neck, hastened out of the Galilee porch of his church and, slipping and slithering, hurried across. He stared piteously at Claypole and Corbett's retinue before crouching beside the fallen man. Jackanapes was not yet dead; his legs trembled, his feet in the pathetic old boots still shifted on the cobbles.

'*Jesu miserere*,' Father Thomas whispered. He stretched himself out on the slush and whispered the Absolvo Te, the final absolution, into the dying man's ear, then opened the small pyx and forced the host between Jackanapes' lips before swiftly anointing the dying man's brow, eyes, lips, hands and feet.

Corbett, astride his horse, cloak gathered about, crossed himself and whispered the Requiem. Ranulf followed suit even as he turned in the saddle to gaze swiftly around the square. Claypole's men were now returning. A search was futile, Ranulf realised that. Slayings like these were not new to the sons of Cain. In London the same happened every so often. A killer on the loose, some skilled archer, a veteran, his soul rotten with old grievances and ageing grudges, hating life and eager for death, would deal out summary judgement. Sometimes from a church tower or steeple, the dark mouth of a stinking alleyway or the window of a deserted tavern. Corbett caught Ranulf's attention and raised a hand as a sign that he should stay.

'He is gone.' Father Thomas clambered to his feet, eyes brimming with tears. 'Why should anyone kill poor Jackanapes?'

'Two shafts.' Corbett leaned over the corpse. 'That's not happened before, has it?' He gazed around. No one answered. 'One to the chest and one to the throat. The killer wanted to make sure Jackanapes was killed.'

'So swift.' Master Benedict forced himself through the throng. 'Master Claypole,' the chaplain turned to the mayor, 'I was waiting for you here. I swear the marketplace was deserted. I saw no one. You came down, you rode towards Jackanapes, then that horn.' He paused, gave the reins of his palfrey to a bystander and walked over to grasp the bridle of Corbett's mount. 'That's how it was, Sir Hugh.' The chaplain stared fearfully up at him. 'That horn, followed by the whistling shafts, isn't that true, Master Mayor?'

Claypole took a deep breath. Old memories were pressing deep upon him, images from a foul nightmare. He was truly fearful, yet he must hide it. 'Lord Scrope did not come?' he asked.

'Apparently not,' Ranulf snapped.

'Then we must go . . .'

Master Claypole paused as Brother Gratian arrived, perched precariously on a palfrey that came trotting across the cobbles, the Dominican's white and black robe flapping about. He clumsily pushed his mount through the bystanders, reined in and glanced down at the corpse.

'God have mercy,' he intoned. 'God have mercy on us all.'

'If we deserve it,' Father Thomas added. 'Look . . .' He briskly summoned forward some of his parishioners, inviting them by name, issuing instructions for Jackanapes to be taken to the corpse house on the far side of God's Acre. He then wiped his hands on his gown, muttering that he would join them, and hurried away.

Corbett decided not to wait, but turned his horse's head and made his way across the market square, up the side streets and ice-covered runnels towards the trackway that led across frozen fields to the dark forest circling the deserted village. Master Claypole pushed his horse alongside but Corbett ignored him. The clerk could make little sense of what was happening; he would just listen, observe, recollect, sift and analyse. Silence was best. Corbett tried to recall Maeve resplendent in her fur-trimmed nightgown, her rich hair tumbling down framing that beautiful face, those eyes full of mischief. He took a deep breath and glanced back. Father Thomas had joined them, urging his hack alongside Master Benedict. The rest, apart from Ranulf and Chanson, were retainers or town levies, a dark host of men, a black cloud moving across the snow-covered fields. Ahead of them a line of trees marked the edge of the forest. Steel-grey clouds pressed down as if they wished to cover the land criss-crossed here and there by hedgerows or long high mounds marking the end of one field and the beginning of another. A flock of birds mobbed an owl caught out in the daylight. Corbett glimpsed a fox, belly low, loping across a field.

The silence grew oppressive, despite the muttered conversations of the men. Father Thomas chanted the Dirige psalm for the dead. Chanson quietly teased Ranulf. The Principal Clerk of the Chancery of the Green Wax truly feared the desolate, forbidding countryside. Chanson was whispering stories about Drac, a hideous monster that lurked in the forest and came out seeking its prey especially on a sombre day like this. Corbett smiled grimly to himself. This was similar to marching in Scotland or along those Welsh valleys; the longer the oppressive silence lasted, the worse it became. He took a deep breath and, much to the surprise of everyone, wistfully sang a favourite marching song about a beautiful girl in a tower. The words were familiar, the tune simple to catch. Within a short while, other voices were raised in song, the melody echoing across the bleakness, bringing some warmth, dulling fears about the future and the memory of Jackanapes in his death throes. Once the singing ended, Corbett reined his horse in and turned to Claypole, who was staring curiously at him.

'There's nothing like a song, Master Claypole. Now, this village, you know the way?'

Claypole pointed to the trackway snaking between the trees.

'There is only one path in, Sir Hugh.'

'And Mordern,' Corbett asked, 'why is it deserted?'

Claypole pulled down the rim of his cloak, eager to impress this clerk.

'About ninety years ago it was totally destroyed in the civil war between the King's grandfather and the barons. A massacre took place around the old church; the place became cursed. Some people claim Lord Scrope's ancestors sowed the earth with salt so the survivors had to move away.'

'And you?' Corbett asked.

'Oh, I think the village lay too deep in the forest. Its inhabitants lacked the means to fell the trees and plough the land. So they simply used the war as an excuse to move away.'

'Lord Scrope allowed the Free Brethren to shelter there?'

'Why not?' Claypole declared. 'Others have. There is very little we can do about it: wandering tinkers, traders, even the occasional outlaw, moon people. Lord Scrope allows them to shelter and snare the occasional rabbit for the pot. As long as they don't start poaching or hunting venison, he leaves them be. In the summer it's different, the children go out there to play. When I was a lad I used to follow Lord Scrope there with his sister Marguerite and their cousin Gaston.'

'This cousin,' Corbett asked, 'what happened?'

'Wounded at Acre,' Claypole replied, 'taken into the infirmary. Sir Hugh, if you read the accounts of Acre, or if you know anything about the fall of that fortress, it was every man for himself. Gaston died. There was little we could do.'

'How do you know he died?' Corbett asked.

'I followed Lord Scrope when we decided to leave. He was determined to take his cousin with us, but when he entered the infirmary, Gaston was dead.'

'And the Templar treasure?'

'Why not, Sir Hugh? We'd fought hard, the infidels had breached the walls. Why should they have what we could take? So we seized what we could and fled.'

'And Jackanapes?' Corbett asked. 'What did he say before he died?'

'Oh, babbling as usual. How the Sagittarius had returned, something about claiming a reward. Nothing but nonsense.'

Corbett reflected on what he had seen and heard in the marketplace.

'I wonder,' he murmured, 'I truly do!'

The conversation died as they entered the line of trees. A different world of tangled, snow-covered gorse that stretched like a chain linking the stark black tree trunks, their bare branches laced against the sky. A secret, furtive place of swift movement in the undergrowth, the ghostly wafting of bird wing, the sudden call of an animal or the crack of rotting bracken. Corbett's hands slid beneath his cloak. He understood Ranulf's fears about such a place. In the cities and towns, the Chancery of Hell dictated its villainy from narrow runnels or darkened nooks. Here it would be different. A shaft loosed from a knot of trees, a knife or axe sent whirling through the air or a cunning rope or caltrop to bring down a horse. A landscape of white menace harbouring God knew what evil that had crawled across the threshold of hell. Here the Sagittarius could hide cloaked by nature. To still his fears, Corbett thought of Maeve and smiled as he recalled the lines of a romance she'd read to him over the Christmas holy days.

A woman in whose face more beauty shown.
Then all other beauties fashioned into one.

'This village, Mordern?' Ranulf, riding behind Corbett, spoke up.

'Haunted and devastated,' Claypole replied. 'As I told Sir Hugh . . .'

His words trailed away as they broke from the forest into a broad glade with clumps of snow-covered trees and straggling gorse under its icy pall. Corbett reined in and stared across at the derelict buildings, their roofs long gone, the wattle and daub walls no more than flaking shells. Here and there an occasional stone dwelling. On the far side of the glade rose the tumble-down, weed-encrusted wall of the cemetery; beyond this the memorials of the long-forgotten dead circled the ruined church. Corbett studied this, an ancient chapel probably built before the Normans came, with its simple barn-like nave, jutting porches and squat square tower. Once an impressive edifice, but the tiled roof had disappeared, the windows were black empty holes whilst no doors or gates protected its entrances.

'Some people call it the Chapel of the Damned,' Claypole whispered.

Corbett glanced at him

'I don't know why,' the mayor stammered.

Corbett just nodded, aware of the growing unease amongst the comitatus behind him.

'Look, master, the corpses.' Ranulf stretched out a black-gauntleted hand.

Corbett strained his eyes, secretly wishing his sight was better. The murmuring behind him rose as others glimpsed the horrid fruit of Scrope's bloody work. Corbett wondered how many of these with him had been present at that hideous assault.

'Sir Hugh?' Ranulf was pointing again.

Corbett narrowed his eyes, searched and stifled a gasp. The snow hid the bloody mayhem, but now he glimpsed the eerily shaped mounds sprawled around the church. Frost-hardened and snow-covered heaps, each a corpse, the only sign being the glint of colour or a booted leg sprawled out frozen in its death throes. Corbett followed Ranulf's direction and stared at the clump of oaks to the left of the church tower, branches burdened down as if with snow. In truth they were hanging corpses, heads skewered, necks twisted, hands tied behind them, feet dangling. Father Thomas and Master Benedict had already intoned the De Profundis. A young man amongst the escort was quietly sobbing; others were cursing.

'You were here, Master Claypole?'

'You know I was.'

'Then you know what has to be done.' Corbett urged his horse forward and reined in before one of the corpses hanging from a branch. Thankfully the decaying face was covered by a mask of icy snow. Corruption and the scavengers had plucked all dignity from it. He dismounted, leaving Chanson to hobble his horse, and went across into the church porch. A woman's corpse, garbed in a long red gown, sprawled nearby. Corbett glimpsed the headstone Brother Gratian had mentioned. Its surface had obviously been used to sharpen blades. He crouched beside the corpse. It lay face down, the once blond hair all matted with thick dirt, part of the outstretched arm gnawed clean to the bone. Despite the freezing chill, Corbett caught the stench of corruption. He swallowed hard, crossed himself and stood up.

'Cut down all the corpses,' he shouted. 'You, sir,' he beckoned to Robert de Scott, leader of Scrope's retinue, 'organise your men, collect dry kindle, build a funeral pyre. You've helped clear a battlefield before?'

The grim-faced captain nodded. 'Aye,' he slurred, then took a mouthful of wine from the skin looped over his saddle horn. He almost choked as Ranulf swiftly urged his horse forward and pressed the tip of his drawn dagger against the captain's throat.

'Sir Hugh speaks for the King!' Ranulf's voice was thick with anger. 'You, sir, do not gobble wine when he speaks to you.' He leaned forward and knocked the wineskin from the man's hand. 'No drinking!' He stood high in his stirrups. 'No eating, nothing until my lord Corbett says.'

The captain pushed back his cloak, hand going for his sword.

'Come then!' Ranulf teased. 'Draw, sir, but I'm no unarmed madcap sheltering in a deserted church.'

Robert de Scott's hand fell away.

'How many of you,' Ranulf shouted, 'were here at the attack?'

Most of the escort raised their hands.

'Well you've sown the tempest; now reap the whirlwind. Collect the corpses of those you killed.' Ranulf ignored Robert de Scott and joined Corbett in the narrow porch of the church. 'A bully-boy,' he whispered. 'In God's name, Sir Hugh, what was Scrope thinking of, to attack, to kill but then to leave these dead—'

'True,' Corbett interrupted, putting a hand on Ranulf's shoulder. 'Well done, good and faithful servant,' he teased, quoting from the scriptures.

'Sir Hugh?'

'Ranulf, you are correct, why did Scrope leave them here? I can understand hot blood running, but later? Surely one of the great acts of corporal mercy is to bury the dead. Even the King does that,' he added drily. He steered his companion into the church. 'Despite our threats we'll not get the truth from them.' He indicated with his head. 'I suspect Scrope came here to punish but also to search, but for what? I suspect whatever he was scouring for, he never found, so he left those corpses to frighten away the curious.'

Corbett peered around and whistled softly. 'Truly named,' he murmured. 'The Chapel of the Damned!' The walls of the ruined church were covered with creeping lichen, its floor a dark, squalid mess littered with the dung of fox, bat and all the wild creatures of the forest. The air smelt rank and fetid. Outside, the men were now busy under the shouted orders of Robert de Scott and Master Claypole. The three priests were chanting the psalms for the dead: Corbett paused and listened to the sombre words:

That you may be correct when you give sentence.
And be without reproach when you judge.
Ah, remember in guilt was I born.
A sinner was I conceived.

'True, true!' he whispered. 'Sin stalks this Chapel of the Damned, Ranulf. Ghosts gather, pleading for vengeance. Blood, spilt before its time, demands Christ's retribution!'

Gloomy and shadow-filled, the church had been stripped of all movables, reduced to a mere skeleton of mildewed stone. The light pouring through the lancet windows did little to disperse the ghostly aura. Corbett walked slowly up the nave and paused where the rood screen must have stood.

'Nothing!' He gestured around. 'Nothing at all,

Ranulf! Yet the Free Brethren must have had baggage, panniers, baskets.'

'Plundered by the rogues outside,' Ranulf murmured. 'Master, what is all this? What else are you searching for?'

'I don't know.' Corbett walked into the darkened sanctuary and stared up at the small, empty oriel window. 'I truly don't.' He walked into the sacristy, a long, narrow chamber, its walls plastered and fairly clean. He prodded at the dirt on the floor with the toe of his boot, then walked further down.

'Master?'

'I suspect this was the refectory of the Free Brethren.' Corbett crouched down and sifted amongst the dirt. 'See, Ranulf, the imprint of table legs, and look, here're those of a bench. I am sure Scrope's men must have plundered everything.' He rose and walked to the door at the far end. He lifted the latch and opened it. Ranulf glimpsed Scrope's retainers, dragging a corpse from a ditch near the crumbling cemetery wall. Corbett slammed the door shut. 'They mended this door to make it secure. They met here to sit and discuss. I wonder what?'

'Sir Hugh?'

Corbett walked over to where Ranulf was peering at the wall. He pointed at the thick black etchings painted there. Corbett opened the door to allow in more light. At first they could not make out the words – several attempts had been made to obliterate them – but eventually Corbett distinguished the verse inscribed there:

> Rich, shall richer be,
> Where God kissed Mary in Galilee.

Beneath these words were drawings, though most of them had been cut away with a knife. Corbett glimpsed a tower, a siege machine, a man on a couch.

'I wonder,' he whispered, 'is this the work of the Free Brethren or someone else? They've certainly been done recently, not years ago.' He walked back into the sanctuary, staring at the dirt-covered flagstones. From outside drifted the shouts and cries of those collecting the dead. Corbett continued his scrutiny, telling Ranulf to do likewise.

'What are we looking for?'

'You'll know when you find it,' Corbett murmured.

Father Thomas came in and said that the dead were now collected and the funeral pyre was being prepared. Corbett went out. The corpses, fourteen in all, lay along what was the old coffin path. The retinue from Mistleham now stood about, faces visored against the seeping stench of rottenness. Corbett moved from corpse to corpse. Decay as well as the forest creatures had wreaked their effect, shrunken flesh nibbled and gnawed, faces almost unrecognisable. Corbett crossed himself and murmured a prayer.

'Beautiful they were, Sir Hugh.' Father Thomas stood next to him. 'Like angels, and so full of life. God curse Lord Scrope! Endowed with all God's gifts, they could sing beautifully and dance like butterflies.'

'You are sure they are all here?'

'Oh yes.' The priest indicated two of the corpses. 'Adam and Eve, their leaders and the painters.'

Corbett remembered the scrawl on the sacristy wall.

'Father, does this mean anything to you: "Rich, shall richer be, Where God kissed Mary in Galilee"?'

'No.' The priest shook his head. 'Where's it from?'

'I found it written on the sacristy wall. You said they were painters, Father?'

'You must visit St Alphege's and see their work. Do so quickly. Lord Oliver has promised the whole church will be repainted and regilded, the same for St Frideswide. Perhaps it is reparation for this, but come, Sir Hugh, the rest are waiting.'

'Let them!' Corbett turned. 'Master Claypole, Robert de Scott.'

The mayor and the captain of the guard left the huddle of men. The captain was no longer swaggering. Corbett gestured at them to follow him a little further. They did so, pulling down their visors.

'You were involved in the attack on this place?'

'You know that.'

'And afterwards?'

'We searched the church and other buildings,' Master Claypole replied.

'You took all their possessions?'

'Yes.'

'But those are King's goods.'

'Sir Hugh, there was next to nothing,' Claypole replied.

'A matter Lord Scrope must account for.' Corbett studied the aggressive faces of these two men: hard of soul, hard of heart and hard of eye, they would show little mercy to any enemy.

'Sir Hugh.' Master Benedict, with a doleful Brother Gratian trailing behind, approached. 'The men are freezing cold.'

'And so am I.' Corbett stared at the gentle-faced chaplain; he looked pale, distinctly unwell. The clerk glimpsed streaks of vomit on the front of his gown.

'We must say the prayers, Master Benedict and I, then be gone,' Gratian murmured. 'Sir Hugh, this is a haunted, benighted place. I am hungry and freezing cold. I feel the ghosts about me. I understand Father Thomas has brought the holy water and sacred unguents.'

'And I have the oil.' Master Claypole spoke up. 'Sir

Hugh, beneath the snow we've found dried kindling. We have also brought faggots, dry wood sheltered from the damp.'

Corbett nodded. He ordered the pyre to be completed as swiftly as possible and the corpses laid out. He glanced up at the sky; the day was drawing on. He and Ranulf returned to the Chapel of the Damned and continued their search. Although Ranulf was close to him, Corbett felt a prickly unease: the shifting shadows, the pallid light, the sense of ominous brooding and lurking menace. A mood not helped by the odd scrap of wall painting depicting the horrors of hell or the battered, snarling faces of babewyns, gargoyles and exotic beasts carved on corbels and plinths.

'Sir Hugh,' Ranulf was kicking with his boot at a paving slab just beneath one of the narrow windows, 'there's an iron ring here.'

Corbett hurried across. The ring was embedded near the edge, rusting but still strong and secure. He tugged and the entire stone loosened. Assisted by Ranulf, he pulled it free, sliding it across the next stone as a gust of musty air made them cough. Corbett grasped the lantern and glimpsed the steep, narrow steps leading below.

'Ranulf, there're more lantern horns outside. Take one, get it lit and come back.'

A short while later, the lantern horns glowing, Ranulf shouting at the curious now congregating in the porch to busy themselves elsewhere, Corbett led the way down. At the bottom of the steps he lifted the lantern and quietly whistled.

'A crypt,' he murmured. 'Look, Ranulf.' He pointed to cresset torches, still thick with pitch, fastened in their sconces. Ranulf hurried across and lit some of these. The light flared, illuminating the long, sombre chamber with its curiously bricked walls and the remains of battered pillars that must once have reinforced a ceiling above. The floor was of shale, patched here and there with faded tiles; crouching down, Corbett studied the elaborately intricate designs, then the ledge that ran either side of the chamber. More torches were lit. The light glimmered. Ranulf shouted; Corbett glanced up. At the far end of the room, piled against the wall, rose a heap of shattered skeletons. Corbett hurried down to inspect the grisly pile of cracked dark brown bones, a hideous sight in the dim light. The stench was noisome. He drew his sword and sifted amongst the shards; sharp ribs, leg and arm bones and cup-like skulls.

'God rest them. These have been dead a long time,' he muttered.

'And the stench?' Ranulf asked.

Corbett sifted the dust with the point of his sword.

'Herbs thickly piled on but now decayed. Rosemary, withered hyacinths, cypress leaves and new shoots. This is an old charnel house, Ranulf, a place of gloomy midnight. All that is missing,' he glanced over his shoulder, 'is a screeching owl, a cauldron of bubbling mandrake, and it could be a warlock's cavern, but no.' He sheathed his sword. 'The truth is that the soil outside is hard to dig, hence the village's eventual decay. Accordingly, every so often the inhabitants of Mordern would empty God's Acre for fresh burials and bring the bones of their long-departed down here. I suspect the church above was built on something more ancient still, when Caesar's people ruled this island.' He walked round, pausing near the ledge, and, in the light of the lamps, studied the ground. 'Food and wine?' He picked up scraps of bone and hardened bread. 'Why should anyone eat or drink in such macabre surroundings?'

'Unless they were hiding.'

'John Le Riche,' Corbett replied. 'And richer still? I wonder if that verse applies to him. Did the Free Brethren hide him here? Which,' he got to his feet, 'brings us to a more pressing problem, Ranulf. If you were a member of that Westminster gang, fleeing through the wilds of Essex with treasures stolen from the King's own hoard, you would be very careful, surely?'

'Of course.'

'And you wouldn't proclaim the fact. Yet Le Riche, cunning enough to break into the royal treasury, astute enough to escape the King's searchers, finds sanctuary in Essex but then becomes a babbling infant. He actually turns up at Mistleham guildhall offering to sell a dagger belonging to the King. A dagger not of English origin but Saracen, which would certainly arouse suspicion. Master Claypole and Lord Scrope are not telling us the truth, but that will have to wait. What I do suspect is that this crypt was used to house Le Riche; he hid here, the Free Brethren fed him. They probably also stored their weapons here against the curious. They made mistakes . . . No, no,' he shook his head, 'no they didn't, at least not then.'

'What do you mean, master?'

'Scrope's story – that a verderer was wandering in the woods and by chance came across some of the Free Brethren practising archery – that doesn't ring true; it's not logical, is it? Here are a group who were planning a secret attack, yet practised with their weapons in the greenery where verderers, foresters, beggars, wandering tinkers and chapmen could see them.' Corbett pointed down the chamber at the pile of bones. 'They were collected,' he said, 'and piled there deliberately.' He went back and moved the bones away to reveal the great beam embedded in the wall beyond. 'Ranulf, bring the lantern closer.' His companion did so. 'Look.' Corbett pointed at the countless fresh marks in the thick dark beam.

'Archery,' Ranulf whispered. 'A target post.'

'It's possible.'

'Sir Hugh,' Ranulf gestured at the far end of the crypt, 'they came down here and used this central pillar as a target. If they could hit that in this murky place, they would strike anything in God's own daylight.'

'So,' Corbett declared, 'if they were practising their archery down here, and I think they were, why go out in the greenwood where the world and his wife might come upon them? One lie after another, eh, Ranulf? We will have to start again. Question Scrope and Claypole closely, show we are not the fools they think we are . . .' He paused abruptly. 'Did you hear that, Ranulf?' He put a finger to his lips, then the sound came again: the long, chilling blast of a hunting horn.

'It could be Master Claypole or Robert de Scott,' Ranulf said hurriedly, 'calling in their men.'

'I doubt it!' Corbett declared.

They hastened up the steps into the church and out of the nave. As they did so, another horn blast trailed away. Corbett stared round. The funeral pyre was almost prepared, the corpses lying between layers of kindling, bracken and dried wood. One of the comitatus was already pouring oil but the rest were scattering, looking for arms. Claypole came round the church towards them, his white face all sweat-soaked.

'Sir Hugh, the Sagittarius is here.'

'Who called him the Sagittarius?' Corbett asked.

'Sir Hugh, that's the name given to him.'

'But that's not the name, is it?' Corbett glimpsed Father Thomas emerging from the trees with a pile of kindling in his hand. 'That's not the name that was told to Father Thomas when he was visited in his church.'

'Sir Hugh, what does it matter?'

'Yes, yes, I agree.' Corbett drew his sword and stepped out of the porch. 'Ranulf, for the love of God tell those men to use their wits. If the Sagittarius is here, the church is their best defence.'

Both clerks went out calling to the escort to fall back. Corbett tried to ignore the thought of that nightmare killer, bow drawn, arrow notched, slipping through the trees searching for a victim. For a while there was chaos and confusion. Corbett organised some of the men to watch the treeline, whilst the others fell back to the church.

'Nothing!' Robert de Scott called out. 'I can see nothing at all.'

Corbett chose ten men and led them out into the

trees, spreading out, moving forward towards what he considered to be reasonable bowshot, a perilous walk through the coldest purgatory: trees and gorse soaked with ice and snow, all shrouded by that heart-chilling silence. Eventually he summoned the men back, strode out of the trees and ordered that the pyre be lit. Sacks of oil drenched the wood and bracken, the corpses hidden between. Father Thomas blessed the pyre once more, sprinkling it with holy water using the asperges rod and stoup he'd brought. One Pater and three Aves were recited, then the torches were flung. Everyone withdrew as the flames roared and plumes of black smoke curled above the trees.

'They'll see it in Mistleham,' Master Claypole declared.

'Then they'll know what is happening,' Corbett replied. 'God's judgement, and that of the King.'

6

We wish a hasty remedy for this outrage.
Letter of Edward I, 6 June 1303

Lady Hawisa was tending her extensive herb garden in its walled enclosure at the manor. Despite the snow and ice, the grey skies and sharp air, Hawisa loved to come here, to be by herself. She had already visited the kitchen, inspecting the trenches of beechwood, the pewter jugs and drinking horns as well as the knives, fleshing blades and cutters of the cooks before moving to scrutinise the ovens and hearths. She wanted to ensure all was clean and safe, including the ratchet used for the huge cauldron and the bellows for encouraging the flame. Everything had to be neat and precise. Lady Hawisa prided herself on that: being busy like a nun marking the hours, moving from one task to another. She'd also visited the butteries and store chambers where the bitter fruit of last autumn's harvest was stored, stirred and mixed into potted jams, jellies and preserves. Finally she'd supervised the preparation of the evening meal, taking special responsibility for the blancmange of veal, mixed with cream, almonds, eggs and some of these herbs all dried and chopped. Lady Hawisa did not want to think, to give way, to reflect on the passions seething in her like black smoke trapped in a stack. She smiled at the thought of Ranulf-atte-Newgate then blushed. Ranulf was so handsome, so courteous!

'Ah well,' she whispered. 'I wonder when the clerks will return from Mordern.'

A royal messenger carrying letters for the sheriff at Colchester had stopped at the manor with a chancery pouch for Sir Hugh, issuing strict instructions that it must be given to the clerk as soon as he returned. Lady Hawisa abruptly startled at the cries from a maid standing in one of the casement windows overlooking the herb garden. She followed the direction of the girl's gaze and saw the dark cloud of smoke rising above Mordern forest like some demon, shapeless but swift, as if eager to escape into the grey sky.

'They are burning those corpses,' the maid cried.

Lady Hawisa nodded, indicating with her hand for the maid to withdraw. She stared at the drifting, ominous cloud and the curdle of hate, resentment and fury welled within her. She walked down the path and found herself standing by the Hortus Mortis – the Garden of Death – a special herb plot housing plants that in very small portions, could heal, but used unwisely could also kill in a few heartbeats. Her especial favourite was belladonna or deadly nightshade, a plant that fascinated her and plagued her nightmares. She crouched and stared at the herb: it was midwinter so there were no purple violet trumpets, no dark glossy berries, yet it still remained deadly. Lady Hawisa stretched out her hand as if to caress the plant and stared again at that filthy cloud spreading over the trees like some malevolent miasma. That smoke she thought, bore the flesh and blood of Adam, the beautiful leader of the Free Brethren, with his kissing mouth and laughing eyes, now dead like the rest, all sent into eternal night by her husband. Lady Hawisa breathed in slowly. She recalled Father Thomas' description of the mysterious stranger who'd come to threaten her husband. He had called himself Nightshade. Well, if that was true, Lord Scrope was Mandrake incarnate, body and soul! Again she stretched out her hand and caressed the belladonna. Some of this would serve! She thought of the blancmange she'd mixed. Just a scattering of powder on his portion . . .

Lady Hawisa jumped to her feet, staring wildly around as she realised what she was thinking. She glimpsed the clump of coppice aspens trembling in the cold breeze on the far side of her garden. Were they trembling? Or was it something else? Legend had it how the aspen shivered, breeze or not, because it housed the secret guilt of being the wood used for the Saviour's cross. Yes, Lady Hawisa thought, she was like the aspen, furtively cherishing malevolent thoughts and desires. She'd come here to soothe her soul, but now she was tempted, she had to be free!

Forgetting her basket, Lady Hawisa fled the garden through the coffin-shaped door and down the passageway. Servants stopped and stared curiously at her. She paused and drew a deep breath. She must not betray herself. She walked slowly along the passageways and galleries to her own chamber. Once inside, she tried to control her seething rancour. She lay on her bed, staring across the chamber, and slept for a while, eventually wakened by sounds from the yard below as Sir Hugh and the others returned. Lady Hawisa still felt ill-humoured; she could not meet him, not now. She needed to shrive herself, to pray. She rose, made herself presentable and went out along the passageway to the manor chapel. The door was off the latch. She wondered if someone had entered, so she called out, but there was no one. She closed the door and leaned against it, staring at the beautiful jewelled pyx hanging above the altar, shimmering in the red glow from the sanctuary lamp. Beside this was the crucifix, the lowered head of the dead Christ crowned with a ring once owned by Gaston de Bearn, her husband's cousin. Hawisa idly wondered what this kinsman of her husband, this crusading hero, had truly been like. On the wall of the chapel was a marble plaque to his memory, the valiant Christian warrior who had perished in Acre. She moved down to the place of pity by the lady chapel to the left of the altar. Here the visiting priest would sit in the mercy chair while she knelt on the quilted prie-dieu to confess her sins. She did so now; no one could hear her, she was alone with God. The chapel was dark, brimming with shadows that filled the corners and alcoves. Lady Hawisa stared up at the crucifix.

'Like my soul,' she whispered, 'full of shadows.' She crossed herself. 'Absolve me, Father,' she intoned as if Father Thomas was sitting there. 'Absolve me from my filthy sins. My last shriving was at Advent. I have sinned as follows: I have committed horrid murder many, many times here in my heart.' She struck her breast. 'My husband, Lord Scrope; in my dreams I kill him, time and time again, with rope, dagger and poisoned cup. He is a demon who forsakes my bed except for his lusts, refuses me comfort, hates and despises me as he does every living soul. He has murdered and butchered to hide the dark secrets locked fast in that grim iron soul of his. He dare not sleep with me lest he babbles in his dreams about old sins now ripe to full rottenness. Father, I truly hate him. I loathe his touch, his lifeless eyes like those of a crow. He killed the young ones, beautiful Adam, for what? I have given him a cup, Father, fashioned out of yew, but told him it's of beech; a gift, in truth a curse. It will bring him ill fortune in that cell he's had built for himself, the dark hidden corner of a dark hidden life. I dream of feeding him poison, filling that yew cup with some noxious potion.' Hawisa felt the anger drain from her. She relaxed, bowed her head and, as she muttered the Confiteor, let the tears come. Eventually she composed herself and rose. She felt slightly guilty. A whole host of guests awaited her.

'*Mea culpa, mea culpa*,' she whispered. 'I have neglected my duties.' She thought of the chancery pouch sealed with the royal warrant awaiting Corbett. She quickly dried her eyes and left the chapel, oblivious to the watcher hiding in one of the recesses of the sanctuary. A watcher who had observed and heard her secret confession . . .

Corbett lay on the bed, his boots, cloak and war belt piled on the floor beside him. Ranulf was sitting at the chancery desk laying out a writing tray. He glanced across and smiled. Master Long Face would now be grinding, like an apothecary with his mortar and pestle, all he'd heard, seen and observed. Ranulf was pleased to leave that haunted, lonely forest, away from that macabre village with its ruined church full of ghosts, the funeral pyre, as Sir Hugh said, blazing away the effects of sin but not its cause. They'd ridden swiftly back through the breath-catching cold to the warmth of the manor, a delicious dish of stewed venison, soft white bread and goblets of the finest claret whilst they sat in the buttery warming themselves in front of a roaring fire. Master Benedict, who'd returned to Mistleham Manor like a ghost with his dark-ringed eyes and pallid face, had slowly recovered. He'd asked Ranulf and Sir Hugh if they could wait on Dame Marguerite, who'd stayed at the manor the previous evening and wished to have words with them. Corbett promised he would go to her later in the day, but first he wanted to rest and reflect. Ranulf wondered when his master would begin. He was about to sharpen a quill when there was a loud knock on the door. Corbett swung his legs off the bed and indicated with his head. Ranulf crossed, opened the door and smiled at Lady Hawisa.

'I am sorry.' She stepped out from the shadows. Ranulf noticed the distress in her eyes and face. 'I apologise, but . . .' He stood back and courteously ushered her in. Corbett apologised for not being suitably dressed to greet her. Lady Hawisa brushed this aside, still smiling at Ranulf's obvious pleasure at seeing her. 'Sir Hugh, I must apologise.' She stared unblinkingly at him.

Corbett noticed her red-rimmed eyes. She held up the chancery pouch. 'This arrived while you were gone. I should have brought it earlier, I . . .'

Corbett thanked her. Lady Hawisa, hastily recollecting where she was, immediately backed towards the door. Ranulf followed her out into the gallery; when he returned, Corbett was sitting at the chancery desk, his cipher book open as he hastily translated the missive.

'It's from Drokensford in the Royal Chancery.' Corbett smiled. 'The court is moving to Colchester, and two other items. A spy in New Temple claims the Templars have someone here in Mistleham to collect the Sanguis Christi.' Corbett pulled a face. 'He, or she, is under the strict instructions of the Master of the Temple not to wait for Lord Scrope to hand it over but to seize it whenever possible.'

'Who, why, when?'

'Drokensford does not know, but apparently the Temple will take what they regard as theirs and not twiddle their thumbs waiting for either Scrope or the King. They must also know we are here.' Corbett grinned. 'Perhaps they have spies in our own chancery, or suspect our real purpose for visiting here.'

'Lord Scrope himself could have told them about our arrival and what we intend.'

'Possibly,' Corbett conceded. 'Out of sheer malice Scrope might want the Sanguis Christi returned to the Temple rather than to the King.'

'And the second item?'

'Drokensford doesn't know if this is relevant or not, but according to the records, our plunderer of the royal treasury, John Le Riche, hailed from Caernarvon and served amongst Edward's royal troop of Welsh archers.'

'So he was a master bowman. He could be the Sagittarius.'

'Correct,' Corbett breathed. 'That is, if he is still alive. Now, Ranulf, let's put pen to paper.'

Corbett rose and gestured at the chair he'd left. Ranulf sat down and busied himself. He watched as Corbett began to walk up and down. You love this, Ranulf reflected, you adore the Lady Maeve and your children but this is different. You want to resolve problems and mysteries, dig out the truth, apply logic as sharply as a farmer prunes a plant with a knife.

Ranulf opened one of the pots and stirred the red ink with the tip of his pen. He recalled the King's eyes at Westminster, that writ hidden away in a secret coffer, then Lady Hawisa's beautiful face. Would the King grant him Mistleham if they were successful? he wondered. If Lord Scrope died? Such a prize, only a knife-thrust away: to be a great manor lord! For a brief moment Ranulf thought of himself as a boy in a ragged tunic, racing along the foul runnels of Cheapside. So much had changed. A brief moment of time and all was different; a sudden act of mercy by Corbett. But that was how the dice fell. Life could change so abruptly. An arrow or dagger brought death or, there again, riches and preferment.

'Ranulf? Ranulf?'

He glanced up. Corbett was staring at him curiously with those sharp dark eyes.

'What are you thinking?'

'Time, master.' Ranulf laughed. 'How time can change someone's fortune so abruptly.'

'Strange, I was thinking the same. Ranulf, you must read the Venerable Bede's work *On the Nature of Time*.' Corbett recommenced his pacing. 'A great scholar, Ranulf! Bede was a Saxon monk who lived in a monastery close to the Roman wall. Anyway, he wrote this work, in which he demonstrated how in God's eyes there can be no time.'

'Sir Hugh?'

'Easily understood, Ranulf. Look at that tapestry.' Corbett pointed at the hanging on the wall that vividly portrayed the death of Priam during the fall of Troy. 'You look at that and you understand it at one glance. However, what if you could only understand it by taking each section at a time? Bede, as did the great

Aquinas after him, talked of the "eternal now". In God's eyes there is no past, present or future, just the eternal vision.'

'But we . . .'

'We fashion time, Ranulf, because we have to. We must make sense of one moment following another. We are compelled to create order. Now it is midday, and the Angelus bell will soon ring to remind us of truths beyond time, otherwise we'll forget or ignore them. We have to move across the tapestry of life very carefully so we constantly define time, naming it, dissecting it, making it part of a week or a certain month or a certain year. We create sun dials, hour candles and other mechanisms to assist us.'

'And here at Mistleham?'

'Time is like the seasons outside, Ranulf. They run parallel to each other. We sow in autumn, watch in winter, tend in spring and reap in summer. Here at Mistleham a bloody harvest has sprouted, but the seed . . . Time is the answer to all the mystery. When did that begin? Why? And who was responsible? So, Ranulf, Principal Clerk in the Chancery of the Green Wax, take up your pen and let us impose our own horarium, our own book of bloody hours on the mayhem at Mistleham.'

Corbett walked over to the window.

'Today is Wednesday the thirteenth of January, the

Feast of St Hilary in the Year of Our Lord 1304. It's also harvest time, Ranulf, for what happened in the past, the fruit of seeds sown at least thirteen years ago, perhaps even earlier.' Corbett paused as Ranulf began to write using the secret cipher his master had taught him. 'In 1291,' Corbett continued, 'a company from Mistleham, fired by religious fervour no doubt,' he added sardonically, 'journeyed to Outremer under two young knights, Sir Oliver Scrope and his cousin Gaston de Bearn. Others accompanied them, including Master Henry Claypole, now Mayor of Mistleham; during that expedition he acted as Scrope's squire. Now Acre fell on the twelfth of September 1291. We don't know what really happened, but according to reports . . .' Corbett paused in his pacing. 'I left messages with Drokensford to send me an account of events, what the chronicles tell us. However, what such a document will not divulge is what happened to the company from Mistleham. Acre fell, Scrope and Claypole escaped. Gaston, Scrope's cousin, died of his wounds in the infirmary, the rest were killed. Now all that could be suspect but we possess no evidence to the contrary. By 1292 Scrope had returned to England with treasures looted from the Templars, particularly the Sanguis Christi. He became lord of the manor, rich and powerful, hailed as a crusading hero by king and council. Already wealthy with his loot and his inheritance, he was given a rich heiress in marriage and settled down to a life of peace and plenty.

'Between 1291 and 1292 his blood sister Marguerite had entered the Benedictine order, a capable woman who, with the support of Church, Crown and Lord Scrope, was appointed Abbess of St Frideswide, the nearby Benedictine convent. All at Mistleham lies quiet and fallow. Father Thomas returns from the wars in Wales; a reformed priest, he takes up residence at St Alphege's. Again, all is quiet. In the autumn of 1302 Master Benedict Le Sanglier becomes Dame Marguerite's chaplain, yes? In the following January, Brother Gratian arrives as Lord Scrope's confessor. The harmony continues until Lent last year and the arrival of the Free Brethren of the Holy Spirit. Now the Free Brethren were one of those wandering groups of religious. Carrying letters from the papal curia at Avignon, they land at Dover, are given safe passage into Essex and settle in the ruins of Mordern.'

'Why should Scrope allow that?'

'He viewed them as no danger. They were patronised by Father Thomas, who, late last summer and early autumn, asked them to devise a painting for his parish church. Dame Marguerite also took a liking to them. The Free Brethren were undoubtedly eccentric, not heretic or schismatic, though they adopted a rather original interpretation of certain Church doctrines. We do not know who they really were; French undoubtedly, but they assumed Old Testament names. They proclaimed themselves as free as the air. It would take years, if ever, to establish who they really were and where they came from. Then, in November of last year, John Le Riche, one of the gang who plundered the crypt at Westminster, arrives in Mistleham with at least the dagger used on Edward by the assassins in Outremer. Master Claypole and Lord Scrope capture him, seize the dagger, try Le Riche and hang him, but almost immediately Le Riche's corpse disappears. Now,' Corbett paused, 'harvest time arrives. God knows why, but the relationship between the Free Brethren and Mistleham becomes malignant. Weeds, rotting and corrupt, spring up and spread blight in the community. Allegations of theft, poaching and rampant lechery are levelled against the Free Brethren. Suspicions about their true purpose emerge when Lord Scrope, through Brother Gratian and others, discovers they are well armed and practising archery deep in the forest.

'After the attack Scrope undoubtedly discovered evidence that the Free Brethren were planning to attack his manor as well as secure swift and easy passage abroad. He may have suspected that Le Riche was somehow involved with them. Le Riche might have sheltered in that crypt that the Free Brethren also used in their secret designs. Scrope never found that crypt. Or did he, but just ignored it when he discovered it contained nothing he was searching for? I must reflect on the secrets held by that Chapel of the Damned, but not just yet.' Corbett paused.

'Anyway, Scrope decides to wipe out the Free Brethren root and branch and does so late last year. All are killed. He leaves their corpses to rot. He seizes whatever possessions they had, including incriminating documents and weapons, and, to all appearances, harmony returns to the community. At least until the New Year, when the Sagittarius emerges blowing his horn and dealing out death indiscriminately amongst the people of Mistleham. The same killer destroys Lord Scrope's guard dogs. He also pays a midnight visit to our parish priest Father Thomas, where he describes himself not as the Sagittarius but as Nightshade, and warns Scrope to make a public confession of all his sins before the market cross within a certain time or suffer the consequences. Now what else is there? Well, we know Lord Scrope has been threatened by two different sources, the Temple and one other. He has decided to deflect this by handing over the Sanguis Christi to the King, though not through us but Brother Gratian. That is a matter I will have to decide for myself. Well, Ranulf, is that a fair summation?'

The Principal Clerk in the Chancery of the Green Wax, as nimble with his wits as he was with his pen, nodded in agreement.

'There are other mysteries, such as the horn-blowing last night as well as today out at Mordern, though no Sagittarius appeared. Then there's Jackanapes, killed by not one but two shafts . . .' Corbett paused as Chanson knocked on the door. The groom stumbled into the chamber trying to straighten a buckle and wanting to know when they would next eat. Corbett made him sit by the fire, poured him a goblet of wine and offered the platter of bread and cheeses the servants had left under a piece of linen. Chanson made himself comfortable, ignoring Ranulf's glare as Corbett returned to his pacing. 'Now that's the story being peddled, Ranulf, but is it the truth? *Primo*: what truly happened at Acre, the Year of Our Lord 1291? Why are events that occurred during the fall of that last Christian fortress in Outremer the root of all this malignancy? *Secundo*: those warnings sent to Lord Scrope: is it the Temple, some other enemy or both? The threats refer to time, about the Mills grinding slow, a reference surely to a long period of justice being planned, but for what and by whom?'

'The Sanguis Christi?' Ranulf asked.

'Oh, I think there's more to it than that, Ranulf. *Tertio*: the Free Brethren of the Holy Spirit, who were they? Why come to Mistleham in the first place? Where did they obtain their weapons? Were they truly planning an assault on Lord Scrope at Mistleham Manor or elsewhere? Why such violence? There were fourteen in number; all were killed during the assault, no one disputes that. However, what was the real reason for the deaths? Why did Scrope lie about them practising archery in the forest? That would have been foolish, surely? A great deal of evidence indicates that the Free Brethren hid their weapons and exercised their skill in that gloomy crypt in the Chapel of the Damned.

'*Quarto*: the Sagittarius – is he killing out of revenge for the slaughter at Mordern? If so, why? Was there a fifteenth member or a sympathiser here in Mistleham who wants vengeance for Lord Scrope's victims? Now, there is no doubt that the people of Mistleham were involved in the assault, so they will pay, but for how long? Until fourteen are dead? The Sagittarius kills indiscriminately, yet it is strange that Jackanapes was murdered by not one arrow but two. Why? Apparently the madcap was befriended by the Free Brethren, and if Dame Marguerite is correct, and I do not see why she should lie, and he was a witness to the massacre at Mordern, he may have been able to help us. The townspeople call the killer the Sagittarius, the Bowman, but when Father Thomas' sinister visitor appeared, he called himself Nightshade. Why? What is that a reference to?'

'Who created the name Sagittarius?' Ranulf asked. 'It must be a scholar, someone educated, knowledgeable in Latin.'

'True, true,' Corbett murmured. 'Then there's John Le Riche, former royal archer, an outlaw, a man of wit and sharp intelligence, so why did he blunder so foolishly into Master Claypole's trap? Did the Free Brethren shelter him? Why? Out of charity, or some other reason? And when he was captured, why the swift trial and even swifter execution? Was he truly hanged or did he escape? Is he the Sagittarius? If he did die, why steal his corpse? Who would do that? Then there's that verse, "Rich, shall richer be, Where God kissed Mary in Galilee."' Corbett paused. '*Quinto*: Lord Scrope.' He drew a deep breath. 'So many, many questions to ask of him: Acre, Le Riche, the Free Brethren, the Sagittarius, Nightshade, his secret sins; Scrope has much to hide. He is now threatened on every side. Above all, why did he organise that massacre? What was he searching for? Why did he leave those corpses to frighten off the curious? Does that mean he never found what he was searching for?'

'We must question him, master.'

'Eventually,' Corbett replied, 'but I doubt if he will tell the truth. He knew we were coming, Ranulf, he is well prepared and advised. Not even the best lawyers of the Exchequer could trap him . . .' Corbett paused at the sound of feet running along the gallery outside, followed by a pounding on the door, Chanson hastened to open it and the servant almost fell into the chamber.

'Sir Hugh, my lord Corbett,' he gasped, 'Lord Oliver beseeches you to come. The Sagittarius has returned to Mistleham . . .'

The chronicler of the nearby Convent of St Frideswide as well as the town clerk Walter Bassingbourne recorded the terrifying events surrounding that hideous incident late on Wednesday 13 January 1304 just as the beadles and bailiffs prepared to ring the market bell, the signal for the closure of business. A good day, though the frost had hardly thawed and an icy breeze kept nipping at the skin. A thin mist had seeped in as daylight faded and stall-holders ordered their apprentices to put away stock in barrels and casks. The beggars crept out to search for scraps outside the bakers, cookshops and taverns. Pedlars, chapmen and tinkers stored away their precious pennies in hidden purses. Pilgrims on their way to St Cedd's hermitage on the Essex coast stowed their bundles in stables after reaching agreement with the tavern masters. A group of whores in their tawdry finery had been released from the stocks to the jibes and jeers of a gang of roisterers who were trying to encourage four blind beggars to fight for a goblet of wine and a piece of juicy crisp pork. Apprentices and shop boys followed their masters to the goldsmiths to lodge their day's profits safely away, all unaware that death had entered Mistleham and was stalking them with a sharp eye for suitable prey.

Robert de Scott, captain of Lord Scrope's retinue, was the first to die. Full of resentment at Corbett, he had adjourned to the Honeycomb tavern, then on to the Portal of Heaven, which also fronted the market-place. There he had drowned his sorrows in cheap ale, then bought the favours of a slattern to entertain him in a grubby garret upstairs. He came lurching out of the Portal of Heaven even as three long blasts of the hunting horn announced that bloody mayhem had once again returned to Mistleham. Robert was so drunk he could only stand staring bleary-eyed whilst others fled. He swayed on his feet, meaning to move just as the yard-long iron-tipped ash shaft pierced him in the heart. A deadly shot, which threw him on to his back to quiver gargling on his own blood. Chaos engulfed the marketplace as traders fled or hid beneath their stalls. Women grabbed their children and ran shrieking into alcoves, doorways and runnels. Two brave souls raced across to help Robert de Scott, but he was dead and all they could do was drag his corpse into the tap room of the Portal of Heaven, locking the door behind them. A short while passed. People peeped out of their hiding places, the light greying, the air turning colder as evening set in. William Le Vavasour, another of Scrope's men, died next. Confident that the danger had passed, he crept out of the runnel where he'd hidden, glimpsing another of Scrope's retainers emerging eager for the warmth and shelter of the tavern. Vavasour moved first and was struck in the throat, the iron barb piercing skin, muscle and bone. Mutwart, the second retainer, had reached the door to the tavern and was thumbing at the latch when the arrow came thudding into his back and out through his chest, pinning him like a fly to the wood.

The townspeople were still hiding when Corbett and Ranulf, accompanied by Scrope and the rest of his henchmen, thundered into the marketplace. Scrope's retainers had brought long oval shields from the manor armoury. Corbett and his companions dismounted and hid behind the shields as the henchmen formed a protective screen around them. Corbett peered over the rim of the shield-wall and saw a corpse almost floating in a puddle of blood as well as the body of the last victim still sprawled gruesomely against the tavern door. He ordered the shield-wall to hold, telling Chanson and others to keep the horses quiet. Scrope, beside himself with rage, was glaring around. He glimpsed Claypole waving agitatedly from a window.

'How many?' Scrope bellowed.

Catchpole lifted a hand, three fingers extended.

'Vavasour and Mutwart,' declared one of Scrope's men, with a keener sight than the rest.

'Robert de Scott is also dead.' Claypole's voice carried across the marketplace.

Scrope gave vent to a litany of curses. Corbett ignored him as he gazed at the entrance to the Portal of Heaven then round the marketplace. He admired the skill of the assassin. This was a good place for a master bowman to move and hide. He studied the empty doorways, the dark mouths of alleyways and runnels; the killer could lurk in any of these, not to mention the houses, four or five storeys high, with their garrets, narrow windows, ledges and roofs. Nevertheless, Corbett sensed the Sagittarius would not strike again. Time had passed. It would be too dangerous now; a flurry of movement or a flash of colour might betray the killer. The Sagittarius not only hid in the dark but used panic and fear to disguise himself.

'In God's name, I beg you cease this!'

Corbett spun around. Father Thomas, preceded by Master Benedict Le Sanglier carrying a cross, processed across the marketplace. In one hand the parish priest carried a lighted candle capped against the breeze, in the other a hand bell, which he shook vigorously.

'In God's name,' the priest shouted, 'I adjure you to cease this.' He paused in the middle of the square. A dog came snuffling over. Corbett ordered the shield wall to stand aside and walked across.

'I think the danger has passed,' he said softly.

'It will return,' Father Thomas retorted, face all concerned. 'As it has in the past . . .' He broke off abruptly. 'I was closeted in my house.' The priest's anger drained away. 'Master Benedict came running through the church to tell me what had happened.' He blew out the candle and pointed at the Portal of Heaven. 'I must see to the dead.'

7

On that day 13 January 1304,
the Judges began their deliberations.
Annals of London, 1304

Father Thomas hurried away even as people began to emerge from their hiding places. Doors were flung open, shutters removed. A boy came racing across the cobbles, ignoring the shrieks of his mother. Lord Scrope's retinue broke up. The manor lord became busy talking to Master Claypole, who'd emerged from his house looking rather ridiculous, a dagger in one hand, a large pan in the other to serve as a shield. A bell sounded. The market returned to business, but Corbett sensed the mood had grown ugly. There were dark looks, mutterings and mumbles. The people of Mistleham now believed that the Sagittarius and his dreadful acts were connected to those hideous events out at Modern. Corbett told Chanson to guard the horses, plucked Ranulf by the sleeve and gestured towards the Portal of Heaven. 'The Bowman must have stood directly opposite.' He turned and pointed to the line of houses across the square, facing the tavern.

'Search the alleyways, alcoves and runnels, Ranulf. Go literally from house to house and room to room, see what you can find.'

'He must have carried his bow,' Ranulf murmured.

'Or had it hidden away, ready for use. There again,' Corbett chewed the corner of his lip, 'a bow can be unstrung, it can look like a stave, whilst the quiver of arrows remains hidden under a cloak. See what you can find.'

Ranulf nodded and walked across. Corbett went over to where Scrope and Claypole were deep in conversation. He paused. He hadn't noticed it before, but now the more he stared at these two men with their harsh, pugnacious faces, the more he could see the blood tie between them. What was more important was that both the manor lord and the mayor were in heated conversation. Corbett wondered what it was about, whilst he was eager to question both about that strange half-finished remark by Father Thomas about the Sagittarius returning as he had in the past.

'Sir Hugh,' Scrope turned, a bland smile on his ugly face, 'this is damnable.'

'So is the cause, Lord Oliver! The Sagittarius, who gave him that name?'

Scrope glanced at Claypole; the mayor just pursed his lips, shrugged and glanced away.

'I asked a question.' Corbett paused as a crowd of townsmen headed towards them, carrying clubs, faces full of resentment. Corbett drew his sword in a slashing curl of light. Scrope also drew his, whilst his men-at-arms began to drift back, uncertain about what was happening.

'I am the King's man.' Corbett advanced to confront the angry mob. 'You will see justice done. This is not your business! Go about your trade.'

'This is Scrope's doing!' a voice shouted. 'Those young ones out at Mordern, it should never have happened.'

'In the King's name,' Corbett repeated loudly, 'go about your business.' His hand went behind his back, he pulled his dagger from its sheath and walked closer to the hostile traders. 'Don't be foolish,' he said softly to their leader, a burly faced, popping-eyed man, apparently a butcher from the bloody apron wrapped around him. 'Go back to your business, sir; take your friends with you. This will end and justice will be done, I assure you.'

The butcher glanced at his companions. Corbett lowered his sword.

'As you say,' the man muttered, 'this must end.' He gestured with his hands; the tradesmen broke up, drifting back, muttering and cursing over their shoulders.

'Sir Hugh,' Scrope declared, 'these murders must be brought to an end.'

'And so they will be, Lord Oliver, though I suspect it will end in a hanging.'

'What do you mean?' Claypole queried, eyes narrowed, lower lip jutting out, ready to take up the argument.

'That's how it always ends,' Corbett added cheerfully, sheathing his sword. 'A hanging! Someone, some day, somehow will have to die violently for all this. However, I do not predict the future, I just use logic and evidence. I asked you a question, sirs. This bowman, the Latin name, the Sagittarius, who gave it to him?'

He stared up at the sky, trying to hide his nervousness. If he wanted to, that deadly bowman could return, and what better target than the King's own man? He felt a stab of fear. He was hunting a true killer, a soul dedicated to inflicting as much destruction as he could. He was right, there was no other way, this business would end in heinous violence.

'Lord Scrope, I asked a question. Indeed, I have so many questions to ask you.'

'Father Thomas,' Scrope replied testily. 'He first used the word Sagittarius.'

'When?'

Both men looked at each other.

'When? Lord Oliver, Master Claypole, I want an answer. I am losing patience. The King's own subjects have been killed, whilst you show little respect for the corpses of men who served you.'

'I'll see to my own dead, Corbett.'

'*Pax et bonum* . . .' Corbett whispered. 'I wish you well, but watch your tongue, Scrope. You can speak to me here man to man or I'll summon you to Westminster. One question: why the Sagittarius? Father Thomas also hinted that such an assassin has been here before.'

'He's a prattling priest.'

'A good priest, Scrope. So do you and Master Claypole wish to appear on oath before the King's justices?'

'Tell him,' Claypole grated, turning his face against the biting breeze. 'For God's sake, Lord Oliver, tell him! What does it matter now?'

'Sir Hugh!'

Corbett turned.

Master Benedict, neat and precise in his long woollen robe, cowl pulled full across his head, came striding across.

'Sir Hugh, Dame Marguerite would like to speak to you.'

'Master Benedict, give your mistress my kindest regards. Tell her I shall do so when I return to Mistleham Manor.'

'Sir Hugh.' Master Benedict took a deep breath and bowed. 'If you can, sir, remember me at court.' The chaplain wrung his hands. 'Here in Essex, this violence, the bloodshed . . . Sir Hugh, that is one of the reasons I entered the priesthood. I detest what is happening here. I do not wish to carry a sword, pluck a bow . . .'

Master Benedict was still shocked by what he had witnessed.

'Go back.' Corbett gently patted him on the shoulder. 'Do not worry.' He smiled. 'I shall do what I can.'

The chaplain, thanking him profusely, walked away. Corbett turned back.

'Now, Lord Scrope, Master Claypole, the Sagittarius?'

'I returned here in 1292.' Scrope measured his words. 'I settled down. All was peace and harmony, but in the autumn of the following year, for a few weeks I was stalked, hunted, Sir Hugh, by a bowman. Oh, he must have loosed six or seven shafts at me. He always missed.'

'At no one else?'

Scrope smiled thinly. 'No, Sir Hugh, just me. Father Thomas called him the Sagittarius; he warned his parishioners from the pulpit that whoever was responsible was committing a great sin.'

'But the Sagittarius never did any harm, he never struck you?'

'No, Sir Hugh, then it stopped as mysteriously as it began.'

'And you never found out who or why?'

'Of course not. If I had found the culprit, I'd have hanged him! Sir Hugh, you said you had many questions, so ask me, though I do not have many answers. I have told you what I can. I know nothing else. I cannot help you. I have agreed to return the Sanguis Christi and the dagger. What I have done here I did for my own protection and for the good of the Crown. I kept the peace.'

'And this Sagittarius,' Corbett persisted, 'do you think he is the same person as the last?'

Scrope just pulled a face. Corbett stepped closer.

'Whatever you say, Lord Oliver, or you, Master Claypole, I tell you this, not as a King's clerk, but as one soul speaking to another. This violence will continue blazing like a fire; only the truth can douse its flames.'

Corbett spun on his heel and walked over to St Alphege's Church. A group of young men and women sheltering inside the porch informed him how the three corpses had been taken to the death house.

Father Thomas was busy tending them there with the Guild of Magdalene, a group of pious townswomen dedicated to such tasks as collecting the dead, dressing them and preparing them for burial. Corbett nodded. He asked about the painting done by the Free Brethren. One of the young men led him in along the transept and pointed to the fresco.

'Vividly done,' he said. 'Look, sir, the colours.'

'And the story?'

Corbett's guide screwed his face up in concentration. 'Father Thomas did tell us. He preached about it and used the painting to explain. Ah, that's it! The Fall of Ba—'

'The Fall of Babylon.' Corbett, staring at the fresco, finished the word. 'Of course, thank you very much.'

He examined the painting closely. The theme had been cleverly depicted, the colours specially chosen to stand out in the poor light, particularly the reds and greens. He studied it curiously, moving from scene to scene. The great dragon in the sky; the towers and walls of the city; the attackers in their white cloaks; a man in bed; a banquet scene; the flight of Judas and other traitors down the Valley of Death; the strange symbols and plant-like shapes decorating the fringes of the painting. He broke from his study as voices further down the church near the front door began to sing a hymn.

'Oh pure Virgin! Come ye with tapers of wax. Come forth here and worship this child both God and man, offered in his Temple by his mother dear.'

Corbett smiled and glanced down the nave. Despite the hideous killings out in the marketplace, the young men and women in the porch were still intent on preparing for the Feast of Candlemas. He walked back and watched the troupe rehearse their play: Simeon and Anna the prophetess waiting for Mary and Joseph to bring the baby Jesus into the Temple. They finished with a rendering of the Benedictus. Corbett asked if he could participate; they cheerfully agreed and gathered around the baptismal font to rehearse. Corbett sang the first verse so he could set the pitch and tone; the others replied with the second stanza, the choristers staring shyly at this King's man who seemed so interested in what they were doing. Eventually the cadence and tone were agreed and Corbett led them in song, opening with the beautiful line of the hymn: 'Blessed be the Holy Child, Mary's own son . . .'

The choir joined in lustily. Corbett soon forgot the dangers, chanting the verses with the rest. He was so pleased with the result, he asked if they would sing it a second time, handing over a piece of silver for them to share afterwards. The choir quickly agreed. Once again Corbett became lost in the rise and fall of the beautiful plainchant. After they had finished, the choir made their apologies but said they must go, adding that Father Thomas would not be returning to give them a blessing. They left, closing the door behind them. Corbett crouched at the foot of a pillar and stared down the nave. Darkness was creeping in. Candle glow from the chantry chapels and the lady altar provided meagre light. He glanced towards the transept and glimpsed those wild figures on the battlements of the wall painting. A cold night mist was seeping under the door. Corbett shivered. He was approaching his nightmare, one that always haunted him on expeditions such as this, that he'd be caught vulnerable by an arrow or knife speeding through the darkness. He shook himself and got to his feet. The Christmas season was now over; perhaps if Father Thomas did return, he would hear Corbett's confession and shrive him. Corbett returned to the painting, studying it carefully, marvelling at its ingenuity and imagination. He felt a pang of pity for the young people who had done this, now nothing but black ash in that dark, damned forest at Mordern.

He heard the corpse door open and whirled round. Father Thomas came striding across.

'Sir Hugh, one of the young men you were singing with,' the priest stepped out of the shadows, 'he came and said you were here. What can I do to help?'

'I admire the painting.' Corbett gestured at the wall. 'You must be very proud of it?'

'I am.' Father Thomas smiled.

Corbett stepped closer. The light was poor and he wanted to watch this priest's eyes. 'It's a pity,' he said, 'they were killed.'

'Aye.' The priest sighed. 'And if Lord Scrope has his way, the painting will disappear. He has agreed to refurbish both St Alphege's and a great deal of St Frideswide's Convent, perhaps contrition for his sins.'

'We all have reparation to make.'

'Is that true, King's clerk?'

'It is true, priest. You asked if you could do anything for me. I would like you to shrive me, hear my confession.'

Father Thomas looked surprised, but agreed. He led Corbett up the church and gestured to him to kneel on the prie-dieu before the mercy seat. Then he went to the sacristy and returned with a purple stole around his neck. He sat down on the chair, turning his face away from Corbett.

'In nomine Patris et Filii et Spiritus Sancti . . .'

Corbett blessed himself and intoned the formula.

'Father, it is three months since I was last shrived. These are my sins . . .'

Father Thomas tried to hide his surprise and concentrate on what Corbett was saying. It was virtually unheard of for such a leading royal clerk to make his confession to a simple parish priest. Nevertheless, the more the priest listened, the more perturbed he became. Corbett he recognised as a just man, trying to pursue the right: the clerk turned in on himself, confessing not so much sins as all the opportunities to do good he had ignored. How he'd showed irritation to his wife and children, impatience to others in the Chancery where he worked, a lack of compassion towards his companions. Father Thomas never interrupted, just nodded occasionally as his own apprehension deepened. If this man could criticise himself so clearly, so accurately, what would happen when he turned on the inhabitants of Mistleham, himself included, with his keen wit and sharp eye? If this clerk had his way, all the evil mystery swirling around the town and manor would be resolved. Once Corbett had finished, Father Thomas sat in silence for a while, then turned to face the clerk squarely.

'You shouldn't belabour yourself, Sir Hugh. You should also,' he smiled, 'think of the good you've done. That is what being shrived is about: recognising your true state before God. For your penance, what can I give you, what would you like to do?'

Corbett smiled. 'Let's sing, Father. The day is ending, bloody work has been done. I came into this church to be shriven, to be cleansed.' He stared round at the dancing shadows and pointed to the lady altar. 'Do you have a good voice, Father?'

'I once sang in the royal chapel.' The priest laughed. 'Come then.'

They both went and stood in the lady chapel, staring up at the statue of the Virgin. For a few moments they practised, then both men intoned the Salve Regina, the Church's evening hymn to the Virgin.

'*Salve Regina, Mater Misericordiae, Vita Dulcedo et Spes Nostra* – Hail Holy Queen, Mother of Mercy, Hail Our Life, Our Sweetness and Our Hope . . .'

Father Thomas was a lusty singer with a powerful voice. Corbett thoroughly enjoyed himself, not only in giving praise but in purging himself of the terrors of that day. After they'd finished he lit three tapers, one for Maeve, one for Edward and one for Eleanor, and then, feeling guilty, a fourth for the King.

'I must be gone,' Father Thomas declared, but then paused as the door was flung open and Lord Scrope, accompanied by Brother Gratian, came marching up the nave like anger incarnate.

'The corpses are in the death house?' Scrope made no attempt at courtesies.

'You know they are.' Father Thomas gestured at the door on the far side of the church.

The manor lord stared round. 'I promise you this,

Father, by midsummer the renovation work will have begun. I'll give you a church to be proud of.'

'I am proud of it now.'

The manor lord didn't even bother to answer, but continued on. Brother Gratian, his bony white face shrouded by a deep cowl, nodded courteously and followed him out.

'I had best go with him,' Father Thomas murmured.

'No, Father, I don't think you should.' Corbett caught him by the sleeve.

The priest glanced up in surprise.

'Father, you served in the King's forces in Wales?'

'You know I did.'

'And you met Lord Scrope there?'

'Yes.'

'You were a priest in the royal chapel?'

'I was.' Father Thomas tried to keep the nervousness out of his voice.

'And you decided to abandon Crown preferment to become a faithful pastor, a good shepherd?'

'I strive to do my best. I was in the war in Wales. I saw people murdered, killed in more ways than any man could imagine. Afterwards I felt sick. What does it profit a man if he gains the whole world but suffers the loss of his own soul? I was party to that. I had to make reparation. I met Lord Scrope at the beginning of the campaign, years before he went to Acre. He promised me that if I wanted, he would use his influence, persuade the Crown to appoint me to a benefice here.'

'But you did not like him?'

'No, I didn't.'

'Do you have a longbow, Father? Please, the truth, here before Christ.'

The priest turned abruptly and walked away. Corbett realised that he intended to return and did so a short while later, hurrying back with a longbow and a quiver full of arrows.

'Of course, I keep it close. We live in violent times, Sir Hugh. A priest may have to protect himself, his church or his flock.'

'And your aim is as good as ever?' Corbett asked.

'Lord, do you want to put me to the test?'

Corbett smiled thinly. 'I'm no fool, Father. If you are trained in the longbow, you will eventually hit your mark.'

'Why are you asking this, Sir Hugh?'

Corbett walked past the priest, paused, then turned.

'The Sagittarius, the one who appeared almost ten years ago: you were that man, weren't you, Father? You served with Lord Scrope in Wales. You saw him butcher Welsh prisoners, and when you arrived here, you saw him high on the hog, feasting himself, a man of blood acting the great lord. Isn't there a psalm about God drawing back his bow and aiming at the wicked?'

'What makes you think it was me?'

'Oh,' Corbett walked back, carefully measuring his footsteps, 'a master bowman never misses, Father. Maybe once, but two, three times, no! The bowman of almost ten years ago was a man who wanted to frighten Lord Scrope. The only person who'd want to do that, at least according to the evidence, would be you. You called yourself the Sagittarius – God's archer. It's true, isn't it, Father? You've heard my confession; now I'll hear yours. What I have said to you is covered by the seal; what you say to me is also covered by the seal.'

'I hate him!' the priest whispered. 'Sir Hugh, I felt guilty. I secured this benefice through his good offices, but I truly hate Lord Scrope. Yes, I was in Wales. A group of Welsh rebels, tired and hungry, came down from the hills carrying a cross, ready to surrender. Scrope was in charge of a vexillation of mounted archers and footmen. I was there. It was late in the evening, on a day like this, cold and bitter. They came into our camp barefoot and unarmed, one of them carrying that cross. Before anyone could do anything, Scrope had drawn his sword and moved amongst them, stabbing and hacking; others joined in. They'd seen their friends and comrades killed by the Welsh so they showed no mercy. By the time I'd reached that part of the camp they were dead, sixteen or seventeen souls, Corbett, young men, some of them mere boys, corpses awash with blood, Scrope leaning on his sword, the others holding axes, daggers, clubs, bloodied up to their elbows. I cursed him. I shrieked at him. You served in Wales, Corbett, you know what it was like. No mercy asked, none shown. A fight to the death.' Father Thomas breathed in.

'Afterwards, I left the royal service; I served in this village or that. Scrope is a strange man. Part of his soul is not yet fully rotten. He sinned but he wanted to purge himself. Anyway, he remembered me and I was invited back here.' Father Thomas abruptly caught himself. 'The people of Mistleham are good, decent and God-fearing. Oh there are individuals like Claypole and Robert de Scott, but you met those young men and women preparing the play for Candlemas. I enjoy serving them. Anyway, I was appointed just after Scrope returned from Acre. He came back more steeped in sin than ever. He brought treasures and waxed fat as the wealthy manor lord. He married Lady Hawisa, a true beauty. I'll be honest.' He smiled. 'We priests are supposed to be celibate, chaste in thought, word and deed, but Lady Hawisa . . .' He shrugged. 'I sometimes dream of her, my fair, fair lady. I was angry with Scrope, I recalled those corpses. He seemed to be gaining everything; no ill could befall him, living proof that Satan does look after his own. So I decided to frighten him. I brought out my longbow and, for a while, taunted, baited and terrified him. I realised I was doing wrong so I stopped. Yes, I was the Sagittarius. I preached against my own sin. I was the one who used that name, but I tell you this, Corbett.' He grasped Sir Hugh's hand and squeezed it. 'Not in my nightmares did I ever imagine another Sagittarius would emerge, the archer of death, the bowman from hell!'

Corbett heard the door open and Ranulf calling his name. 'I must go.'

'God's peace stay with you, Sir Hugh. I'll see you tomorrow morning for the Jesus Mass at the manor. Dame Marguerite and I have business with Lord Scrope. He has invited us to the reclusorium, so we'll meet again soon. Remember, I've heard your confession and you've heard mine. I have nothing more to add.'

Corbett joined Ranulf out on the porch.

'Master, I did as you asked. On each side of the square run needle-thin alleyways, really nothing more than holes between the houses.'

'And the houses themselves?'

'Well, as you know, some are four, five storeys high. Some are lived in, some are not. Others are single-room tenements used by travelling chapmen and tinkers.

One thing I did learn, many of those tenements are actually owned by Lord Scrope; he draws rent from them.'

Corbett nodded. 'What I suspect, Ranulf, is that our Sagittarius may have a bow and quiver of arrows disguised or hidden away, or,' he shrugged, 'he may have stored his weapons in one of those garrets or rooms.'

'Not to mention stairwells, Sir Hugh, and a host of windows. Some are mere arrow slits open to the wind, others are casements that can be unlocked. I stood at a few of these; they give a good view across the marketplace. For a skilled archer, it would not be difficult to bring down three or even more men.'

'And all those killed were from Lord Scrope's retinue,' Corbett declared.

'They were with us at Mordern this morning. The killer knew they'd adjourned to the taverns; he simply waited for the right time.'

'Did you question anyone?' Corbett asked.

'Servants, maids, boys, but they could tell me nothing. Master, those houses are gloomy and shadow-filled; you could hide an army there. Oh, by the way,' he added, 'Chanson claims he's freezing to death. If we don't return soon, we'll find nothing but a pillar of ice.'

Corbett nodded. 'We've finished here, Ranulf.

Father Thomas will visit the manor early tomorrow morning. I suppose he has to return here to sing the requiem masses for those slain. God's Acre at St Alphege's will soon become full.'

They went out into the now silent marketplace. The day's trading was completely finished. Stalls had been put away. Lantern horns gleamed from hooks on door posts, candles glowed in windows. A dog barked, beggars flittered like shadows in the poor light. Chanson had led their horses over to a tethering pole while he and some beggars grouped around a pitch cask in which some good citizen had kindled a fire to keep them warm during the night. Chanson muttered and groaned about how cold and hungry he was, but soon cheered as Corbett swung himself into the saddle, saying that they'd return to Mistleham Manor for some good food, ale and, perhaps, even another goblet of that mulled wine. They turned their horses to leave. Corbett was glad he'd been shriven; as they made their way across the icy cobbles into the dark lane leading back to the manor, he sensed he was now moving to the heart of this murderous mystery.

8

He along with others, was accustomed to enter houses of different people at twilight and plunder them.

H.T. Riley, *Memorials of London*

Once he'd returned to Mistleham Manor and made himself presentable, Corbett went into the Antioch Wing of the house where a servant led him to the abbess' chambers. Despite the roaring fire, the warm hangings and shuttered windows, Dame Marguerite was still garbed in her thick black gown and cloak, her sweet face framed by a white wimple. She was sitting in a high-backed chair before the fire, her feet resting on a stool. Master Benedict, dressed in a cambric shirt and dark blue hose, feet pushed into slippers, a sleeveless gown over his shoulders, sat next to her, a book on his lap.

'Ah, Sir Hugh.' Dame Marguerite made to rise, but Corbett shook his head. 'Master Benedict was reading from *The Romance of the Rose*. I so like the story. A work of art, don't you think, Sir Hugh?'

Corbett nodded in agreement.

'Master Benedict, please?' the abbess whispered.

The chaplain rose, smiled at Corbett and pulled across another chair, positioning it between himself and Dame Marguerite. Corbett sat down. For a while the usual pleasantries and courtesies were exchanged. Dame Marguerite looked composed but Master Benedict was still pale and pinched from the horrors he'd witnessed.

'I've given Master Benedict two goblets of claret,' Dame Marguerite remarked, following Corbett's gaze. 'My brother is truly a man of blood, Sir Hugh. Perhaps Master Benedict should not have gone there. But look, I thank you for coming.' She paused as Corbett sipped from the goblet of white wine Master Benedict served. The chaplain also offered a platter of comfits, which he refused.

'Dame Marguerite, I have some questions for you. Perhaps it is best if I ask them before you tell me the purpose of this meeting.'

'Of course.' She smiled. 'No, no, Master Benedict, please stay. You are my confessor, you know everything I say and do.' She laughed prettily. 'Even think! Sir Hugh, your questions?'

'You call your brother a man of blood; was he that before he went to Acre?'

'You can answer that yourself. My brother had a

fearsome reputation as a warrior, in Wales and elsewhere, a man who relished the fury of battle. He took to fighting like a fish to swimming. He did not come back changed, just harder, angrier.'

'And he brought back treasures?'

'Yes, he brought back a hoard of precious items looted from the Temple, what he called the spoils of victory.'

'And Master Claypole too?'

'Yes, he profited. Strange you mention his name, Sir Hugh, because that's the reason for my asking to meet you.'

'But first you, Dame Marguerite. You're so different from your brother.'

'God knows why!' The abbess laughed, leaning back in her chair. 'When we were children I was a little frightened of Oliver. He could be violent, but we had a cousin, Gaston, he kept Oliver in check. The three of us would play. Our estates were much smaller than they are now, but where this manor house stands, the Island of Swans, the fields and meadows around, they've always been in my family. Our parents were distant, rather cold. Father was always busy on king's business. Our mother died young so we were left to the care of good servants as well as to our own devices. Mistleham, Mordern Forest, the deserted village, the Chapel of the Damned, they became our places of dreams where we fought dragons, the infidel or the King's enemies. Always the three of us,' she commented, 'but life changes, children cease to be innocent. Oliver and Gaston went off to the King's wars, Wales, Gascony and the Scottish border. Then they came home. Father had died, profits from our estates had fallen off. I admit, and so would Lord Oliver, that he journeyed to Outremer not only to fight for the cross but also for his own purse. By the time he came home I too had changed.' She drew a deep breath. 'While he was away I decided to enter St Frideswide as a Benedictine nun. Life continued to change. Oliver became what he wanted to be and I am what God wants me to be.'

Corbett glanced at the chaplain. He sat head down as if listening intently. Corbett felt just for a moment a profound sadness about the abbess, even though she was half smiling at the memories she'd evoked.

'And Gaston?'

The abbess just shrugged. 'From what I gather, he was sorely wounded at Acre after the walls were stormed. He was taken to the infirmary where he died of his wounds. Oliver and Master Claypole did what they could.'

'But isn't it strange,' Corbett insisted, 'that only two from Mistleham returned? Lord Scrope and his squire Master Claypole.'

'Sir Hugh, in some communities no one returned. Only a few went out, some died on the voyage, others of illness or wounds. My brother himself was wounded, as was Master Claypole.'

'But he came back a rich man.'

'Oh, definitely.'

Corbett startled as Master Benedict sprang to his feet, hand to mouth, and rushed towards the door.

'Poor boy.' Dame Abbess stared at Corbett. 'What he saw this morning has deeply upset him.' She waited for a while, until Master Benedict returned, wiping his mouth on a napkin.

'I am sorry,' he apologised, 'my stomach is queasy.' He retook his seat. 'This talk,' he whispered. 'Acre, the slaughter in the dragon courtyard, hideous killings in Mordern, threats and menaces.' He shook his head. 'I did not think it would be like this.'

Dame Marguerite asked whether he wanted anything to eat or drink, but Master Benedict simply held up a hand.

'Sir Hugh,' the abbess lifted the Ave beads wrapped around her fingers, 'I've come to ask you for two favours. First, when you return to London, please mention Master Benedict to the King. He must enter the royal service, he deserves preferment. He is a very good priest, a most erudite clerk, but I'll leave that to you. Second, however, a much more serious matter.

I call my brother a man of blood, and so he is. He is now being threatened whether rightly or wrongly, but he is still threatened. Even the King is displeased with him. The Sagittarius has appeared. In my view, that murderous archer is pursuing vengeance for those deaths at Mordern. I am sure you would agree with me; there's no other logical explanation. What I believe is that sooner or later my brother is going to meet his God. Scripture says that those who live by the sword die by the sword. I fear for my brother, I truly do.'

'Madam,' Corbett replied, 'how does that concern me? I am here to serve your brother's interests as best I can. You quote scripture: what a man sows, his soul reaps. Are you saying your brother is in mortal danger?'

'My brother is always in danger,' she replied. 'He is the heart of the problem. Our family, Sir Hugh, have owned this land since the Conqueror. We are the last Scropes. I am a virgin dedicated to God, my brother is married but has no legitimate heir. If he dies suddenly without issue . . .'

'Then surely the lands would go to his wife, Lady Hawisa?'

'I am deeply concerned,' the abbess cut in, 'as is Master Benedict, with whom I've discussed this on many occasions. If my brother dies without heir, true, his estates would go to Lady Hawisa. I would receive my portion; some would also go to Master Claypole and others. However, you must have heard the rumours? You must have looked at Claypole and my brother and seen the likeness?'

Corbett just stared back.

She took a deep breath. 'Some people claim,' she continued, 'that Master Henry Claypole is a by-blow, the illegitimate son of my brother. Many, many years ago, before he took to fighting and serving in the King's forces, my brother became enamoured of a certain Alice de Tuddenham. She was the daughter of a local wool merchant. Alice became pregnant shortly before she married a local trader, and the rumour persists . . .'

'That Claypole is your brother's son rather than that of Alice and her husband?'

'Precisely, Sir Hugh. Now, my brother Oliver and Master Henry Claypole have always been close. I am sure that in his will Lord Oliver has remembered Henry Claypole's good and faithful service. However, I am deeply concerned that when my brother dies without a legitimate heir, even though his estates should go to his widow, Master Claypole may well argue in the King's courts that he is not only my brother's son but a legitimate one.'

'How can that be?' Corbett was now genuinely puzzled.

'There are rumours,' the abbess continued, 'that Lord Scrope secretly married Alice de Tuddenham, which makes her second union invalid according to canon law. Both she and her husband have now gone to their reward, whatever that may be. Now, Sir Hugh, according to the law of the Church—'

'Henry Claypole could prove that he is the legitimate heir of Lord Oliver,' Corbett declared. 'And, by right of that, claim his estates, yet to achieve that, he will need proof?'

'I have visited Father Thomas,' Dame Marguerite declared. 'We have both searched for the blood books, the marriage registers, whatever documents the church might hold. However, for the period in which my brother may have married Alice de Tuddenham, the blood registers have mysteriously disappeared.'

'You think Master Claypole has stolen them?'

'He's an ambitious, avaricious man, Sir Hugh. He has fingers in many pies in Mistleham. It is possible that he stole them, keeping them against the evil day. At the same time, perhaps, the absence of those blood books is just a mishap. My brother and Alice de Tuddenham may have married in another church, another parish, though I doubt it.'

'Have you questioned your brother on this?'

'On a number of occasions over the years, but he

has always shrugged it off. He claims he is not responsible for the sins of his youth.'

'And Lady Hawisa?'

'I have never spoken to her directly about the matter. I feel a kinship for her, a virtuous woman. She's probably heard the rumours but nothing definite.'

Corbett stared into the fire. He had heard of similar cases coming before the chancery courts where an illegitimate child argued that he was in fact born within wedlock and, according to the law of both church and state, should receive a man's inheritance.

'Is your brother frightened of Master Claypole? Is that why he has favoured him, supported him in his appointment to mayor?'

'Over the years their relationship has changed,' Dame Marguerite conceded. She paused and stared round the comfortable chamber as if searching for a memory. The fire crackled and sparked. Outside, the wind had picked up, flapping at the shutters. Corbett could hear the creak and groan of the timbers of the manor, so full of riches yet also a place of dark memories, grudges and grievances. He was right to be cautious, to be wary. An intricate game was being played out here; more blood would be spilt.

'Yes,' Dame Marguerite nodded, 'I would say their relationship has changed. Claypole was always the servant; sometimes now he regards himself as an equal, as if he has . . .'

'A claim against your brother?'

'Exactly, Sir Hugh.'

'Is Lord Oliver frightened of Master Claypole?' Corbett repeated.

'My brother is a warrior. Publicly he is frightened of no one, but of course you haven't visited the reclusorium?'

Corbett shook his head.

'I've heard about the first Sagittarius,' he declared, 'the bowman who appeared, what, some ten years ago, and loosed shafts at your brother, though none ever found its mark.'

Dame Marguerite smiled. 'Yes, that frightened Lord Oliver, frightened him deeply, but there are other terrors lurking in his hard heart, like wolves in the darkness of the trees. He had been back scarcely two years when the reclusorium was built. He'd always liked the Island of Swans. When we were children he and I would go across there, turn it into what we called our own little kingdom. Now it is his refuge, so yes, my brother is frightened, perhaps of Henry Claypole or of others, shadows from the past.'

Corbett glanced at Master Benedict, who sat like a scholar in a schoolroom, all patient and attentive.

'And what do you think of this, sir?'

'I understand my lady abbess' concerns. I too share them. Nonetheless, as I've said to you, Sir Hugh, Mistleham is not my manor or the place I want to be. I believe that should I be appointed to some benefice in London, perhaps gain preferment in the royal service, then if, as she says, that evil day comes, the lady abbess would have—'

'Friends at court?' Corbett asked.

'Precisely!' Master Benedict pulled a face. 'Sir Hugh, when you return to London, when this business is finished, perhaps you can raise the matter of Claypole's secret desires and ambitions before the King.'

'I have heard of similar cases.' Corbett closed his eyes. 'I cannot quote chapter and verse, but even the King himself cannot set aside the law. If Master Claypole can prove he is Lord Scrope's legitimate heir, there is little anyone can do.' He opened his eyes and smiled. 'But of course, you want more, don't you?'

'Yes, Sir Hugh, I want my brother to live.' Lady Abbess swallowed hard. 'He must live. I pray for his safety. What I would like to do, through you, is to challenge Master Claypole about these rumours whilst my brother is still alive, to establish whether or not he is Lord Scrope's legitimate heir.'

'Of course,' Corbett whispered. 'I now understand why you wished to see me, Lady Abbess. If Henry

Claypole is summoned to the King's council, put on solemn oath and asked to produce whatever proof he has whilst Lord Oliver is alive and has no heir, your brother can rebut or support such claims. Of course, once your brother is dead, the one person who knows the truth is silenced for ever. But surely you have raised this issue with your brother, the dangers you and Lady Hawisa face?'

'I have, but my brother just scoffs at me, and says that time will take care of everything. Sir Hugh, I do not put my trust in time but in God and you. The sooner this business is done, the better.'

Corbett finished his wine and made his farewells. He rose, bowed to both Dame Marguerite and Master Benedict and went out closing the door behind. He'd reached the top of the stairs when a shadow slipped out of a window embrasure, so swift, so unexpected, Corbett stepped back, hand going round for his dagger.

'*Pax et bonum*, Sir Hugh.'

Corbett relaxed. 'Brother Gratian, I beg you, in the dark, at a time like this, in a place like this, you should be more prudent about stepping out of the shadows.'

'I wanted to see you, Sir Hugh. I have a favour to ask. You'll be finished here, surely? Can I accompany you back to London?'

'You'll be carrying the Sanguis Christi?'

'Of course!'

'Why the haste, Brother? What about your care for the spiritual life of your patron?'

'Sir Hugh, such a matter, between him and me, is covered by the seal of confession.'

'I will answer your question, Brother, when you answer mine.'

'Which is?'

'Were the Free Brethren such a threat to Holy Mother Church and the King's peace?'

'I've told the truth, Sir Hugh.'

Corbett shook his head.

'No you haven't, Brother! I don't think anyone has told the truth. I bid you good night . . .'

Corbett watched as Father Thomas finished the Jesus Mass with the final Gospel, the first twenty-two verses from St John beginning: '*In principio erat Verbum* – in the Beginning was the Word.' At the phrase 'the Word was made flesh', Corbett, together with the rest of the small congregation in the manor chapel, genuflected and kissed his thumb as a mark of respect. He rose and stared round. Ranulf, Chanson, Lady Hawisa, Dame Marguerite and Master Benedict were present, with servants and retainers from the manor. Brother Gratian was undoubtedly celebrating his own dawn mass in his chamber whilst Master Benedict, according to Dame Marguerite's hushed conversation before mass, had spent most of the night in the manor infirmary. Corbett rubbed his own eyes. He'd slept well but fitfully, his rest plagued by nightmares.

After the mass, Corbett had a few words with Lady Hawisa, then joined Ranulf and Chanson in the buttery for bread, cheese, butter and light ale. He hadn't decided what to do that day. He discussed with Ranulf the possibility of convoking a formal court of oyer and terminer, acting as Justices of the King and summoning people on oath. He considered the possibility of the priests, Master Benedict, Brother Gratian and Father Thomas, pleading benefit of clergy, that they answered to the church courts rather than those of the King. Nevertheless, he thought such a way forward was possible. One thing he had decided on: to interrogate Lord Scrope again and try to establish logical answers to his questions. He and Ranulf were about to leave the buttery when he heard a distant clanging. A groom sprang to his feet.

'What's the matter, man?' Ranulf asked.

'It's Lord Scrope,' the fellow replied. 'That's the alarm from the reclusorium!'

Corbett and Ranulf joined the rest as they streamed from the buttery across the yard, through the Jerusalem Gate and down the icy, slippery hill towards the Island of Swans. Corbett paused halfway and took in the scene in the grey morning light. On the jetty

Father Thomas was busy clambering from a boat; on the other side of the lake Dame Marguerite was busy beating the gong hung outside the reclusorium, the door to which was flung open. Corbett hurried down, now and again slipping on the ice, Ranulf following behind. Once they'd reached the jetty, Ranulf turned, telling the servants to stand back. Corbett grasped Father Thomas, who was still labouring to catch his breath.

'What is it?' he asked.

The priest looked haggard, wet-eyed from the cold. 'Sir Hugh, it's Lord Scrope, he's been murdered. You'd best come.'

Corbett clambered into the boat; Ranulf followed with Father Thomas. The boat itself was small and bobbed dangerously. The oarsman told them to sit down. He too was pale-faced, startled at what he'd seen. He pulled on the oars and the wherry cut its way through the cold water to the far side.

'Be careful,' the oarsman said as he pulled the oars in and slid his boat alongside the landing place. Corbett and Ranulf clambered out and walked up the steps to where Dame Marguerite was standing just inside the doorway. The lady abbess was whey-faced, eyes enlarged, and could hardly speak as she led Corbett into the reclusorium. The clerk immediately stared around. The windows were shuttered behind their drapes of velvet and leather. The room smelt of wine and fragrant beeswax; two or three candles still spluttered against the darkness. Corbett was aware of richness and luxury, costly items, rugs on the floor, heavy tapestries hanging against the walls, beautifully carved stools, tables and chairs, a large bed in the far recess, light glinting off silver and gold ornaments. He also noticed the window immediately to his right. Its drapes had been torn away, the wooden shutters smashed.

'It's where we forced an entry,' Dame Marguerite whispered.

Corbett held his hand up. The reclusorium reeked of wealth, but something else lurked in the gloom, an evil Corbett had pursued all his adult life: sudden, brutal murder. He had to go forward to see, to inspect the horror waiting deeper in the darkness. He crossed over to the dark shape outlined in the poor light, slumped in the great high-backed chair. Lord Scrope sat there, dead hands grasping its sides, his head slightly back. The look of mortal horror made his ugly face more gruesome in death, eyes popping, mouth slightly opened, nose and lips crusted with blood. In his chest, thrust deep to the hilt, was the assassin's dagger, the King's property, the faded red ribbon still attached to the handle.

'By Satan's feet!' Ranulf murmured.

Corbett studied the dead man's corpse closely. Scrope's tawny bed-robe was drenched with congealed blood. Ranulf brought across a candelabra, the weak flames deepening the hideousness of that corpse, gruesome in death, the face like a gargoyle mask. Some blood stained Scrope's fingers; a little more was on the floor.

'The bed chest!' Ranulf whispered.

Corbett walked over. The curtains to the four-poster bed had been pulled back, the counterpanes and sheets also; the bolsters were slightly pressed. Scrope had apparently adjourned to bed before murder came visiting. The trunk at the foot of the bed had been ransacked. The metal-rimmed caskets and coffers inside were empty, their lids thrown back. Corbett returned to the corpse. He leaned over, trying to avoid that popping, glassy dead glance. He felt beneath the rim of the bed-robe and gently lifted the silver key-chain up over the head, then went back to the chests and coffers. Sounds from outside echoed through. He glanced over his shoulder. More people had crossed to the Island of Swans, including Lady Hawisa. Dame Marguerite recollected herself and went out to help. Servants were also milling about; apparently both ferries had been used to bring them across. Corbett quickly tried the keys in the chests; they all fitted. He handed them to Ranulf and went outside. The island now thronged with the gawping and the curious, with more gathering on the far bank. Lady Hawisa stood at the foot of the steps, leaning on the arm of a maid. Scrope's widow was half listening to a silver-haired man with a wan face, bushy eyebrows over deep-set eyes, his shaven cheeks sharply furrowed.

'Lady Hawisa?' Corbett came down.

'Ah, you must be Lord Corbett.' The silver-haired man blinked and smiled, though his face and eyes remained keen. He stared over Corbett's shoulder into the darkness of the reclusorium.

'I am who you say I am, and you, sir?'

'Physician Ormesby late of Balliol Hall, Oxford, now spending my autumnal days on the outskirts of Mistleham. In brief, sir, I am or was,' Ormesby added, 'physician to Lord Scrope. My main care now is for Lady Hawisa.'

Corbett glanced around. Dame Marguerite was ordering servants here and there. Father Thomas was walking backwards and forwards, Ave beads strung from one hand. Brother Gratian stood on the jetty, fingers to his lips, like a man who'd lost his wits. Across the water Corbett glimpsed the arrival of Master Claypole and members of the town's council, resplendent in their ermine-lined robes and glittering chains of office. He groaned and plucked at Ormesby's sleeve.

'Physician, I want you to stay here. Father Thomas and you, madam,' he gestured at the abbess, 'must also stay, together with the servant who rowed you across.' Corbett then grasped Lady Hawisa's hand, listless and ice cold. Eyelids fluttering, she opened her mouth to speak but then shook her head. 'Lady Hawisa,' he urged, 'you must leave.' He gently squeezed her hand. 'No, no, your husband, God assoil him, is dead, cruelly murdered. You must not see him like that. You,' Corbett turned to the maidservant, 'look after your mistress. My lady, you must leave.'

Lady Hawisa nodded in agreement. Corbett strode up the steps beckoning to Ranulf, who quickly joined him outside. Corbett drew his sword and banged on the bronze gong dangling from its chain beside the door post. Eventually he obtained silence.

'Good people,' he shouted, 'I am Sir Hugh Corbett, King's man. I have authority here under the royal seal. Lord Scrope, God pardon him, is dead, cruelly murdered. I must ask you to leave the Island of Swans immediately, except for those I ask to stay.'

People looked askance at him. There were shouts, a few catcalls and mocking cries. Ranulf drew his sword. The clamour died and people drifted towards the jetty. Corbett called across Physician Ormesby, Dame Marguerite, Father Thomas and the servant who'd rowed them across, a small beetle-browed character who rejoiced in the name of Pennywort. Corbett respectfully asked all these to stay outside whilst he and Ranulf returned to inspect the corpse, the chests, the windows and the only door. All the windows except one were firmly shuttered, their bars down, the pegs on each shutter at top and bottom firmly in place, their velvet and leather drapes undisturbed.

'There is no other entrance,' Corbett breathed. 'The main door is secured by bolts at top and bottom, its lock definitely the work of some guildsman.'

He inspected the broken window. The shutters were smashed, the lintel scuffed and scraped. He and Ranulf went outside, apologising for the delay to those waiting. They walked round the reclusorium. Corbett admired what Scrope had done. A ring of vegetation ran along the rim of the island, with clumps of trees, including beautiful bending willows, but the area immediately around the house itself had been provided with a clear view, no other obstacle except for a narrow channel dug from under the reclusorium to carry waste down to the lake. The icy ground was now pitted with the footprints of those who'd come across. Corbett glanced down at the lake. It must be, at every point, at least six yards across and undoubtedly deep. He could see no other landing place or sign of any bridge, raft, ferry or boat. He and Ranulf returned inside. He covered Scrope's face with a cloth, instructed Ranulf to build up the meagre fire and then invited his guests, Dame Marguerite, Father Thomas, Pennywort and Physician Ormesby, to the stools he placed in front of the fire. The physician excused himself and went across to scrutinise the corpse. He removed the face cloth, exclaimed in horror, then busied himself near the table on which Corbett had glimpsed the exquisitely carved wooden goblet brimming with red wine. The physician picked this up, sniffed at it, then muttered a prayer.

'What is it?' Corbett went across.

'Smell but don't drink, Sir Hugh.'

Corbett did so. Beneath the rich odour he caught a bitter tang.

'Belladona,' Ormesby murmured. 'Deadly nightshade. But look, Sir Hugh, the cup seems untouched, the wine not drunk. I've observed Scrope's face, and it betrays no symptoms of poisoning.' Again that cold, knowing smile. 'Sir Hugh, I know poisons. If nightshade had killed him, its effects would be obvious; he would have died in frenzied convulsions.'

Corbett nodded and handed the goblet back. 'Was Scrope first poisoned before being stabbed?'

'I doubt it.' The physician stepped closer. 'We only smell it now because it has fermented, being mixed with the wine for hours. That's why the victim drinks it and physicians like myself later detect it. Belladona is a cruel assassin; Lord Scrope would have convulsed like an imp in hell. Of course I need to inspect his corpse more closely. There are other symptoms.' Ormesby patted his own stomach. 'Discoloration of the belly, stains on the flesh.'

He paused and went back to sniff at the silver-chased wine flagon.

'The same,' he declared. 'The flagon, I suspect, was poisoned, the wine later poured into the goblet. Oh, by the way, the goblet is fashioned out of yew, an ill-omened wood.' He lifted the cup. 'I know the texture of woods. My father was a verderer in these parts.'

'Very well,' Corbett replied. 'Give the goblet to Ranulf to keep.'

The physician obeyed and joined the rest at the fire, handing the goblet to Ranulf and whispering at him to be careful. The clerk placed the cup on the floor.

'What happened?' Corbett asked.

Father Thomas glanced at Dame Marguerite, then fearfully over his shoulder as if he expected the corpse to stir.

'I was repelled by him in life,' the priest murmured, 'and so in death, Sir Hugh. Must we stay here with his corpse?'

'The dead are beyond us now,' Corbett replied. 'What I must do, Father, is discover who murdered this loyal subject of the King, and, more importantly, who plundered those coffers and caskets. I believe, Dame Marguerite, though I have yet to establish this, that the Sanguis Christi and other precious items were kept here.'

The abbess, eyes closed, nodded in agreement.

'According to what I see,' Corbett continued, 'Lord Scrope came over here last night. You, sir,' he pointed to Pennywort, 'brought him across?'

'Oh yes.' Pennywort was pleased at the importance being shown him. 'Oh yes, Sir Hugh, ever since his hounds were killed, Lord Scrope ordered some of his men out beneath the trees. I suppose I was in charge, Robert de Scott being killed in the marketplace. My task was to row him across. I did so.'

'When?'

'Oh, late last night, sir, after he returned from the town. It must have been well after Compline.'

'And how was Lord Scrope?'

Pennywort closed his eyes and smiled, his teeth nothing more than little stumps. 'I would say he was morose, withdrawn. He said we would have visitors in the morning, Dame Marguerite and Father Thomas. We reached the jetty. As usual he did not thank me but went straight up the steps.'

'Did you follow him?'

'Yes, yes, I did,' Pennywort replied. 'I always had to. Lord Scrope wanted to make sure there'd be no disturbance. He unlocked the door and went inside. I helped build up the fire as I always did, made sure everything was as it should be. Lord Scrope sat in that chair drumming his fingers on the arm, impatient for me to go. I lit the candles. Lord Scrope growled at me to keep a close and careful watch that night with the rest. He missed his two dogs, Romulus and Remus. Perhaps he felt wary. I left. Now as I went down the steps, I definitely heard him draw the bolts and lock the door behind me. As I rowed across, I could see lights glowing between the shutters. I then joined the rest of the guards in the clump of oak trees further up the hill; you know, sir, where the dogs used to lie. We built a fire. There was a full moon last night. It was bright.'

'Did you patrol the banks of the lake?'

'No, we watched,' Pennywort replied, glancing away, 'but we saw nothing.'

'And there is no other way across,' Corbett insisted, 'between the two jetties, except by boat?'

'None, Sir Hugh.'

'Dame Marguerite, you know this island – you came across as a child?'

'There was a bridge where the jetties now stand. A rickety wooden affair more dangerous than useful. My brother totally destroyed it.'

'And the lake,' Ranulf asked, 'how deep is it?'

'Very deep indeed, sir,' Pennywort replied. 'I would say at least three yards in places. It would swallow you up. It is weed-encrusted, a dangerous stretch; not even Satan himself could swim across such an icy lake at the dead at night. If someone crossed they would have to use one of those boats. If they did, I would have seen them. I would certainly have noticed something wrong this morning but I didn't.'

'Did you observe anything untoward?' Corbett asked. 'Anything at all, Pennywort?' He opened his purse and took out a coin.

Pennywort almost sighed with pleasure, and his fingers went out. 'Sir, I could make up lies and stories, but if you put me on oath in Father Thomas' church, my hand placed over the pyx, I would swear I saw nothing, I heard nothing, nor did any of my companions. True, we kept ourselves warm, true we ate our dried meat and drank our ale, but we kept close watch, sir. Nothing happened.'

9

I have been an enemy to his enemy.
Annals of London, 1304

'About this morning?' Corbett stretched a hand out to the flames and glanced across at Ranulf, who was listening intently.

'You know what happened, Sir Hugh.' Father Thomas spoke wearily. 'I finished the Jesus Mass. I intended to go back into town to celebrate the funeral rites for those who'd been murdered. However, Dame Marguerite and I had agreed with Lord Scrope to visit him here after mass.'

'And when was this arranged?'

'Oh, about two days ago. As you know, Lord Scrope intended to refurbish and renew the convent buildings as well as St Alphege's. Of course the events of the last few days had rather dimmed the prospect.'

'Father, tell the full truth,' Dame Marguerite intervened. 'I am sorry, there was something else. Sir Hugh, we were not only going to ask about our churches and buildings. My brother was a very wealthy man and, only God knows, he had reparation to make. We were also going to make a plea that he'd be a little gentler with everybody.'

'Including me,' Ormesby spoke up cynically. The physician leaned forward, playing with the rings on the fingers of his left hand. 'Sir Hugh, I've heard of your reputation in Oxford. I know you work in the Secret Chancery. You'll find the truth here. I must be honest. Very few liked Lord Scrope. You'll probably discover that I certainly did not.'

'Who told you about the murder?'

'The news spread like God's breeze,' the physician replied. 'Scrope is dead. The word went out, servants tell servants, people hurried into town. I was in the marketplace and came immediately.'

'Lady Hawisa, have you tended to her?' Ranulf asked. 'I mean in the past?'

'Oh yes, but as to what happened and why, Hawisa should tell you that.' Ormesby nodded. 'Just like the priest here, I have my confessional, covered by its own seal.'

'This morning,' Corbett insisted, pointing at Pennywort, 'Father Thomas and Dame Marguerite came down to the jetty.'

'I saw them come,' the boatman replied, 'and hastened to meet them. I remember telling you,

Father, to wrap your cloak firmly about you because the water was icy cold and the oars would splash.'

The priest nodded, half smiling.

'I rowed them across,' Pennywort declared. 'I brought my oars in. I tied the rope to one of the posts and helped Father Thomas out, and then we both assisted Dame Marguerite. They went up the steps. I decided to wait just in case Lord Scrope had a task for me. Some of my companions came drifting down . . .'

'We knocked on the door, but there was no reply.' Dame Marguerite took up the story. 'We knocked and hammered to no avail. Outside, Sir Hugh, you'll find an axe. I picked this up and handed it to Pennywort. I told him to break the shutters.'

'So I did,' the boatman replied. 'I hacked the shutters; the bar across is metal but the shutters themselves are wood.'

'I've noticed that,' Ranulf said drily.

'I lifted the bar and scrambled in. Lord save us, sir, Lord save us.' Pennywort shook his head. 'I've seen sights in my life, Lord Corbett, oh yes, sir, I have fought in the King's wars, I have seen—'

'Tell us what you did see.' Corbett handed over the silver coin. Pennywort grasped this, a look of supreme pleasure on his face. Corbett sensed the boatman would use the money and what he'd seen to regale all of Mistleham before the week was out.

'It was dark, Sir Hugh. The fire had burnt low. Most of the candles had guttered out. I called out to Lord Scrope but there was no answer, then I saw him sitting in the chair. At first I thought he was glaring at me as he did in life. I went across. Lord, sir, the blood, dark like some witch's potion splattering his mouth and nose! Hands gripping the sides of the chair, those eyes glaring. He must have been visited by some demon.' Pennywort recollected where he was and, fingers to his mouth, stared at the floor, shaking his head and whispering to himself.

'Pennywort,' Corbett said gently, 'you saw Lord Scrope and then what?'

'I hastened to the door.'

'Tell me precisely what you saw,' Corbett intervened.

'Sir, the bolts at the top and bottom were pulled firm across. The key was turned. I had to pull back both bolts and unlock the door to allow Dame Marguerite and Father Thomas in.'

'And the other shutters?' Ranulf asked.

'All clasped shut,' Pennywort replied.

'That's true.' Dame Marguerite spoke up. 'Sir Hugh, I was shocked when I saw my brother. I couldn't believe it. Father Thomas went and whispered the words of absolution in his ear. I ordered Pennywort to stand guard outside. I searched round; perhaps the assassin might still be there, or, if the windows were all shuttered, the door locked . . . I mean . . .' Her voice faltered.

'We checked all the shutters.' Father Thomas spoke. 'Sir Hugh, I have been to the reclusorium before; there are no secret entrances or tunnels. The lake is wide and deep, every entrance was locked and bolted, except for the shutter Pennywort broke.'

Corbett thanked them. He asked Father Thomas to bless the corpse then help Pennywort and Physician Ormesby remove it to the manor.

'There is a death house there, isn't there?'

Ormesby nodded. 'A small room in the cellars. I'd best dress the corpse there. I'll tell you faithfully what I observe, Sir Hugh.'

Corbett rose and crossed to inspect the corpse. He studied it most closely, asking Ormesby and Ranulf to lift it up so as to scrutinise the seat of the chair.

'In my perception,' he murmured, 'Lord Scrope was in bed but moved to sit here when the assassin struck. He drove that dagger into Scrope's heart; Scrope's right hand went up to grasp the blade and was splashed with blood; he leaned forward, hence more blood on the floor, then fell back.'

Physician Ormesby agreed.

'Very good, very good,' Corbett murmured. 'Sirs,

Dame Marguerite, please excuse me.' He beckoned Ranulf to join him, and once again they searched that chamber, the shutters, the floor, the walls, the ceiling, the door, but Corbett could find nothing amiss. He sat on the bed and watched Ormesby, assisted by Pennywort and Father Thomas, lift the corpse up and carry it out to the waiting boat. Dame Marguerite came over, eyes brimming with tears.

'Sir Hugh, his soul?'

'Gone to God now, Dame Marguerite. I suggest that you also return to the manor. You must have pressing business at your convent, but Lady Hawisa will need some comfort.'

The abbess nodded in agreement and went outside.

Corbett followed her and stood at the top of the steps watching them place the corpse in one boat whilst Ormesby, the priest and Dame Marguerite clambered into the other now brought across.

'Tell Lady Hawisa,' Corbett called, 'I am going to seal the reclusorium. No one is to be allowed in.' He returned inside. He and Ranulf did their best with the broken shutter and stretched a rug across the gap. Ranulf fetched the chancery bag and Corbett sealed the edge of the rug fixed against the wall. He then scrutinised the chamber once more and left, locking the door and placing the key in his belt. He impressed his seal along the rim of the door then went around the outside of the reclusorium and did the same on every shutter.

'I doubt,' he declared, stamping his feet against the cold and blowing on his fingers, 'whether anyone will come across here. I'll give strict instructions to Pennywort that no one except you or I is to visit this place. Ranulf, I feel ice in my veins. I must thaw my blood and reflect on what we've seen.'

When they reached the jetty, Pennywort, full of the highest estimation for this generous royal clerk, was already waiting for them. He brimmed with news. The manor was in complete disarray. Brother Gratian and Dame Marguerite were already issuing instructions about doors being locked and sealed against any possible thefts; Master Claypole was also busy on this. Corbett nodded as Pennywort leaned over the oars and pulled away, still chattering about the effect of Lord Scrope's death and wondering what would happen. Once on the other side he gave the boatman strict instructions and immediately adjourned to an eerily silent manor house, its servants slipping like shadows along the galleries and passageways. He found his chamber already prepared by Chanson, who'd built up the fire, lit candles and ordered some dried meats, bread, cheese and butter from the buttery along with tankards of ale. Corbett thanked him. He and Ranulf sat in front of the fire, hands out to thaw their frozen figures.

'I'm so cold,' Corbett murmured. 'I'll be glad when winter's past and spring comes.'

'Last night's mayhem?'

'Well, Ranulf, certain facts are established. First, Lord Scrope went across to the Island of Swans by himself. No one was waiting for him, Pennywort confirmed that. The boatman left. Lord Scrope locked and bolted himself inside his reclusorium: a small fortified house on an island surrounded by an icy lake. Second, that lake can only be crossed by boat; according to the evidence, there was no sign of that happening once Lord Scrope locked himself in. Third, however, during that night someone did cross the lake, entered that locked and secured hermitage and stabbed Lord Scrope to the heart. Fourth, Lord Scrope was a warrior, he was a killer, yet the evidence indicates that he offered not the slightest resistance. He was sitting in that chair when the assassin plunged the blade into his heart. Fifth, the dagger belongs to the King. Now there's a riddle! Lord Scrope must have had that precious item locked in his treasure chest. He must have opened it and actually given his murderer the weapon that was later used against him. Strange, Ranulf.' Corbett stretched his feet towards the flames. 'Those chests and coffers were not prised or broken open. Scrope must have opened them for his would-be murderer then put the key-chain back round his own neck. Why? Someone he truly trusted? A person who could kill him in the twinkling of an eye? As the psalmist says, death was sprung like a trap! How could a devious, suspicious man like Scrope be so easily trapped? Ah well . . .'

Corbett grasped his tankard. 'Sixth, at no time did Lord Scrope show any anxiety or try to raise the alarm outside, nothing at all. Seventh, once Scrope was dead, the assassin plundered the treasury and escaped unscathed and unnoticed, going through locked shutters, brick walls or a fortified door, not to mention crossing a freezing lake without any assistance, no boat, raft or any other wherry. Guards were sitting close by, yet they saw nothing untoward. Eighth, according to Pennywort, no one crossed that lake until Dame Marguerite and Father Thomas approached him early this morning. They only gained access by breaking in. Now, it is possible that all three are accomplices in a conspiracy to murder, but I consider that's nigh impossible; not a shred of evidence exists to indicate it. Moreover, Lord Scrope appears to have been slain in the early hours, long before his guests arrived. Ninth, that cup of poison? What does that mean? If someone went across to murder Lord Scrope, why take poison with them? However,' Corbett put his tankard down and, taking a pair of iron tongs, moved one of the crackling logs so that it burst, giving off more flames and heat, 'we do know the murderer.'

'Master?'

'The Sagittarius, it must be,' Corbett declared. 'That's why the mastiffs were killed, as well as Robert de Scott. They weren't just acts of revenge; the assassin was preparing for last night's bloody work. Imagine, Ranulf, the freezing cold darkness; the guards would stay close to the fire. Now and again they'd glance towards the reclusorium or the lake. Dogs are different: they wander, they pick up scent, and they notice things we humans don't. They had to go, and so they did. The same with Robert de Scott, a man close to his master's dark doings. The Sagittarius learnt that Robert was roistering in that tavern. He took up position and killed him. Robert de Scott was Lord Scrope's man body and soul. He wasn't there last night; the usual vigilance of bodyguard and dog was removed. The important thing about assassination, Ranulf, is that to murder the likes of Lord Scrope, you must first remove the guards. The Sagittarius did that. However,' Corbett placed the iron tongs down, 'who the Sagittarius is and how he actually killed Scrope – I don't know.'

'How will you resolve this, master?' Chanson brought across a platter of bread, cheese and dried meat and served out portions on to the pewter plates

Ranulf held. The Clerk of the Stables was fascinated by what had happened. He wondered how Sir Hugh would deal with it. He loved to observe Corbett question people; it was better than watching lurchers chase a hare!

'How shall we resolve it, Chanson?' Corbett cut himself a piece of meat and tore off some bread. 'We'll leave it for the time being; let evil have its day. I want to move and move quickly. The King will be displeased that Scrope is murdered; he'll be even more furious that his dagger was used and the Sanguis Christi and other items stolen. We have so many questions to ask so many people. Accordingly, tomorrow morning we'll establish a court of oyer and terminer: myself and Ranulf, with Physician Ormesby sworn in as the third justice. We will hold it in the manor hall and summon them all on oath. That will be best. For the time being I have to reflect.'

In the days following, Corbett decided against convoking his court of oyer and terminer so soon. He deemed it best just to observe and listen carefully for a while. Moreover, the manor was in mourning and Lady Hawisa still in shock, yet obliged to deal with all the funeral preparations. Lord Scrope's corpse was hastily prepared for burial. Father Thomas, Master Benedict and Brother Gratian solemnly promised to sing chantry masses every day up to the final interment for the repose of his soul. The Dominican in particular became very busy. He held one copy of the tripartite indenture that laid out Lord Scrope's will, the other two copies being held by Father Thomas in his parish chest and Scrope's attorney in Mistleham. Corbett was sure that the manor lord must have kept his own master copy. This might well have been in one of the caskets or coffers held secure in the bed chest, yet no such manuscript was found. Corbett, recalling Father Thomas' words about the blood registers, wondered if any manuscripts had been stolen from the reclusorium. According to rumour, Brother Gratian often mentioned the will, as if eager for the funeral preparations to be completed, loudly announcing that now Lord Scrope was dead, he must return to Blackfriars in London. Ranulf, very solicitous for Lady Hawisa, made his own careful inquiries about the will. Its clauses still had to be read, published and approved by the Court of Chancery, though it seemed that the bulk of Scrope's estates would go to his wife, with the most generous bequests to Master Claypole, Father Thomas, Dame Marguerite, Brother Gratian and Physician Ormesby.

The old physician himself cheerfully proclaimed the good news when he visited Corbett to report on what he'd discovered when he'd dressed Scrope's body for burial.

'The flesh was marked with old bruises and scars. Scrope was definitely a man of war, his skin bore ample witness to that. For the rest his right hand was stained with blood. He was definitely killed by one dagger thrust to his heart. I detected no signs of resistance, fresh cuts or blows. True,' the physician spread his hands, 'deadly nightshade was found in the wine. God knows why, as Scrope never drank a drop. And that, my royal clerk, is all I can tell you, except that the funeral is arranged for the day after tomorrow. A small service in the manor chapel followed by a procession down to St Alphege's for the solemn high requiem mass. Our good manor lord will be interred for a while in God's Acre whilst his tomb is built in the south transept of St Alphege's, a beautiful table monument with an exquisite canopy.' The physician smirked. 'Few will make pilgrimage there! Lady Hawisa is much recovered.' Ormesby bowed sardonically in Ranulf's direction. 'Your colleague and comrade has been a great source of help and comfort to her.'

Ranulf stared coldly back.

'As far as the rest are concerned,' the physician continued blithely, 'Dame Marguerite, with her little shadow the chaplain, has taken up residence here. Lady Hawisa is distressed, so the good abbess has taken over the running of the manor. Master Claypole looks thunderstruck, weighed down by all the cares of high office.

Brother Gratian is impatient to leave but still insists on distributing the Mary loaves three times a week at the manor gates.' Ormesby noticed Corbett's surprise. 'Yes, our good Dominican's one Christ-like task. Anyway, Father Thomas is busy with funeral matters, the burials of those killed by the Sagittarius. I suppose it's true what he says.'

'Which is?' Corbett asked.

'Hell must surely be empty because all the demons have come to Mistleham. God be thanked,' the physician rose to his feet, 'the Sagittarius has not returned. Perhaps he's finished his bloody work now that Scrope is dead.' Ormesby made his farewells. Corbett thanked him and the physician left.

For a while the royal clerk just stared at the door.

'Master?' Ranulf asked.

'Father Thomas' mysterious visitor, the one who threatened Scrope: he called himself Nightshade, the same poison found in Scrope's wine. The same sinister visitor ordered Scrope to creep to the market cross and confess his sins. He didn't, so he was killed. Now Brother Gratian wishes to leave.' Corbett stared at the table. The letters he'd received from the Chancery still lay there.

'What are you thinking, master?' Ranulf rose and placed another log on the fire. 'By the way, that's your job,' he teased, turning towards Chanson, who was perched on a stool in the corner, busy whittling at a piece of wood.

'I have another task for you, Chanson.' Corbett beckoned him forward. 'It's simply this.' The groom came over.

'Master?'

'Work at last,' Ranulf whispered.

'At least I'm not frightened of the countryside, Ranulf!'

'Enough of that.' Corbett pointed to the door. 'I want you to mix with the servants, Chanson, but keep a very close eye on Brother Gratian. Every time he distributes the Mary loaves, go down with him, act as if you're just gawping around.'

'That won't be difficult,' Ranulf interjected.

'No, no, listen,' Corbett continued. 'Just watch him distribute the loaves.'

'What am I looking for, master?'

'I don't know.' Corbett grinned. 'But you'll know when you see it. Come back and tell me.'

Corbett spent the rest of that day sifting through the evidence, but he could find nothing new. Now and again he'd leave his chamber and wander the manor. Chanson was gossiping with the other grooms, Ranulf was taking special care of Lady Hawisa during her mourning. Corbett smiled to himself. He knew what Ranulf was plotting. The Principal Clerk in the

Chancery of the Green Wax was extremely ambitious; he had yet to decide which road to take: marriage to the likes of Lady Hawisa, or any other heiress who attracted his attention; or entry into the church, receiving clerical status and seeking preferment along that path. Other clerks did the same. Corbett's colleague John Drokensford had remained a bachelor and accepted clerical status; rumour at court whispered that the next bishopric which fell vacant would be his. Corbett eventually decided to visit the manor chapel and, in its silence, sat and reflected on the problems facing him. He eventually concluded there was very little he could do, not until the funeral was over. He returned and closeted himself in his own chamber, writing to Maeve and the children.

The following morning, when a royal messenger came thundering up to the manor flecked with muddy snow and cursing the state of the roads, Corbett received more chancery pouches. Most of these were business reports from his spies and agents in various ports, such as a letter from the Mayor of Boulogne complaining about the infringements of the French. The pouch also included a personal letter from the King expressing his anger at Scrope's death and his fury at the loss of the Sanguis Christi. Corbett simply tapped this against the table and put it to one side. Edward's anger would have to wait. Finally there was a letter from Drokensford saying how he'd searched the records but had discovered little of note about the fall of Acre or Scrope's involvement in it.

On the eve of the funeral Corbett summoned Ranulf and Chanson back to his chamber. The Clerk of the Stables had little to report except how Scrope was savagely disliked and people now hoped Lady Hawisa would be a more benevolent and kind seigneur. They also prayed that the Sagittarius, having wreaked his vengeance, would not re-emerge. People wanted to close the door on the past and get on with their lives. As for Brother Gratian, he had not distributed any Mary loaves but apparently intended to do so once the funeral was over. Corbett heard Chanson out, then turned to Ranulf, laying out his plans for the commission of oyer and terminer. He declared he would announce it at the end of the funeral banquet tomorrow, with Ormesby being sworn in as the third member of the commission.

Lord Scrope's funeral day proved to be bitterly cold. No snow fell, but an icy breeze stung the faces of mourners as they processed solemnly down the trackway, across Mistleham market square and into St Alphege's. Scrope's coffin rested on an ox-drawn cart, covered with thick purple and gold drapes and surrounded by altar servers carrying funeral candles capped against the breeze. The harness of the oxen gleamed a golden brown. Black banners flapped alongside standards, and pennants emblazoned with Scrope's arms. On top of the coffin rested the dead knight's crested helmet, shield, war belt and sword. The air grew sweet with the incense smoke trailing from swinging thuribles as Father Thomas vigorously chanted the psalms for the dead. Scrope's body had lain in state in the manor chapel, so once they entered the welcoming warmth of the nave, the townspeople drew aside to allow the funeral cortège to pass. The requiem mass began immediately, celebrated by Father Thomas, assisted by Brother Gratian and Master Benedict as deacon and subdeacon respectively. Lady Hawisa led the mourners, escorted by Dame Marguerite and Ranulf, on whose strong arm she securely rested. They took up position just within the rood screen, whilst Corbett stood outside in the nave. Once everyone was settled, he moved back into the transept, his gaze drawn by that vivid wall painting done by the Free Brethren.

Father Thomas intoned the introit, leading the choir with the powerful words '*Dona ei requiem aeternam, Domine* . . . Eternal rest grant to him, oh Lord.' The rest of the mass followed its usual beautiful rhythm. The gradual hymn was sung, its sombre words echoing around the nave: '*Dies irae, dies illa* – oh day of wrath, oh day of mourning, see fulfilled Heaven's warning, Heaven and Earth in ashes burning.' Corbett joined in lustily, then listened to the epistle and gospel being read, followed by Father Thomas' brief homily on the final resurrection. The priest's words cut through the incense-filled church where the carvings of saints, angels, demons and gargoyles gazed down in stony silence. The solemn part of the mass then ensued: the consecration, the distribution of the singing bread and the final benediction. Corbett only half participated, his attention fully taken up by that wall painting: the colours used, the strange symbols and plants: the scene of a man lying in bed, the banqueting chamber, the flight of Judas, and that cross dominating the Valley of Death displaying the five wounds of Christ. He felt a tingle of excitement – was this truly a drawing of the Fall of Babylon or something else?

'Let him be taken to a place of rest and not fall into the hands of the enemy, the evil one . . .' Father Thomas' strident voice caught Corbett's attention. The coffin was now being blessed with holy water, incensed and prayed over. The funeral party lined up; the coffin was raised and taken out through the corpse door into a bitterly cold God's Acre. Snow clouds were gathering. The cemetery looked bleak and stark. A scene from purgatory, Corbett decided as he watched the coffin being lowered into the ground.

Father Thomas continued his litany of prayer. Corbett leaned on a headstone and gazed around the various memorials. He was still thinking about the wall painting when his attention was caught by a headstone of recent origin to one 'Isolda Brinkuwier, spinster of this parish'. On either side of the woman's name was a carved stone medallion illustrating the Annunciation, when the Angel Gabriel asked the Virgin Mary to be the Mother of God.

'Nazareth in Galilee,' Corbett whispered to himself. '*Where God kissed Mary*.' He thought of the refrain etched on the sacristy wall of that lonely church. *Rich, shall richer be, Where God kissed Mary in Galilee*. 'I wonder,' he murmured, '*si mortui viventibus loquntur* – if the dead do speak to the living.'

Father Thomas had finished. The funeral party began to disperse, first the curious amongst the townspeople then the party from the manor. Corbett glimpsed Chanson mingling with the servants. Ranulf was still being supportive of Lady Hawisa, who was dressed completely in black, a veil drawn over her face. She walked away from her husband's grave, both hands grasping the arm of Corbett's companion. The bells of St Alphege tolled, the signal that another soul had gone to God blessed and hallowed. Corbett wondered what judgement awaited Scrope, before deciding to make his own way back to Mistleham Manor. He left the cemetery by the wicket gate, going across the square, ignoring the dark looks and grumbles of the townspeople he passed. In their eyes the King's man was busy, but it seemed as if God was going to settle matters rather than the King at Westminster. Corbett ignored them. To show he was not cowed, he paused on a corner of the marketplace where a wandering story-teller had set up his stall. He'd hobbled his donkey and driven his standard, as he called it, into the dirt, the pennant fluttering from it indicating which way the cold breeze was blowing. Children and young people were gathering round. The story-teller, dressed garishly in motley rags, was reciting well-known stories about 'Madam Lyabed' and 'Madam Earlybird' as well as 'Madam Gobblecherries', characters whom his audience would recognise as people perhaps living in their own town or even along their own street. Corbett stopped and stared at the story-teller's worn face; such a man might be one of his own agents wandering the streets and lanes of England. He did not recognise the face, so he moved on out of the town and up the deserted trackway.

He was only a short way along when he began to regret his decision. The line of trees on either side rose stark and black, the undergrowth still covered by an icy canopy, the sheer loneliness of the place becoming all the more oppressive after the noise and bustle of the town. To lighten his spirit Corbett began to sing a Goliard chant: 'I am a wandering scholar lad full of toil and sadness. Often I'm driven by poverty to madness. Literature and knowledge I fain would be learning . . .' He paused and laughed softly at the doleful words. He was about to continue when three figures slipped like shadows on to the trackway, hooded and visored; they raised their longbows, arrows notched, pointing at Corbett. The clerk stopped, his hand going beneath his cloak for his sword. He tried to control his seething panic. This was his nightmare, to be trapped, killed on a lonely road. Would it be here that he'd receive his death wound? Would it be here where he would rise on the last day?

'Friends,' he called out, 'what business do you have with me? I'm the King's man.'

'We know that, Sir Hugh, we simply want something from you.'

'Then ask, friends. Why not pull back your hoods, lower your visors, speak like Christian folk. Why do you threaten the King's man on the King's highway? That is treason, punished immediately by death.'

'We mean you no harm, Sir Hugh. We ask you this: the Sanguis Christi, do you have it on you?'

'Do you think I would wander these lanes with a precious relic belonging to the King in my pouch?'

Corbett spread his hands. 'Search me! I have no such item, and before you ask, nor do I have it at Mistleham Manor. You've heard the news. Lord Scrope is dead, his treasure coffer raided; the Sanguis Christi is missing. I do have a letter from the King expressing his anger at what has happened.'

The archer on Corbett's right lowered his bow, as did the one in the centre, but the one on his left still kept aim.

'Friends,' Corbett walked forward, 'you've asked me a question, so I'll ask you one. What is the Sanguis Christi to you, why do you demand it of me?'

He received no reply. The archer to his left still had his bow drawn, arrow notched, the barbed point directed at Corbett's chest. The man in the centre spoke swiftly, some patois Corbett had never heard before. The bow was lowered. The man in the centre was about to walk forward when Corbett heard shouts and yells behind him, and a crossbow bolt came whirring over his head, smacking into a tree. He whirled round. Ranulf and Chanson were hastening towards him, the Clerk of the Green Wax already fitting another bolt into the arbalest. When Corbett glanced back, all three assailants had disappeared. He took off his gloves and wiped the sweat from his face, then stared down at the trackway, trying to control his breathing. His stomach was pitching and he felt as if he wanted to vomit, but by the time Ranulf and Chanson reached him, he'd regained some composure.

'Master.' Ranulf grasped him by the shoulder and spun him round, then drew him close, his green eyes like those of a cat, cold and hard. 'Do not do that again!' he whispered. 'For the love of God, master, have I not told you, you are a King's man! Walking along a lonely country trackway! We are surrounded by enemies on every side and you wander as witless as a pigeon!'

'Ranulf is right,' Chanson piped up. 'Especially out here in the country, master, where all sorts of beasts and dreadful creatures lurk.'

'Shut up!' Ranulf snarled.

Corbett was glad of Chanson's interruption. He winked at the Clerk of the Stables, took away Ranulf's hand and clasped it between his own.

'Ranulf, I apologise. I become lost, brooding in my own thoughts. I wandered away. Even before those outlaws stepped out from the thicket, I realised I had done a stupid and dangerous thing.'

'But they weren't just outlaws, were they?' Ranulf asked.

'No, they weren't,' Corbett agreed. 'They wanted the Sanguis Christi. God knows who they were. It has opened the possibility that there might be more than one Sagittarius!' He grinned. 'Now my two stalwart companions have come to the rescue, what danger can afflict us?'

Corbett kept up the brave front, but as soon as he was back in Mistleham Manor, he excused himself, went up to his chamber and sat on the edge of the bed. Then he moved to a stool in front of the fire, pulling off his gauntlets and his boots, warming his hands and feet, closing his eyes and quietly reciting a prayer of thanks. Ranulf came up with a platter of food and drink. Corbett sipped at the bowl of hot pottage from the kitchens, where they were preparing the funeral feast.

'Master, I leave you to your thoughts.'

'To look after the Lady Hawisa?' Corbett spoke over his shoulder.

'Master, that's my business; your safety is ours and the King's. I beg you not to do that again.'

Corbett gave him assurances and Ranulf left. Corbett sat staring into the flames, wondering who those three strangers were. He tried to recall every word and gesture. They were not assassins; they truly meant him no harm. They simply wanted something. He wondered what would have happened if Ranulf and Chanson had not emerged. He recalled the wall painting in the church, the carving on that headstone in the cemetery. Slowly, surely, he was gathering the pieces of the mosaic. He must gather some more. He recalled Master Plynton, a wandering artist who visited Leighton manor. Plynton had executed a small mosaic for the village church just near the baptismal font, the head of St Christopher and that of the infant Christ. Corbett had watched fascinated as the skilled craftsman had assembled the coloured stones. Jumbled together they made no sense, but as Plynton put them in place, a beautiful picture began to emerge. This puzzle was similar, though the conclusion would be horrid and dreadful. The face of an assassin, a murderer, who, if Corbett could prove he or she was guilty, must hang.

Corbett heard sounds from downstairs. He sighed, put on his boots, took off his war belt and walked to the door. He would go down, observe the pleasantries, but before the day was out, he must tell Lady Hawisa and all the rest what was planned for the morrow.

10

Nor would they, without the advice of their ecclesiastical superiors, submit themselves to secular Judges.

Annals of London, 1304

Corbett had his way. The commission of oyer and terminer met just after the Angelus bell the following morning. Corbett took over the great hall, its high table and the dais being transformed into King's Bench. He displayed the royal warrant, the King's seal giving him the power 'to act on all matters affecting the Crown'. Across the warrant he laid his sword. Nearby stood a crucifix flanked by two candles. Three high-backed chairs were placed behind the table. On the wall above these Corbett displayed the King's standard, emblazoned with the royal arms, golden lions against a scarlet and blue background. Before the table stood a row of stools. Near the dais was a lectern bearing a Book of the Gospels bound in reddish leather with a gold-embossed cross on its front; those summoned would take the oath on that. The fire had been kindled, candles lit, cresset torches flickered. Physician Ormesby had agreed to be included and was taken up to the chapel to render the oath.

Corbett had announced the sitting during the funeral collation the night before. Lady Hawisa had immediately demurred. All three priests voiced their clerical status, pleading benefit of clergy, which Dame Marguerite supported, whilst Master Claypole claimed the rights of the town. Corbett swiftly silenced the protests, pointing out how the King wished to establish the truth about so many issues, including the murder of a manor lord, not to mention the theft of royal property, whilst a refusal to co-operate could mean the Court of Chancery might find it difficult to approve Lord Scrope's will. Corbett even hinted that, as in certain cases, such a delay might take years. They all agreed, more or less, the three priests, Brother Gratian particularly, reminding Corbett that they were clerics and could not be tried before a secular court.

'You're not being tried,' Corbett retorted, 'but asked the truth about certain questions.'

Father Thomas replied that he had no difficulty with that and the three priests promised to present themselves before the commission when summoned. Corbett also issued warrants under a subpoena to the town hangman, boatman Pennywort and others of Scrope's retinue. He began with these. Pennywort could add little to what he had already said. He took the oath standing at the lectern beside Chanson, then recited what had happened. Corbett thanked him, asked Chanson to return Pennywort's belt then gave the boatman a coin to stand on guard outside the door whilst Chanson secured the inside. The rest of Scrope's retinue could say little about the night their master was murdered. Corbett quickly established how these men had sheltered amongst the trees around their fire. The weather had been freezing cold. They had been reluctant to leave the warmth yet they individually swore that the jetties, the boat and the approaches to the reclusorium had been carefully watched, and they had seen no one or anything untoward. Verderers and huntsmen were questioned about the Free Brethren practising archery in Mordern woods, but memories were indistinct and no one could say who actually saw what. Corbett then summoned the hangman Ratisbon, a dirty, dishevelled character dressed in faded leather breeches and jerkin over a tattered grimy shirt. His hair was lank and greasy, moustache and beard badly clipped, his face rubbed raw by the wind, his watery blue eyes reluctant to meet Corbett's gaze. He was unable to read, so had to give the oath word by word after Chanson had repeated each one at least twice. He slouched down on the bench, glared at Corbett then looked away.

'I've done nothing wrong,' he mumbled. 'All I do is the odd job here and there. The mayor pays me to execute felons, so I do.'

'Do you remember John Le Riche, the thief who plundered the King's treasury at Westminster?'

'Course I do! Hanged him in November I did, a very expert job too, sir. He was on the cart, I pushed him up the ladder. I put the noose around his neck, the knot tied tight behind his left ear. I climbed down the ladder, then turned it. He dangled and kicked as they always do.'

'Are you sure he died?' Ranulf asked.

'As sure as I am sitting here.'

'How do you know that?' Ranulf insisted.

'I've seen enough men hang. I know when they are dead. They lose control over bladder and bowels. It's a filthy business. John Le Riche died, his soul has gone to God. When I'm given a job, I do it well.'

'You collected him from the prison,' Ormesby asked, 'on that morning?'

'Yes, yes, I did.'

'And he was the prisoner Le Riche?' Corbett asked.

'Oh, of course.'

'What was his disposition?' Corbett asked. 'How

was he?' He explained. 'Le Riche? Some men protest, others are quiet.'

'Well, I tell you this.' Ratisbon leaned an arm on the table and spoke in a gust of ale-sodden breath. 'I like a drink, and so did Le Riche. Master, if he'd drunk any more he'd have fallen down.'

'He was drunk?' Corbett asked.

'Drunk? He could hardly stand, but I tell you this, drunk or not, he's dead.' Ratisbon could say no more. Corbett thanked him, gave him a few pennies and the man shuffled from the hall.

Lady Hawisa arrived garbed in her widow's weeds. She took the oath, sat down, lifted back her veil and immediately smiled at Ranulf, who became so solicitous Corbett glared at him.

'Lady Hawisa,' Corbett began, 'I thank you for coming here despite these distressing times. Certain questions must be asked and the King requires answers.'

'Sir Hugh, ask your questions.'

'How long were you married to your husband?'

'About eleven years.'

'And you had no child?'

'None whatsoever, Sir Hugh, God's will.'

Corbett studied her pale face, eyes large and dark, lips pressed together. Lady Hawisa had a slightly nervous movement of the head as if the left side of her neck pained her. Despite the circumstances, Corbett decided bluntness was the best path to follow.

'Did you love your husband?'

'No, I hated him!'

Corbett ignored the gasps and muttering of his two companions.

'Why did you hate him?'

'He had a midnight soul, Sir Hugh, dark as the deepest midnight. He was cruel, he was cold.'

'Lady Hawisa.' Corbett stooped down for the leather sack under his chair and drew out the cup he'd taken from the death chamber. 'You recognise this cup?'

'Of course I do. I gave it to my husband as a present.'

'It is fashioned out of elm?' Corbett asked.

'No, Sir Hugh, I think you know what it's fashioned out of. Yew. I gave it to him as a curse. To bring yew into a house creates ill luck. I hoped ill luck would befall my husband.'

'Lady Hawisa, you tend the manor herb garden. It's richly stocked with all kinds of plants, some beneficent, others malevolent, yes?'

Lady Hawisa just stared back.

'And in that herb garden you grow belladonna – nightshade?'

'Yes.'

'I've been down there.' Corbett leaned forward.

'I've looked at a certain plot where the nightshade grows; the soil has been disturbed, a plant has been plucked.'

'It may well be, Sir Hugh, but I did not do that.'

'You do know what was found in your husband's chamber?'

'I've heard the rumours: wine tainted with deadly nightshade.' Lady Hawisa glanced quickly at Physician Ormesby. 'Enough poison to kill him, but he never drank it and I never put it there! Neither the plucking of the herb nor the poisoning of the wine was my doing. Ask the servants. Lord Scrope took his own wine there. He chose it himself from his cellar, filled the jug and took it across; he would always sample it. Lord Scrope was a man with many enemies. He feared the past, God knows why; he was most cunning in all his dealings.'

'Did your husband know you hated him?'

'My husband did not care a whit about what I felt, what I thought or what I did. I was a rich heiress, Sir Hugh. I did not marry out of choice. I was a ward of the Crown. My husband married me not because of my fair face but for my rich estates.'

'Did you ever plot to murder your husband?'

'In my mind, many, many times. Why not? As I've said, he had a soul as black and as deep as midnight. He was not brutal or cruel to me, just cold, dead!

He had a heart of stone, no soul. He had no real lusts except for wealth. However, much as I loathed him, I did not kill him. I will not act the hypocrite, Sir Hugh. I will not swear on the Book of the Gospels and say we had a marriage made in heaven. We simply didn't have a marriage. I was a stranger to him, as he was to me.'

'And how can you explain the nightshade?'

'I cannot. I had nothing to do with it. Anyone can enter that herb garden. Anyone can pluck a plant.'

'Sir Hugh?' Ormesby protested.

Corbett raised a hand. 'Very well, and the night your husband was murdered?'

'I was asleep in my bed. My husband had decided to withdraw to the reclusorium.'

'Why did he do that?'

'To think, to talk to himself. Yes, I think he conversed with himself as if another person was really with him. I suspect the conversation was about the past, though he never talked about that to me. As for my movements that night, Sir Hugh, you've seen the lake, for the love of God, yards wide, yards deep; the water is so icy, the very shock of it would kill you.'

'And your husband's past, did he ever refer to it, even obliquely?'

'No, though I suspect it troubled him deeply. He was a knight. He fought in Wales, Scotland and

Gascony, then he took the cross. He led a company from Mistleham. Sir Hugh, I swear I know nothing of what happened out there except that Acre fell, and my husband seized a great deal of treasure and brought it back to England.'

'And these warnings?'

'I can add nothing to what has already been told you.' Lady Hawisa shook her head. 'Nothing,' she whispered. 'Some hideous legacy, I suppose, from a hideous past.'

'And the Free Brethren of the Holy Spirit?'

'At first Lord Scrope tolerated them; he did so at my request and that of his sister. I was much taken by them, especially the leader, Adam, a merry soul with laughing eyes.' She glanced archly at Corbett. 'No, Sir Hugh, there was no dalliance. I regarded Adam as the brother I would have liked or the son I would have loved.'

'Then your husband changed his attitude?'

'God knows why. He never discussed the matter with me. I only knew about the massacre after it occurred. I remember him summoning the men in the courtyard below. They were armed, chattering about going out to Mordern to overawe the Free Brethren. As God is my witness I did not think he intended to slay any of them. On reflection it was inevitable; by the Feast of All Saints Lord Scrope truly hated the Free Brethren. He called them vermin in his barn and wanted to have done with them. My husband,' Lady Hawisa laughed sharply, 'kept his word. They were wiped out like you would a nest of rats.'

'And Lord Scrope was pleased?'

'Like any farmer who'd cleared his property of a nuisance. He celebrated with Master Claypole and Robert de Scott, a few more cups of wine than usual.'

'And Master Le Riche, the thief?'

'Again, Sir Hugh, I have told you what I know. My husband was summoned to the guildhall, where Le Riche had been seized and detained. I was with him because I wanted to make certain purchases from the market. We entered the guildhall; Le Riche was already bound. He looked a folorn, abject creature. I thought he was inebriated, drunk.'

'You are sure of that?'

'Sir Hugh, I tell what I saw.'

'Lady Hawisa, your husband and Master Claypole?' Corbett straightened himself in the chair, ignoring the disapproving looks of both Ranulf and Master Ormesby. 'A delicate, sensitive matter . . .'

'No, a rather feckless matter!' Lady Hawisa retorted. 'True, now that my husband is dead, the stories about Claypole being his legitimate son could play a prominent part in my life. I've heard all the rumours, but the truth? If Claypole is Lord Scrope's son, then he's a by-blow, illegitimate, with a bar sinister across his arms. He has no more right to these lands than the Great Cham of Tartary.'

Corbett smiled at Lady Hawisa's bluntness.

'If Master Claypole wants to try his case in the courts, then let him. I shall vigorously challenge any such claims.'

'And before your husband died?' Corbett asked. 'He betrayed no anxieties?'

'I did not know my husband's business. He resented you being here and wished you were gone. He bitterly regretted having to hand over the Sanguis Christi. He believed the King had judged him unfairly over his treatment of the Free Brethren, but more than that? Lord Scrope was as much a stranger to me as he was to you. When he spoke it was about minor matters, the care of the manor, what the cooks were doing. He showed more concern for his horse and his dogs than he did for me.' She paused. 'Only one thing, and he mentioned it more as a source of irritation. The day before he died, Lord Scrope asked if I had noticed anything missing from the chapel. I said I hadn't, what was he talking about? But that was his manner. He just glared at me and walked away.'

'Something missing from the chapel, here in the manor?'

'Yes, Sir Hugh. I still don't know what he was talking about.'

'Sir Hugh,' Ranulf intervened, 'I believe her ladyship has told us all she can.'

Lady Hawisa beamed at Ranulf, who just coughed and glanced away. Corbett studied the woman. Sometimes in court or during an interrogation he would scrutinise something that could not be put into a logical framework. If Lord Scrope was a mystery, so was Lady Hawisa. Was it because she had spent her long years of marriage living like a nun, hiding behind a veil against her cold-hearted husband, or was she concealing something else? Nevertheless he sensed that he'd questioned her enough, at least for today. He rose, thanked her, and Lady Hawisa took her leave. She nodded at Ormesby, smiled dazzlingly at Ranulf and swept out of the hall. Corbett sat down, drumming his fingers on the tabletop.

'You are hard, master.'

'Ranulf, this is hard business. We are dealing with treason, murder and theft. Let us not forget why we are here. Lord Scrope, whatever he was as a man, was a manor lord holding his lands directly from the King. He also held certain goods which rightly belong in the royal treasury at Westminster. More importantly, a murderer prowls Mistleham; he has killed time and time again and might do so again. Our task is to resolve these mysteries. We'll question Master Claypole next.'

The mayor swaggered up to the dais resplendent in his fur-lined civic robes, a chain of office round his neck, its gilt medallion shimmering in the light. He stood at the lectern, his mean face screwed up with annoyance. He placed one hand on the Book of the Gospels, lifted the other and gabbled the oath. Afterwards he took the chair directly opposite Corbett, one hand clutching the edge of the table, the other his beaver hat. He glared at Corbett as he wiped his mouth on the back of his hand.

'Say it,' Corbett rasped. 'Come on, say your piece, Master Mayor! How you object to these proceedings. How you are a mayor of a town with its own liberties. How you object to being summoned here.' He shrugged. 'All nonsense! You either answer here or before King's Bench in Westminster Hall. I assure you, Chief Justices Staunton and Hengham will have little patience with your petty claims.'

Claypole cleared his throat and waved a hand as if wafting away a foul smell.

'Sir Hugh, your questions. I am here.'

'Your service in Outremer?'

'In 1290,' Claypole gabbled as if reciting a poem, 'we learnt how hard pressed the Christian kingdom in Outremer had become. Lord Scrope convoked a meeting of every able-bodied man in the nave of St Alphege's Church.'

'Yes, yes,' Corbett intervened. 'You went as his squire along with others; they never returned, you did.'

'You are skilled with the longbow?' Ranulf asked.

'Of course!' Claypole retorted, face all flushed. 'As are many in Mistleham.'

'Why did Scrope appoint you as his squire?' Ormesby asked.

Corbett hid his smile. The rumours about Claypole's possible parentage would certainly intrigue this inquisitive physician.

'Why shouldn't I be his squire?'

'Is it true,' Ormesby persisted, 'and remember, sir, you are on oath. What you say can be used elsewhere either for or against you.' He paused. 'Are the rumours true that you are a by-blow, the illegitimate son of Lord Scrope?'

Claypole's face suffused with rage, red spots of anger blotched high in his cheeks, eyes glittering, and for a moment Corbett thought he was going to rise and strike Ormesby.

'Master Claypole,' Corbett soothed, 'we only repeat rumours. Are they true?'

'No, they are not true.' The mayor leaned against the table, glaring at Corbett. 'They are not true because I am the legitimate son of Lord Scrope and Mistress Alice de Tuddenham, and I shall prove that.'

'How?' Corbett asked. 'Father Thomas says the blood registers covering the year of your birth are missing. Do you have them?'

'Do you think I would be sitting here if I did? No! I asked Lord Scrope about that. He believed Father Thomas stole or destroyed them.'

'Why should he do that?'

'Because Father Thomas hates me as he hated Lord Scrope. Do you think it's a coincidence, Corbett—'

'Watch your tongue!' Ranulf snapped.

'Oh, I am watching my tongue,' Claypole assured him. 'But do you think it's a coincidence that Father Thomas came here to serve in a parish church the lord of which was a man he hated? No, no, no! He came here for other reasons.'

'Which are?'

'Ask Father Thomas,' Claypole retorted. 'He is from these parts, as was his brother Reginald, who joined us on our expedition to Acre.'

Corbett sighed and leaned back in the chair. 'And what happened to Reginald?'

'Killed with the rest.'

'So you think,' Corbett asked, 'that Father Thomas came here to discover what happened to his brother?'

'I don't know. You must ask him.'

'But why should Lord Scrope,' Ormesby asked, 'patronise a man who hated him?'

Claypole showed his yellowing teeth in a smile. 'Quite simple, physician. Lord Scrope did not hate Father Thomas. He is a good pastor, a priest who looks after the poor; such priests are rare. Moreover, Father Thomas is a local man. Lord Scrope felt sorry for Reginald's loss. My master did have his good qualities, a sense of justice. He was happy to see Father Thomas appointed to St Alphege's.'

'And did Lord Scrope inform you that you were his legitimate son?'

'He never did, but I heard the rumours. I used to question him, challenge him; he said I would have to wait. I decided to institute my own searches, but by then it was too late. The blood registers in the parish chest had disappeared. I remonstrated with Lord Scrope, who said there was nothing he could do for the time being. Father Thomas claimed those documents were not there when he took up his appointment after our return from Acre; that is all I can say on the matter.'

'So,' Corbett declared, 'your legitimacy is a matter still to be proved? Lord Scrope never confirmed it?'

'What does it matter?' Claypole jibed. 'As yet I have no proof. One day I shall find it. In the meantime I will issue a challenge in the Court of Chancery against Lady Hawisa's claims. Sir Hugh, it was only after I went to Acre, when my master and I were fighting shoulder to shoulder, when we expected death at any moment, that Scrope confirmed the rumours and said I was his son. It was my legitimacy he refused to confirm. I think he loved my mother. She married again and died in childbirth; that's all he would tell me.'

'So you served with him in Acre. What happened there?' Corbett asked.

'Acre became besieged by the Saracens and their allies. It was a huge port, sprawling, ill prepared for a siege. The Saracens began to fillet us like a butcher would a piece of meat, taking one section of the city at a time. We retreated into the Temple stronghold overlooking the sea. The Saracens made an all-out assault, the story is well known. Lord Scrope and I decided to fight our way out. The battlements were stormed and taken. Lord Scrope and I retreated down the corridors. We first visited the infirmary where Gaston his cousin had been taken with terrible wounds. Lord Scrope went in. Gaston was dead in his bed; ill attended, with no medicines and very little to drink, he had died of his wounds. Lord Scrope decided he would seek compensation for all his troubles. The Templar treasury was near the infirmary. We found the door open; one of the Templar serjeants was already helping himself. We simply went in and did likewise, taking whatever treasures we could seize, including the Sanguis Christi. The fury increased. Shouts and screams rang out. We knew the Templar stronghold had fallen and so we fled. Lord Scrope was a skilled fighter, a true warrior. People here will tell you his faults. I saw his courage that day. We reached the shore, found a boat and rowed out to the waiting ships, and took passage home.'

Corbett nodded understandingly. 'So you returned to Mistleham?'

'Yes. Lord Scrope was welcomed as a victorious warrior of Christ.' Claypole couldn't keep the sarcasm out of his voice. 'He was favoured by king, court and Church, granted extensive estates, given Lady Hawisa in marriage. Her family not only owned land but reaped the rich profits of the wine trade with Gascony. Lord Scrope used his wife's money, as well as the treasures he brought from Outremer, to enrich his demesne, renovate this manor hall and build the reclusorium on the Island of Swans. True, his experiences in Acre did change him, but he never cared a whit about what people thought.'

'And the warnings?' Corbett asked.

'Oh, they began about a year ago,' Claypole replied heartily. 'Lord Scrope was not concerned about them. The Templars tried to negotiate the return of the Sanguis Christi, but Lord Oliver would not do business with them, hence the warning about the Mills of the Temple. As regards the warnings about the Mills of God, they began around Easter last year. Again Lord Scrope ignored them. He was used to such menace; it did not concern him.'

'And Master Le Riche?'

'Le Riche appeared in Mistleham trying to sell that dagger. He approached a goldsmith.'

'Which goldsmith?'

'I forget now, but he directed Le Riche to the guildhall and me. As soon as I recognised the dagger, I recalled the warnings the King had issued about the theft at Westminster.'

'But surely,' Ranulf asked, 'an outlaw like Le Riche would be very wary of approaching the guildhall?'

'He was desperate,' Claypole replied. 'He came in. I met him and arrested him for what he was, an outlaw. I sent a message to Lord Scrope, who was visiting Mistleham at the time; the rest you know. Le Riche was put on trial and hanged. We held the dagger and were prepared to give it back to the King. As regards Le Riche's corpse – God knows what happened to that.'

'And the Free Brethren of the Holy Spirit?'

'Sir Hugh, they came into Mistleham. Lord Scrope was most generous in permitting them to shelter at the deserted village at Mordern. They were allowed to barter their labour for food and drink. Time passed.

Allegations were levelled against them of theft, poaching, lechery and heresy. After careful investigation, Lord Scrope decided they were a group of outlaws. He summoned his men and instructed me to do the same in the town. The rest has been told. Lord Scrope was correct; they were outlaws. We found weapons. They were planning villainy, perhaps an attack on this manor house, though God knows the reason why, apart from plunder and whatever other wickedness they could perpetrate.'

'And the Sagittarius?' Corbett asked.

Claypole just shrugged. 'A killer, Sir Hugh. I know nothing of him.'

'And the night Lord Scrope died?'

'Question my neighbours, my wife. I was home in bed. Why, what are you accusing me of?' He leaned forward. 'Creeping from my bed, entering this manor, crossing the snowy wastes, swimming the icy lake, passing guards unnoticed, securing entry into the reclusorium? I don't think so. Why should I kill Lord Scrope? When I returned from Acre it was he who provided me with the wealth, the means to set up my own shop as a goldsmith and enter the guild. I owed everything to him. I am his legitimate son. Sir Hugh,' Claypole half rose, 'if you have no further questions for me, I should be gone. Like you I am a busy man.'

Corbett waited for the door to close behind

Claypole, then straightened up in his chair. 'Now there,' he remarked, 'goes a liar! A man who has perjured himself. I doubt if he has told us the truth about anything.'

'What proof do you have of that?' Ormesby asked.

'Too glib,' Corbett replied. 'Words tripping off his tongue as if he was reciting lines from a mummer's play. He knew what we'd ask. He'd prepared himself well. A man who has a great deal to hide, is Master Claypole.'

Brother Gratian then entered the chamber and took the oath. He immediately declared how he was Lord Scrope's confessor so he could tell Corbett nothing. He then sharply reminded the royal clerk how the seal of confession was strictly covered by canon law; even attempting to infringe it could incur the most damning excommunication. Corbett hid his own anger at this arrogant priest. He entertained the deepest suspicions about the Dominican, who seemed to care for no one yet distributed Mary loaves to the local poor three times a week.

I'll let you float in your own smugness, Corbett quietly decided, and trap you in my own good time. So he nodded understandingly and airily asked where the Dominican was the night Lord Scrope was murdered.

'In my chamber, Sir Hugh,' Gratian replied smugly.

'Ask the servants; they brought me food and drink. I recited my office and went to sleep. I may do many things,' Gratian's bony white face creased into an arrogant smile, 'but walking across icy water unseen by anyone, then passing through stone and wood is not one of them.'

Corbett nodded as if satisfied and courteously dismissed the Dominican.

'Proud priest!' Ormesby muttered.

'Pride blind!' Corbett quibbled. 'Father Thomas will be different.'

The parish priest was. He took the oath, made the usual reference to his clerical status then promised to answer all questions as honestly as his conscience would allow. He made no attempt to hide his deep dislike of Lord Scrope, his disapproval at the slaughter of the Free Brethren and his condemnation of the manor lord's harshness. Corbett murmured understandingly and kept his important questions to last, glancing at Ranulf as if he was more interested in his scribe's copying than anything else.

'Father,' Corbett smiled, 'why did you really come to Mistleham?'

'I've told you, I wanted to be a poor priest and serve Christ and his people.'

'You also come from these parts?'

'Yes, that did influence Lord Scrope to support

me for the benefice of St Alphege's. I am a local man, a former royal chaplain. I am also, after a fashion, scholarly and erudite, whilst my letters of recommendation were excellent.'

'Your brother Reginald, did he play a part in your coming here?'

'My brother is dead.'

'Killed at Acre, I understand?' Corbett glimpsed the flicker, the change in the priest's light blue eyes: grief, anger, resentment? 'Father Thomas, the truth.'

'I loved Reginald.' The priest fought back his grief. 'Always happy, Sir Hugh, a truly merry soul. I loved him deeply. He left for Acre before I could stop him. He died there.'

'And?'

'I always wanted to find out how and why.'

'Did you?'

'No. The only survivors were Scrope and his creature Claypole. They could tell me little.'

'But you were suspicious?'

'Reginald was my beloved brother. I wanted to know about his final days but I learnt nothing.'

'Despite your best efforts?'

'I heard things.'

'What?'

'Small scraps about the fall of the Templar donjon, the last fortification in Acre to be stormed by the

Saracens, about the defenders breaking, scattering, every man fighting for himself. There were also stories of panic and selfishness, but nothing substantial, Sir Hugh, nothing at all.'

'Why do you think your mysterious visitor called himself Nightshade?' Corbett asked. 'Why do you think he took that name; why come to you?'

'I truly don't know, Sir Hugh. Nightshade has a malevolent aura about it. I suspect he wanted to frighten Lord Scrope.'

'And the painting the Free Brethren did in your church: Lord Scrope liked it?'

'I've told you that. He said it had its qualities. Scrope rarely praised anyone or anything under God's blue heaven.'

'Have you studied the painting?'

'Of course!'

'Look again,' Corbett murmured. 'Is it really about the fall of Babylon or somewhere else?'

'Such as?'

'I don't know,' Corbett smiled, 'but it's not an accurate reflection of the Book of Revelation.'

'I hear what you say, Sir Hugh.'

'And the blood registers that Master Claypole so desperately seeks?'

Father Thomas laughed out loud. 'Oh, I am sure,' he declared, 'Master Claypole would love to have those, but even if they were here, I doubt if they would prove anything. He is illegitimate, Scrope's bastard. I do not have them, despite what Claypole thinks.'

'Then where are they?'

'Where do you think, Sir Hugh? I suspect Scrope, for his own secret, malign purposes, had them removed.'

'And the night Lord Scrope was murdered? Where were you?'

'Praying over the corpses of those killed in Mistleham. I did not like Lord Scrope but I did not murder him. I also know about your questions to the others, about the warnings to Scrope, the thief Le Riche, the slaughter of the Free Brethren. Sir Hugh, I have spoken to you already about such matters. I have nothing to add.'

11

Warrant for the arrest of John Le Riche . . .
of bad reputation with a history of felony
in Bedfordshire.

Calendar of Patent Rolls, 1291–1302

After Father Thomas left, Dame Marguerite and Master Benedict were ushered in. Corbett believed it was best to question them together, ignoring Ranulf's whisper to Chanson about how they were both 'cheeks of the same arse', a remark that would certainly have shaken both the abbess and her chaplain had they heard it. They swore the oath and took their seats. Dame Marguerite quietly dispensed with their ecclesiastical status and privileges, thanking Corbett profusely for questioning them together as Master Benedict was not well. Corbett certainly agreed with that. The chaplain was clean-shaven and tidy, but his long, youthful face had a strange colour and his eyes were round and dark. He looked as if he'd slept badly and clutched his stomach as if he'd eaten something bad. He was also distracted and kept glancing away as if fearful of some malignant spectre hiding in the shadowy corners of the dais.

'Sir Hugh,' Dame Marguerite's pretty face was slightly flushed, 'what more can we tell you?'

'I wish to be away from here, royal clerk.' Master Benedict's words came as a rasp. He glanced directly at Corbett. 'This is truly a place of murder.' He quoted from the Gospels. 'Haceldama. The Field of Blood. I would be grateful if you would give me letters of commendation to Lord Drokensford and the King.'

'Please, Sir Hugh,' Dame Marguerite pleaded.

'When this business is over, my lady.'

'We know little,' Master Benedict interrupted. 'The night Lord Scrope was murdered, I was racked with a fever. Ask Dame Marguerite and the servants, I had a fever . . .' His voice trailed off. 'So many killings, Sir Hugh! Who will be next to be struck down?'

Corbett ignored the question and pointed at the lady abbess.

'Do you know anything about these murderous doings?'

'No, sir. My brother was a law unto himself.'

'Even about Acre,' Corbett intervened, 'after so many years?'

'Even about that, Sir Hugh. He never talked about it, at least not with me. I am sure he did with Claypole, as he would about the Free Brethren, the Sagittarius or Le Riche. Sir Hugh, I know as much as you do. To be sure, they were all dreadful events, but remember, though I am lodged here now, I am abbess of a busy convent. The affairs of Mistleham Manor do not really concern me. I regret my brother's death but I am more vigilant about Master Claypole than anything else, and, of course, advancement for Master Benedict. I have been as honest and truthful as I can.' She paused. 'I only wish Jackanapes had survived. He may have told you more. The thief Le Riche does not concern me. The leaders of the Free Brethren, Adam and Eve, together with others of their coven, often came to our convent, to beg, to pray in our chapel, but they did nothing wrong, they were harmless innocents.'

'And the Island of Swans? Dame Marguerite, as a child you played on the manor estates. Was the lake only crossed by boat or bridge?'

'Yes.' She smiled wistfully. 'The water is very deep, clogged with weeds, which makes it highly dangerous. My brother had the old bridge destroyed; it was where the jetties now stand. Some of his retainers were trained to row him across. The lake is dangerous, Sir Hugh. I cannot imagine how anyone could have crossed it without using one of those boats.'

'So how do you think the killer did cross?' Ranulf asked.

'I have reflected about that carefully.' The abbess chewed on her lip. 'I suspect he,' she smiled prettily, 'or she, swam across during the day.'

'They would have frozen to death,' Corbett declared.

'Not necessarily, Sir Hugh. Someone who took a change of clothing, a small skin of wine. I could swim it.' She smiled. 'Despite the dangers, I sometimes did.'

'But how would they gain access to the reclusorium?' Ranulf asked.

'Perhaps the assassin inveighed my brother into admitting him. But,' Dame Marguerite shrugged, 'I know such an explanation poses as many problems as it solves.' She rose to her feet, Master Benedict with her. 'I can tell you no more, truly, Sir Hugh.'

Corbett thanked the abbess and her chaplain. They both withdrew, Chanson closing the door behind them. Corbett straightened in his chair and turned to Ormesby.

'Well, Master Physician, what do you think?'

'I have served as a coroner, Sir Hugh, and my immediate conclusion, well, it's threefold. First,' he held up a stubby finger, 'of course you have not been told the truth here; that's hardly surprising: no one here is going to make a full confession. Everybody has something to hide. What binds them all together is a deep dislike, even hatred, for Lord Scrope.'

'And?'

'Second, Corbett, this is like a disease, a malignancy. The root, in my view, is the past. You keep asking about Acre; that seems to be the radix, the root of it all. Something mysterious undoubtedly happened there. Men from Mistleham went to Acre; only Scrope and Claypole returned. Old soldiers like to talk about their wars and battles, their wounds, the glories, the triumphs. Scrope and Claypole did not – why? We know they escaped. We also know they plundered the Templar treasury, but they haven't really given the people of Mistleham, the likes of Father Thomas, a true and faithful account of how their colleagues died. Third, if Acre is the root, the flowering is what has happened here. We must, or you must, discover how a killer crossed that icy lake in the dead of night, without being seen or disturbed, and gained entry into a small but fortified house. The assassin then murdered Lord Scrope, who offered no resistance, plundered his treasures and escaped unscathed and unseen. I suggest, Sir Hugh,' Ormesby got to his feet, 'you begin there. If you can solve that, then I believe everything else will fall into place.'

'I would disagree.' Ranulf spoke up. 'Master Ormesby, what you say is perceptive and truthful; nevertheless, there are lies we can still pick at. Master

Claypole, for example. I don't believe the story of Le Riche being captured and hanged out of hand; something's wrong there. The same is true of Brother Gratian. He is so glib. He is hiding behind his status and his privileges. If we could only discover a path in.'

'True, true,' the physician murmured, 'but gentlemen, unless you need me, I must be gone. I will visit Lady Hawisa.' He stretched his hand out and clasped Corbett's then Ranulf's. 'Please call on me again if I can be of further assistance but, as for the truth behind this? I cannot explain,' he shook his head, 'perhaps not even ever.' And grumbling and muttering under his breath, the physician left the hall.

Corbett rose, went to a side table, filled two goblets of wine and brought one back for Ranulf.

'Very well, Ranulf. Chanson,' Corbett beckoned the Clerk of the Stables across, 'fill yourself a goblet of wine. This is what we will do. Ranulf, clear the table here then wander the manor. Try and find the truth of what we've been told about where people were, anything untoward. Chanson, keep an eye on Brother Gratian. If you discover anything, come to my chamber.'

Corbett immediately visited the chapel and sat in a chair before the lady altar; then, getting to his feet, he carefully examined everything whilst wondering what Lord Scrope had meant about something being stolen from there. He gazed up at the crucifix hanging above the entrance to the small sanctuary, then at the altar and side tables, but could see nothing out of place. He returned to his own chamber, took off his boots and lounged in front of the fire. The wine he'd drunk had its effect. He half dozed, and darkness had fallen by the time Ranulf and Chanson returned.

'Nothing,' Ranulf declared, slouching down on a stool next to Corbett. 'Nothing at all, master. Everything we heard is true. The servants sang the same hymn. Dame Marguerite, Brother Gratian, Master Benedict and Lady Hawisa were all in their chambers the night Lord Scrope died, whilst of course, Father Thomas and Master Claypole were not even glimpsed here. So what now?'

'I found something.' Corbett turned to where Chanson was standing by the door. 'Brother Gratian is going to distribute more Mary loaves tomorrow,' the Clerk of the Stables reported.

'Be there,' Corbett urged. 'As for you and me, Ranulf, we will sleep late, take our horses and let no one know where we are going.'

'Where to?' Ranulf asked fearfully, half suspecting Corbett's answer.

'Mordern,' Corbett replied. 'It holds a secret and I intend to discover it.'

'And the Island of Swans?' Ranulf asked. 'I talked

to Pennywort; he'd racked his memory and said a bridge once spanned the lake where the jetties now stand. Dame Marguerite was correct, Lord Scrope destroyed it. I asked if anyone could swim between the two jetties. Pennywort laughed. Apparently the lake is at its deepest at the crossing point.'

Corbett half listened and nodded. 'First Mordern, Ranulf,' he murmured, 'and when we have collected enough to sift the gold from the dross, we will return to the Island of Swans. Until then it can keep its mystery.'

The following morning Corbett and Ranulf attended the Jesus Mass at St Alphege's. Once Father Thomas had left the sanctuary, Corbett returned to scrutinise the wall painting.

'Master?' Ranulf asked.

'Look,' Corbett replied, 'the defenders of that city, they wear russet and green livery.'

'The colours of Lord Scrope?'

'Precisely! Though only some of the figures do, and you have to study the painting closely to distinguish them. Now is this fortress Acre or Babylon? These dark figures fleeing, are they Scrope and Claypole? Who's the figure in the bed? Is this Gaston, Scrope's cousin? And the banquet scene with Judas celebrating, what does that mean?'

'And these.' Ranulf pointed to the plants or herbs the artist had drawn round the edges of the painting. 'Is this deadly nightshade?'

'Perhaps, and this.' Corbett gestured at the cross and the gleaming wounds of Christ. 'Is it a reference to the Sanguis Christi? Ah well.' He sighed. 'I wish I knew more. Come.'

They left the church, paid the urchin holding their horses and swung themselves into the saddle. Others were also leaving the church, traders eager to have their stalls ready by the time the market bell rang. The cold morning air stank of horse manure and the wet straw strewn across the cobbles; these odours mingled with the savoury tang from the bakeries, cookshops and taverns. Across the square three roist-erers, now half sober, screamed at the beadles to free them from the night stocks. The officials did so, but only after pouring buckets of freezing horse piss over their heads. On the steps of the market cross a crier warned traders that only bread bearing a baker's seal could be bought, whilst everyone should be wary of jugs of watered wine, milk or oil, not to mention bread containing too much yeast, stale fish drenched with pig's blood to make it seem fresh, and cheese made to look richer by being soaked in cheap broth.

'That reminds me of a funny story.' Ranulf leaned over. 'A man once asked a butcher for a reduction in price, bearing in mind that he'd been a customer for seven years. "Seven years!" the butcher exclaimed. "And you are still alive?"'

Corbett laughed and urged his horse across the square towards a stall set up in front of a cookshop. It offered platters of pastries filled with chopped ham, cheese and eel, all seasoned with pepper and other spices. He bought two pastries hot from the oven. He and Ranulf moved their horses into the mouth of an alleyway and ate as Corbett stared round the sprawling marketplace. He noticed the many windows and doorways as well as the ribbon-thin alleyways and runnels between the houses. He was certain that the Sagittarius must have used one of those windows above the forest of brazenly coloured signs: a bush for the vintner, gilded pills for the apothecary, a white arm with stripes of red for the surgeon-barber, a unicorn for the goldsmiths and a horse's head for the saddlemakers. He bit into the pastry carefully, his other hand grasping the reins. He was oblivious to the hum of noise, cages and pens being opened to release ducks, chickens, capons and screaming piglets, which were then tied to the stalls, waiting for customers to choose one.

Ranulf glanced at Corbett and sighed. His master was lost in one of his reveries. He looked back towards the church, where carts were lining up. A wandering players' troupe was busy preparing to stage a play.

Their leader had already set up his makeshift pulpit panelled in green and gold and covered with a black pall. He now stood there exhorting the bemused traders and their customers. 'Brothers and sisters,' he intoned in a bellowing voice. 'You who love this age and desire its joys, think of death, of judgement, which our play will describe.' One of the drunks recently released from the stocks came staggering across bellowing a tavern song to drown the man out:

> One for the buyers of the wine
> Twice they sup for those in jail.
> Three times for the girls with their kirtles
> raised . . .

The troupe leader didn't object, but simply waited for the drunk to draw closer then smacked him over the head with a skillet, much to the merriment of the gathering crowd.

'Ranulf!' Corbett had broken from his reverie. 'Let's be gone.'

Ranulf finished what he was eating, put on his gauntlets and gently urged his horse across the cobbles, following Corbett through the milling crowds and on to the winding path that cut through town towards the road to Mordern Forest. At first they had to ride carefully around the carts and sledges, the sumpter and pack ponies, as well as a party of falconers returning from their hunt, poles heavy with the bloodied corpses of rabbits and quail. Pedlars and tinkers surged along the trackway, eager to reach the market square to do a day's business; these were followed by a group of pilgrims marching on foot behind a banner displaying the likeness of Thomas à Becket, whose shrine they hoped to visit in Canterbury. At last the noisy bustle died. The sea of russet, green, brown and black hoods of other travellers washed around the two clerks and was gone. The clamour of voices died. The odours of cooking, smoke, sweat and the barnyard disappeared as they rode out into countryside. An icy landscape stretched before them, dotted with copses of trees and hedgerows, the occasional farmstead and outbuilding and, in the far distance, the sombre line of Mordern Forest.

Corbett and Ranulf guided their horses carefully along the frozen trackway, hoods pulled well over their heads, mufflers raised against the nipping cold. Ranulf was almost relieved when they eventually entered the bleak, deserted village. The Principal Clerk in the Chancery of the Green Wax was certain that Satan, the Warrior of Hell, did not live in smoky, fire-licked caverns but in the white waste of eternal winter. Armed or not, accompanied only by Corbett humming the tune of a hymn, Ranulf was most wary of the brooding loneliness of the countryside, the crows cawing like demons above him, the ravens floating like dark angels across glades echoing with eerie sounds from the undergrowth. They rode into the cemetery, reined in, dismounted and tethered their horses. A cold wind moaned through the trees, sweeping across the battered crosses and stone memorials.

'The haunt of ghosts!' Corbett murmured.

They walked over to the funeral pyre, now nothing more than scraps of charred wood and layers of grey ash being swept around by the wind. Corbett stared down. He took his sword and sifted through the debris, then crouched, lifted a handful of dust and let it trail away.

'Remember, man,' he murmured, 'that thou art dust and into dust thou shalt return. *Sic transit gloria mundi*; thus passes the glory of the world, Ranulf.' He glanced sadly up at his companion. 'Always remember. Golden boys and golden girls must, in their time, turn to dust.' He beat the dirt from his gauntlets and stared up at the sullen sky.

'Yet it does not end here, Ranulf. Oh no, we are spiritual beings. Souls survive, hungry for the eternal light. Blood remains blood and, in the realm of the Holy Spirit, cries for justice. That is why we are here, where, I suspect, the veil between what is seen and unseen grows very thin.'

Ranulf stared bleakly at his master and gestured around. 'Is this God's justice, Sir Hugh?'

'No, Ranulf, it isn't, but it is the beginning of it. In God's own time, at a place of his own choosing, justice will be restored. Not a tear spilt, not a child abused, not a woman broken, not a man ill used goes unnoticed. All things end well in God's own time, but he uses us, Ranulf. He keeps us close to his right hand for his own secret purposes.' Corbett pulled his hood completely over his head. 'He needs our wits and good sense, those talents he has given us. So look around, Ranulf, what is missing here?'

His companion stared around, then down at the pieces of blackened wood, the slimy grey dust. 'Master?'

'Bones.' Corbett smiled. 'Fire consumes everything but human bone, yet I cannot see a scrap or a chard. Someone has been here to clear the remains.'

'Father Thomas?' Ranulf queried. 'Or some of the townspeople as an act of mercy? The Free Brethren did have their friends in Mistleham.'

'Perhaps.' Corbett shrugged. 'But first that verse: "Rich, will richer be, Where God kissed Mary in Galilee." Ranulf, you begin with the first row of graves; I shall start at the far end of God's Acre.'

'What we are searching for?'

'A carving,' Corbett replied, 'a depiction of Gabriel's annunciation to the Virgin at Nazareth.'

Ranulf walked away, boots crackling on the bracken and gorse that curled across the cemetery. Corbett started at the other end. An eerie experience, the mist seeping through the trees, crawling towards them like the souls of those departed who'd lived and died here, slipping through the air curious as to why the living should be so busy amongst the dead. Corbett moved from one headstone or battered cross to another. Most of them were faded. All of them evoked memories of his own dead, his parents, sister and first wife, those gone before him. He was whispering the Requiem when Ranulf shouted and he hastened over to a tombstone in the middle of the cemetery. It had been carved out of good stone many years before; the names and prayers had been hidden by lichen and moss except for the exquisitely carved roundel depicting the Angel Gabriel, wings extended, hovering over a kneeling Virgin.

'Master, look!'

The lichen had been loosened to reveal the carving whilst the actual grave was almost smothered in frozen gorse and bracken, most of it taken from elsewhere and piled over the grave bed to conceal it as much as possible. They hurriedly cleared away the vegetation and began to hack at the ground using their swords, daggers and a small axe Ranulf kept in his pannier bags. The ground was hard, though it was obvious that the bank of earth had been piled quite recently. The soil beneath was loose, and as they dug, the noisome stench of corruption seeped out, forcing them to cover their mouths and noses. Corbett, recalling advice given to him by his physician friend at St Bartholomew's, hoarsely ordered Ranulf to put on his gauntlets and to remember to scrub both hands and face when they returned to Mistleham. The horrid stench grew worse. At last they reached the corpse of the hanged man, still in his hose and linen shirt: all slimy, seeping with dirt and corruption. The belly had swollen and burst, whilst the face was nothing more than a bloated bag of messy decaying flesh, the noose still tight around the throat. Corbett felt his gorge rise; Ranulf turned to retch. They both had to walk away, pulling down their mufflers to gasp at the clear air.

They returned with fallen branches to prise the corpse free from its resting place. Corbett, experienced as he was in tending the dead on battlefields, found this gruesomely macabre. John Le Riche – and Corbett knew it must be he – was now a hideous mound of putrid flesh. Corbett had to remind himself that this had once been a living soul. They removed the corpse and returned to the grave, where they sifted another layer of gruesomely soaked soil and reached the arrow chest. They pulled this up, tipping back the lid, and drew out several smaller leather bundles. They loosened these and emptied them. Ranulf whispered in awe at the fast-growing pile of rings, bracelets, cups, Ave beads, small jugs and platters, a glittering jewel-encrusted hoard of precious metals and stones. Other pouches held diamonds, rubies and mother-of-pearl, crucifixes, signet seals, brooches, head pins, necklaces and armlets. The last item was a wooden casket containing two rolls of parchment. The first depicted a drawing very similar to the painting in St Alphege's Church. Corbett studied this and handed it to Ranulf.

'See, whatever they devise, they plan first. It's a faithful copy: the castle being stormed, the man lying in the bed, the banqueting scene, the flight, the great dragon soaring above, the strange symbols and plants.'

The second scroll was longer, etched in red and blue ink, depicting a vivid picture of hell consisting of great concentric circles or trenches. Each circle was separated by strange geometric symbols similar to the ones around the painting in St Alphege's. In the first trench, according to the scribble beside it, were blasphemers, who were sent endlessly hopping or skipping by horned demons armed with scourges and horrid whips. In the next trench, sorcerers and witches, who had twisted nature by magic, were now twisted themselves, heads facing backwards so their tears rolled down their buttocks. Crawling about the next pit were horrible reptiles searching amongst the thieves and robbers, who, for having robbed people of their property, were now robbed of their souls in one of two ways: either reduced to ashes by the sting of a scorpion, then reassembled for the torture to be repeated; or melted into wax, mingling into each other so they were not able to recognise who they were as, in their earthly lives, they'd been unable to distinguish between what was their property and other people's. Other trenches were drawn and explained. Each was filled with sinners, but the centre of hell was reserved for Lord Oliver Scrope, bound fast, eternally consumed by the divine fire.

'What does it mean?' Ranulf asked.

Corbett leaned against the headstone, staring at the ruined church. 'Ranulf,' he looked over his shoulder, 'those paintings were a warning to Lord Scrope. The Free Brethren had two ideas: one was to draw on the fall of Babylon, which is really a parable for the fall of Acre. The second was a vision of hell, with Scrope, the greatest sinner of them all, lying at the centre. Apparently they decided on the fall of Babylon, but this begs the important question, one that has been hinted at but never developed. The Free Brethren definitely came here to wreak vengeance on Lord Scrope. They, or some of them, certainly hated him; they had a grudge to settle. Hence the paintings, their weapons. Perhaps they really did plan to storm Mistleham Manor.'

'But why?' Ranulf asked. 'What connection did the Free Brethren have with Lord Scrope?'

'The vital question,' Corbett declared. 'I still don't know, but there was a connection; a hidden, lasting one, formed of blood and riddled with festering resentments and grievances.'

'If that was so,' Ranulf argued, coming up to stand beside Corbett, 'their deaths should have ended the matter.'

'Which begs two possible conclusions,' Corbett replied. 'First, not all of them were killed in the massacre; or second, is there someone else, associated with the Free Brethren, carrying out vengeance on their behalf? I don't know, Ranulf.'

'And the treasure?'

'Ah.' Corbett smiled thinly. 'Master Claypole has a great deal to answer for. This is what I suspect. The King's treasure in the crypt at Westminster was robbed, its contents hauled away. Now I know from Drokensford that many goldsmiths in London were implicated in receiving these stolen goods and selling them on the open market. Now, to do that, Puddlicott and his gang must have made arrangements with goldsmiths in the city to receive what they'd stolen.'

'And goldsmiths elsewhere?' Ranulf asked.

'Precisely!' Corbett retorted. 'John Le Riche didn't come here by accident. Think, Ranulf! Puddlicott and his gang would cast their net far and wide. They would have negotiated with London merchants but they would also look for customers elsewhere. Why not Mistleham, a prosperous Essex wool town? And its mayor, Master Claypole, who appears to have no sense of right or wrong, never mind any loyalty to the Crown. Le Riche wasn't trapped, not in the way Claypole or Lord Scrope described. That devious pair had a more subtle plan. They'd received the proclamations from the King, warning that his treasure had been taken and promising the strictest penalties for anyone who received stolen items. Le Riche turns up in Mistleham expecting a hero's welcome. Instead he is arrested. Scrope and Claypole manage his trial, his imprisonment and his swift hanging.'

'But surely Le Riche would have objected, made allegations against them?'

'What proof did he have?' Corbett asked. 'I suspect he was given drugged wine; from the moment he was arrested his wits would have been dulled. For all we know, Scrope and Claypole might have promised him some form of escape, either from prison or the hangman's noose. We both know, Ranulf, how an understanding can be reached with the executioner, a tight leather collar around the throat to protect it, the body later cut down and the victim revived.'

'But that didn't happen?'

'Ah.' Corbett pointed towards the church. 'Le Riche had to be careful. He couldn't simply go blundering into Mistleham, so he came to Mordern Forest and took shelter amongst the Free Brethren. They would be welcoming hosts. Whatever we think about them, Ranulf, the Brethren seemed quite sincere in their beliefs, with little regard for wealth or treasure. Le Riche hid his ill-gotten gains with them and moved into Mistleham to negotiate with Claypole.' He waved a hand. 'I suspect there was some previous secret agreement between Le Riche, Claypole and Scrope, but it proved false. By then Le Riche would have been desperate: nine months as *utlegatus* – beyond the law – would have exhausted him. In a word, he was ambushed. He was certainly given some opiate; completely drugged, he was hustled off to the scaffold. Perhaps he was promised his life; we'll never know. The Free Brethren, realising that more villainy had been carried out by Scrope, cut down Le Riche's corpse, brought it back to Mistleham and gave him what could be called honourable burial here in this deserted cemetery. They also held on to his plunder.'

'And buried it with him?'

'Together with these two drawings. They also left secret directions on that sacristy wall. Ranulf, I am now beginning to see the motivation behind Scrope's massacre of the Free Brethren. First,' he held up his hand, 'there's that wall painting in St Alphege's. He recognised it as a warning to him. Second, by questioning Le Riche, Scrope may have established that the rest of the treasure was still here in the deserted village of Mordern. He arrives early on that fateful morning, the attack is launched in the grey light of dawn and the Free Brethren are massacred. Now Scrope and Claypole hoped they would find Le Riche's treasure, but they didn't. They acted very carefully. If they conducted a truly thorough search it would arouse suspicion. Moreover, if they were found with such ill-gotten goods they would have to answer for it before King's Bench. If we hadn't arrived, they would have continued their searches, but, of course, the presence of king's men at Mistleham meant they had to restrain their impatience, curb their greed and wait for a better day.'

'But they know we found the crypt.'

'But nothing in it,' Corbett replied. 'I suspect Scrope also searched that.'

'And now?' Ranulf asked.

'What I've said is mere supposition, empty theory,' Corbett declared. 'If we forced Master Claypole to confess then we'd have the truth, but I want to be certain. We'll take the treasure, make no mention of it and give Le Riche honourable burial. When this business is finished, I'll leave coins with some priest to say a requiem mass for him. But the dead don't concern me; the living do. Back in Mistleham a skilled assassin lurks in the shadows, cunning and devious. We suspect part of the truth but cannot yet reveal the full story. We must be patient and logical, not come to judgement till we have all or most of the facts. We must act all innocent yet curious. We must carefully observe and note, because,' Corbett sighed, 'scripture is correct: "The children of this world are more astute in their dealings with their own kind than the children of the light."'

12

Whatever treasure is found in the hands of these malefactors, you must deposit in a safe and secure place.

Letter of Edward I, 6 June 1303

Corbett had scarcely returned to Mistleham when there was a tap on his door. He answered it to find a servant hopping from foot to foot in the gallery outside.

'Sir Hugh,' he declared, 'Lady Hawisa sends her regards and asks you to join her in the chapel.'

Corbett went back into his chamber, picked up his cloak and followed the servant along the gallery, down the steps and into the chapel, where Lady Hawisa sat on the mercy seat near the lady altar. The servant ushered Corbett over, then withdrew, closing the door quietly behind him.

'Sir Hugh.' Lady Hawisa didn't even turn in her chair. 'I'd be grateful if you would bolt that door.' He did so, then walked towards the sanctuary. Lady Hawisa rose to meet him. She was dressed in full black, and as he drew closer, she lifted up her veil and smiled serenely at him.

'You must think I am in mourning, Sir Hugh, but I'm not. I am actually giving thanks for my deliverance.'

'From what, my lady?'

'From evil, from my loveless marriage, from the snare that bound me. I came here early today to give thanks and I walked into the sanctuary.' She took Corbett by the wrist and led him to the foot of the steps leading up to the altar. To the right hung the silver bejewelled pyx next to the glowing red sanctuary lamp and, directly above the altar, a crucifix on the end of a silver cord tied to the rafters above.

'They say the wood of the cross is made from the cedar of Lebanon,' she explained. 'Imported especially from Outremer. However, look at the figure of Christ, Sir Hugh.'

Corbett did so: a beautiful bronze carving of the Saviour, arms extended, body twisted in agony, head drooping, the hair hiding his face.

'You've seen this before, haven't you?'

Corbett nodded.

'Study it, Sir Hugh. What is missing?'

Corbett stared at the figure, the feet nailed over each other, the small sign Pilate had pinned above the cross.

'Nothing that I can see.'

'What does the Saviour have on his head on any crucifix you've seen?'

Corbett stood on tiptoe, peered then gasped. 'There's no crown of thorns; that's what is missing.'

'That's how my husband ordered the figure to be carved,' she explained. 'Instead of a crown of thorns, he put a ring on the Saviour's head.'

'Do you know why?'

'As I've said, Sir Hugh, my husband hardly informed me about anything. When I used to kneel here, I would study that ring and wonder. It was made of silver, with jewels along the rim. I suspect the ring belonged to his cousin Gaston, killed at Acre.'

'And now it's gone?' Corbett turned, sat down on the sanctuary steps and stared up at her.

'I noticed it was missing this morning. On the afternoon before he was murdered, my husband complained that something had disappeared from this chapel. That's what he was referring to.'

Corbett rose to his feet and left the sanctuary. He walked over and stared up at the wooden carving nailed to the wall depicting St George killing the dragon, which writhed under the hooves of his horse.

'Beautiful wood,' he murmured. 'An exquisite carving. Lady Hawisa, I thank you for bringing me here. I don't understand the significance of that ring disappearing. All I do know is that the events here at Mistleham thread back through the years to what happened at Acre. However, I have a question for you. On the morning your husband was found murdered, on the table next to him in the reclusorium was that beautifully carved cup brimming with claret. Deadly nightshade had been mixed with that, as well as with the jug of wine on the waiting table. We know from Physician Ormesby that your husband never drank that poisoned wine. Indeed, I suspect the wine was poisoned not before he was murdered but afterwards.'

Lady Hawisa gasped.

'A nasty trick,' Corbett explained. 'A decoy, a device to distract our attention and perhaps point the blame at you. Think,' he continued. 'It was you who gave him the cup, pretending it was fashioned out of elm but actually made of ill-omened yew. You are also known for being responsible for the herb garden here at the manor, which contains nightshade and other poisons. Now I ask you this, as a matter of confidence between the two of us. Have you ever confessed or told anyone of your secret, murderous desire to poison your husband?'

Lady Hawisa swallowed hard and glanced fearfully at him.

'My lady,' Corbett continued, 'I am not accusing you.

I truly believe you had no hand in the murder of your husband, but that cup was poisoned! You have confessed your secret desires, your temptation to do just that.'

Lady Hawisa closed her eyes, breathing in deeply. 'On the afternoon before my husband was murdered,' she began, 'I was out in the herb garden tending certain plants. I approached what I call the Hortus Mortis, the Garden of Death. I studied those noxious plants and the old temptation returned.'

'Why?'

'I saw the clouds of smoke rising above Mordern. I realised you were burning the corpses of those unfortunates. On that afternoon, Sir Hugh, I truly wanted to kill my husband. Such temptations disturbed the humours of my soul. I fled the garden and came here. I sat in the mercy chair and confessed my thoughts aloud where someone else could have heard.'

'But there was no one here?'

'No, of course not.' Lady Hawisa shook her head. 'It's possible someone was hiding away, but I doubt it.'

'And is that the only time you have ever voiced such murderous thoughts?'

Lady Hawisa nodded.

'Are you sure?' Corbett insisted.

'Sir Hugh, I am, but . . .' Her voice faltered.

Corbett walked over, took her mittened hand and gently kissed the fingertips.

'Lady Hawisa, thank you.' He'd reached the chapel door when she called his name.

'My lady?'

She walked slowly towards him, her lower lip trembling, tears welling in her eyes. 'Sir Hugh, I've just remembered. I have voiced such thoughts to my confessor, Father Thomas, but surely . . .'

Corbett stepped out of the shadows. 'Anyone else, my lady?'

'Yes.' She swallowed hard. 'Only once did I turn on my husband, years ago. We were alone. I had visited him in the reclusorium. I screamed how one day I hoped he would drink the poison I gave him.'

'And what was his reply?'

'As always, the curling of the lip, the shrug of a shoulder as if I was some noisome bird pecking at the window, a matter of little importance.'

'And whom might your husband tell?'

'He may have confided in Brother Gratian. However, if my husband trusted in anyone, it would be his creature Claypole.'

She startled at a sudden tapping on the chapel door. Corbett pulled back the bolt and opened it. Ranulf stood there with a servant beside him.

'Sir Hugh, I apologise,' Ranulf glanced over

Corbett's shoulder and bowed at Lady Hawisa, 'but Chanson has urgent business with us. He has something to report.'

The Clerk of the Stables could hardly contain his excitement. He kept pacing up and down Corbett's room. It took some time for the royal clerk to pacify him. Chanson, full of glee, rubbed his hands and kept grinning triumphantly at Ranulf, who just glared back.

'Master, the Mary loaves and Brother Gratian.'

'Yes?'

'He went down mid-morning, just after Nones, to distribute the loaves. The poor gather at the manor gates. Gratian was there acting the benevolent pastor distributing bread. I watched carefully. Sir Hugh, when the hungry receive food, they eat immediately, but I noticed three sturdy beggars . . . oh, they were dressed in rags, their hair and beards all matted, but when they took their loaves, they simply grasped them and hurried away.'

Corbett held up a hand. 'You said sturdy?'

'They were sturdy enough,' Chanson declared. 'Master, I've begged for food. These looked well fed, and what was truly suspicious, unlike the rest, they simply took the bread, didn't eat it but hurried back along the trackway to Mistleham. I followed. Even more surprising, master, these beggars can afford to lodge at the Honeycomb.'

Corbett beamed with pleasure, extended his arms and embraced Chanson warmly, winking over the clerk's shoulder at Ranulf.

'Well done, good and faithful servant!' Corbett stood back. 'Now, Chanson, let's saddle our horses and visit these beggars who are not so hungry and can lodge in a tavern chamber.'

A short while later, Corbett and Ranulf, accompanied by Chanson, rode into Mistleham marketplace. Afternoon trading was not brisk, as many of the apprentices had adjourned to the nearest cookshop or tavern for a stoup of ale and a platter of food. The wandering troupe of actors was now busy erecting the scenery on the stage so as to encourage people to come and watch. The troupe leader, still standing in his pulpit, was warning all who cared to listen about the dangers of hell, where sinners were served goblets of fiery liquid whilst toads and snakes cooked in sulphur were their daily food. Another member of the troupe had set up a small stool beside the carts, offering all sorts of cures for every ailment known. As Corbett and his companions passed, the mountebank was busy lecturing a poor old woman nursing the side of her face about how vinegar, oil and sulphur mixed together cured mouth sores whilst a candle of mutton fat, mingled with the seed of sea holly, was a marvellous cure for a rotten tooth. The candle, he trumpeted, should be held close to the decaying tooth with a bowl of cold water underneath, and the worms infecting the tooth would simply drop out into the bowl. Corbett smiled as he and Ranulf dismounted. He'd heard such a story before. He was also acutely aware of the other scenes of the marketplace: the stalls being visited, two madcaps, drunk beyond reasoning, dancing together, the bailiffs looking on, a dog and cat noisily baiting each other. A traveller from afar, burnt dark by the sun, was standing on a stone plinth near the church, eager to tell his stories about the wonders he'd seen. Corbett paused for a while, staring around, then glanced towards the Honeycomb.

'Chanson,' he murmured, 'when we reach the tavern, take our horses down the alleyway. Ranulf, you follow me inside.'

The tap room was busy, a spacious low-ceilinged chamber, its beams burnt black, the floor covered in a mushy mess of reeds. Most of the windows were shuttered. Lanterns, candles and oil wicks had been lit, though their glow did little to dissipate the gloom or reveal the shadowy figures sitting at tables. Corbett walked slowly across, grasping the hilt of his sword. He was aware of heads turning, the whispers, exclamations about 'the King's men'. The master taverner came out from behind the counter, wiping his hands on a filthy rag.

'Sirs, what would you like?'

Corbett shook his head. He took off his gauntlet, dipped into his purse and brought out a silver coin, twirling it before the taverner's greedy eyes.

'Three men,' Corbett whispered, 'dressed like beggars. They lodge together?'

The taverner was about to lie; the silver coin was twirled again, Corbett's other hand falling to the hilt of his sword.

'Up the stairs, master,' he whispered, 'in the stair-well, the door before you, there's no lock or bolt. You can just push it open.'

Corbett and Ranulf, swords and daggers drawn, went quickly up the greasy stairs. Corbett didn't pause to knock; he pushed open the door, Ranulf following in quickly behind him. The men squatting inside on the floor, playing dice, tried to scramble for their war belts and longbows piled in the corner. Ranulf moved faster, knocking one aside to stand between them and their weapons. For a while there was confusion as the men backed away, but there was no place to hide in the small, shabby chamber with its cobwebbed corners, flaking walls and small open window. Palliasses lay rolled in a heap against one wall. A jake's pot stood on a small shelf nearby. The room smelt stale, the dirty floor splattered with grease. At first glance the three men didn't seem out of place, dressed in coarse jupons, hose and scuffed boots, but their war belts were of gleaming leather, the hilts of their swords and daggers finely wrought, whilst the longbows were the work of a craftsman. Corbett advanced threateningly, and all three backed away. They looked bedraggled and dishevelled, faces almost hidden by straggling hair and beards, yet they were certainly not beggars but professional warriors, quick of eye, not frightened, just watchful, ready to exploit any mistake by their unexpected guests. Corbett sheathed his sword and squatted down. He pointed a finger.

'Who are you? You're not beggars. You take food that you don't eat. You hide in a tavern garret and, I wager, only leave to meet Brother Gratian. Shall I tell you what you are, gentlemen? You're Templars.' He studied all three of them. The man in the centre was older, hair and beard streaked with grey, green eyes gleaming in a face burnt dark by the sun. 'Yes, Templars,' Corbett continued. 'You, sir,' he pointed to the man in the centre, 'you are a knight; your companions are your squires. You've been sent here from New Temple in London to recover the Sanguis Christi.' He paused; the men remained watchful and silent. 'We have met before,' Corbett smiled, 'on the trackway leading out of Mistleham, only then you were hooded and visored. Your bows were strung, arrows notched at me, the King's man. Templars or not, you do know that is treason? To draw weapons against the King's own envoy? I could take you downstairs and hang you out of hand in the marketplace. You come here disguised as beggars to search for the Sanguis Christi, which you believe belongs rightly to your order. It was in the hands of Lord Scrope but has now disappeared. You thought I held it and tried to frighten me. You failed. Am I correct?'

The Templar on his left gazed longingly over his shoulder at the weapons.

'Please,' Corbett murmured, 'don't do anything foolish. The tavern master and those below, though they dislike me, know I'm a King's man. If I shout, "Harrow, harrow" and raise the hue and cry, what will happen then? What are you going to do, sirs, fight your way out? Kill the King's envoy? Look, I have no quarrel with you. You can go on your way as long as you are out of Mistleham by this evening, but first I want information. You are Templars?'

The man in the centre glanced quickly at his companions and his face creased into a half-smile.

'Yes, Sir Hugh, we are Templars. I am Jean La Marche, formerly of Dijon, now working for the New Temple in London; these are my two squires, Raoul and Everard. We are here on the orders of our master to recover what is rightful Temple property: the Sanguis Christi and other treasures looted from our treasury at Acre by Lord Scrope. He is now dead; whoever killed him probably has the Sanguis Christi.'

'Ah,' Corbett smiled, 'so you've changed your position from when we met last. You thought I had it. Of course, Brother Gratian has now told you different. Lord Scrope is dead and the Sanguis Christi is missing. He communicated with you by inserting a small scroll in one of the loaves he distributed, or even slipping it directly into your hand. You must be well advised about what occurs in Mistleham.'

The Templar stared bleakly back.

'What happened in Acre?' Corbett asked. 'Do you know?'

The Templar shook his head.

'Are you sure?' Corbett insisted.

'None of us were there,' La Marche replied. 'All we know is that our brothers held out to the end; our stronghold was the last to fall. They surrendered, but when the Saracens began to ill-treat the women and boys, the Templars attacked them with their bare hands. The Saracens retaliated by slaying all our brothers. Acre is a matter of history, Sir Hugh. One day we shall return, but in the meantime, we look for what is ours.'

'And why Gratian?'

'Ask him yourself.'

Corbett shook his head. 'That is why I am visiting you here. You can answer my questions now and I will let you go, or I'll arrest you. I will either take you to Mistleham or send you under armed guard to Westminster for questioning by the King's justices, so I ask you again, why Gratian?'

'He is a Dominican now,' La Marche declared, 'but in 1291, the year Acre fell, he was one of us.'

'A Templar?' Corbett exclaimed.

'A novice,' La Marche replied, 'a squire; he hadn't yet taken his full vows. After Acre fell, Gratian returned to England, where he decided to change his vocation and enter the Dominican order.'

'Ah, I see.' Corbett nodded. 'Of course, that is logical. Scrope wanted his own confessor, someone who was with him at Acre, so he asks the minister general of Dominicans for Brother Gratian, who perhaps knows all about his past. Now, sirs,' Corbett rose to his feet and stared down, 'there will be no more Mary loaves for you. I want you out of Mistleham before darkness, and you are never to return.'

'And the Sanguis Christi?' La Marche demanded. 'Where is it?'

'I don't know,' Corbett replied, 'but when I find it, I will return it to its rightful owner, the King. If your master then wishes to do business with my lord, that is a matter for him. Gentlemen, I bid you adieu.'

Corbett slowly backed out of the chamber, Ranulf following. They went down the stairs to the tap room. The taverner came bustling over to solicit custom, but Ranulf raised his hand and followed Corbett out into the marketplace.

'They may know more, master.'

'I don't think so.' Corbett peered up at the sky. 'They are just envoys, sent into Mistleham to collect something. Brother Gratian was to deliver it to them at the appropriate time.'

'But I thought Lord Scrope said that Brother Gratian would take it back to London himself?'

'Oh, I am sure he would,' Corbett smiled, 'and on the way he would have been robbed by those gentlemen upstairs. He would return to London acting none the wiser and the King would have to accept what he said. Now, Ranulf, tell Chanson to bring our horses. It is time we returned to Mistleham. I am beginning to wonder. But first I want to question both Master Claypole and Brother Gratian.'

'You are not concerned about the Templars?'

Corbett shook his head. 'They are soldiers, cooped up in that little garret, obliged to wear filthy rags and eat rancid food. They have been sent here by the Temple to collect something. They have failed; that is why they accosted me on the trackway. They were desperate. They came here in the hope that Gratian would hand over the Sanguis Christi. They must have been curious to hear that Lord Scrope was murdered and the Sanguis Christi had disappeared. Hence their attack. I'm sure their master in London will not be pleased when they report back to him though they'll be only too happy to leave such fetid lodgings.'

'They did accost you, the King's man.'

'As I said, they were desperate. What can we do, Ranulf, arrest them? They'll also claim benefit of clergy. No, as long as they are gone by dusk, they do not concern me. Scrope is dead; there'll be no more warnings sent to him by Brother Gratian. Our Dominican friend has a great deal to account for.'

They mounted their horses and were halfway across the square when Corbett heard his name being called. Pennywort came hurrying across, gesticulating with his hand.

'Sir Hugh, Sir Hugh!'

Corbett reined in.

Pennywort grasped the reins, fighting for breath.

'A message from Dame Marguerite, delivered at Mistleham by a servant whom Lady Hawisa sent back. Dame Marguerite says the Sagittarius has visited St Frideswide's. She begs you to come, at least to comfort her. Lady Hawisa has sent me to direct you. Sir Hugh?'

Corbett closed his eyes and sighed. 'Very well.'

Pennywort raced before them like a greyhound. They crossed the market square through the huddle of houses leaning over them and out on to the pathway that wound through ice-bound fields to the convent of St Frideswide. Every so often Pennywort would hurry back to explain where they were going. After a short ride they turned into a narrow trackway bordered on either side by thick clumps of trees. Pennywort told them that they were now on the convent estates, fields that Lord Scrope had granted to St Frideswide during his sister's abbacy. They rounded a bend and sighted the high grey-stone curtain wall, above which rose the red-slate roofs of St Frideswide. A lay sister let them through a postern gate into the convent grounds. Corbett was surprised at how grand the convent was, with its granges, outhouses, stables, guest halls, lodgings, refectory, infirmary, butteries and kitchens, and, at the heart of it all, an impressive church with a high bell-tower. They passed this going into the stable yard, where smells of every sort wafted across from the wash tubs, kitchens, gardens and spicery. Nuns and lay sisters garbed in black or grey pattered about on their business. A bell tinkled clearly while the music of a flute carried hauntingly across the convent grounds.

They stabled their horses and entered the guest hall,

to be met by a very important-looking nun who greeted them loudly, announcing that she was Dame Edith, the prioress. She spoke so clearly, Corbett suspected she was half deaf. He glared a warning at Ranulf and Chanson not to laugh as they followed the prioress across the peaceful cloisters into the convent church, where, Dame Edith trumpeted, the lady abbess awaited them.

The inside of the church was full of the most fragrant incense, which curled around the statues, the beamed roof and the gilded cornices. A serene house of prayer, the floor of the long nave was a gleaming path of black and white lozenge-shaped tiles. Gorgeous tapestries hung between the pillars, which swept up to a brilliantly painted rood screen and the polished choir stalls beyond. Candles glowed around statues and from side chapels. Dame Edith took them along one of the shadowy transepts. Corbett paused before a wall plaque above a brilliantly hued tapestry. The plaque was carved out of Purbeck marble; the lettering under the crowned stag proclaimed the achievements of Gaston de Bearn and asked all those who passed to pray for this '*Miles Christi, fidelis usque ad mortem* – Soldier of Christ, faithful until death'. The memorial was similar to the ones in the manor chapel and St Alphege's, but larger and more exquisitely rendered.

'Beautiful,' Dame Edith remarked. 'We always pray

for Gaston's soul, and see here, Sir Hugh.' She led them further along to where flagstones had been raised and a deep pit dug. 'Lady Abbess plans to erect a memorial to her family. Even more so now that . . .' The prioress abruptly remembered herself and led them along the transept before turning right into a small chantry chapel with an altar beneath a statue of St Frideswide. The chapel floor was covered in pure wool rugs, well warmed by braziers and lighted by a beautiful stained-glass window. Dame Marguerite and Master Benedict sat on a bench, Ave beads wrapped round their fingers, heads close, whispering to each other. On the floor beside them lay an arrow and a scrap of parchment. The pair drew apart as Corbett entered. The abbess looked frightened, slightly red-faced. Master Benedict acted distinctly uneasy.

Dame Marguerite made to rise, but Corbett gestured at her to remain seated. He pulled across a small stool and sat before her. 'I have been confessing my sins to Master Benedict.' Dame Marguerite smiled through her tears. 'I am, Sir Hugh, *in periculo mortis*, in danger of death, just like our beloved patroness.' She pointed at the painted window that described St Frideswide's flight from her royal would-be husband: the saint sheltering in a convent at Oxford, and God protecting her by striking the pursuing king blind.

'My lady.' Corbett gestured at the arrow and picked

up the scrap of parchment, a coarse yellow, the inscription on it clearly written. 'The Mills of the Temple of God,' he murmured, 'may grind exceedingly slow.' He glanced up. 'The same message sent to Lord Scrope.'

Master Benedict hurriedly cleared his throat. 'We were here in the church,' he stammered, 'when Dame Edith brought in both shaft and parchment.'

'Pinned to the kitchen gate it was,' Dame Edith sniffed, mouth all prim. 'One of the gardeners bringing in the produce saw it there, an arrow from hell!'

'Does the Sagittarius wish my death?' Dame Marguerite moaned. 'Oh, Sir Hugh, I'm so frightened.'

Corbett glanced at Master Benedict, who just shook his head, then at Dame Edith. The prioress stared boldly back.

'Dame Marguerite,' Corbett asked, 'do you have any suspicions about the perpetrator?'

'Yes,' she stammered. 'Claypole! He knows I hate him. I detest his arrogant claims. Now my brother is dead, he dreams of being lord of Mistleham. I have reflected,' she whispered. 'Claypole profits much. Sir Hugh, he owns tenements over the market square, he is skilled in archery. Moreover, like my brother, his reputed father, he is a man of blood.'

'Sir Hugh,' Master Benedict raised his hand, 'are you close to trapping this killer?'

Corbett stared at this soft-faced cleric crouching like a frightened rabbit. 'The solution,' he replied slowly, 'is not here or in Mordern, but in Mistleham.'

'What shall we do?' the chaplain bleated.

'Arrest Claypole!' Dame Marguerite snapped.

'But Lord Scrope's death has not advanced his claim,' Corbett replied. 'The blood registers are missing.'

'Are they, Sir Hugh?' Dame Marguerite nodded. 'Or has Claypole had them all the time, biding his moment. But to repeat Master Benedict's question, what shall we do?'

'Be careful.' Corbett picked up the arrow. 'I shall keep this and the parchment, my lady.' He bowed to the abbess, thanked Master Benedict and allowed Dame Edith to escort them back to the stables, where Chanson and Pennywort were waiting. Once clear of the convent buildings, Ranulf urged his horse alongside that of Corbett.

'Master,' he asked, 'do you suspect anyone?'

'Yes, Ranulf, I do, but only thinly, a few pieces collected together. This is going to be difficult. Not a matter of logic or evidence; more cunning. You see, Ranulf, the Sagittarius, the killer, the murderer, the Nightshade – whatever hellish name he likes to call himself – prowls Mistleham. He has two lives: openly respectable, but secretly he is an assassin. However, I suggest that he cannot continue this for ever. Sooner or later he must disappear.'

'In other words, the fox has invaded the hen coop?' Ranulf asked. 'And he is going to find it rather difficult to leave.'

'Correct,' Corbett declared. 'So, Ranulf, we must concentrate on that.'

Once back in his chamber at Mistleham, Corbett sent Ranulf and Chanson together with Pennywort to collect Brother Gratian and Master Claypole for further questioning. He then sought an urgent meeting with Lady Hawisa and explained that, once again, he must use the hall as a place to interrogate certain witnesses. She heard him out and nodded.

'Do you know, Sir Hugh,' she stepped closer, head to one side as if studying Corbett for the first time, 'when my husband knew you were coming here, he was truly frightened. He called you a hawk that never missed its quarry, a lurcher skilled to follow any scent. I can see why. Are you close to the truth?'

'No, my lady, not yet.'

'What is the cause of these hideous events at Mistleham?'

Corbett sat down on a stool and smiled at her. 'Lady Hawisa, this is all about love!'

She glanced at him in surprise.

'Love,' Corbett continued. 'Even the most loving

couple in wedlock disappoint each other. We constantly fail each other, and the reason is that we want to love so much and be loved so deeply. However, if such love is abused, it can turn rancid, evil and malignant; it seeks revenge. That is what I am hunting here, Lady Hawisa. Not events that happened twelve, thirteen, even twenty years ago, but an emotion, a feeling, some passion of the human heart that didn't burn then die, but transformed into something sinister and monstrous.'

'Will you ever discover what?'

'With God's own help, my lady, and a little assistance from yourself.'

'In which case, Sir Hugh,' she extended her hands, 'my hall is yours.'

'One further thing.' Corbett stood up. 'I wish to question Brother Gratian. When I have finished, may I look at the ledgers, the accounts for Mistleham? Not so much the expenditure, but the income from rents, profits, trading ventures – is that possible?'

'For what purpose, Sir Hugh?'

'My lady, I wish I could tell you the truth, but I cannot. I want to scrutinise them carefully. However, when I see my quarry, I will recognise it.'

Lady Hawisa nodded in agreement, and Corbett made his farewells.

13

They have committed terrible crimes
in clear contempt of us.
Letter of Edward I, 6 June 1303

Chanson ushered a rather nervous Brother Gratian into the great hall and up to the chair before the dais. This time Corbett had not produced his warrants or letters of appointment, simply his sword lying next to the Book of the Gospels on which Gratian had taken his earlier oath. When the Dominican went to take his seat, Ranulf sprang to his feet.

'How dare you!' he shouted. 'How dare you sit without permission before the King's commissioner?'

Brother Gratian grasped the table and leaned against it, pallid-faced, eyes darting to left and right, constantly licking his bloodless lips.

'Sir Hugh, what is this? I am a priest, a Dominican.'

'I know enough of that,' Corbett replied slowly. 'I also know you are a liar and a perjurer, responsible for an attack on the King's representative in these parts.'

'I . . . I . . . don't know,' the Dominican replied.

'You'd best sit down,' Corbett declared. Leaning over, he pushed the Book of the Gospels in front of the Dominican, then, stretching across, took Gratian's right hand and slammed it firmly down on top of the book. 'Now, Brother Gratian, I'll be swift and to the point. I have been in to Mistleham. You might not know this – I am sure they've now fled – but I met your friends from the Temple, lodged at the Honeycomb disguised as beggars; the same men whom you used to meet at the distribution of the Mary loaves. You exchanged messages with them, including threats to pass on to Lord Scrope. They've confessed.'

'I don't know . . .'

'If you continue to lie,' Corbett declared, 'I shall arrest you and personally take you to Colchester to be interrogated by the King and his ministers, who have now moved there. You also failed to tell me that you were at Acre in 1291.'

'You never asked. I did not think it was relevant.'

'We shall decide,' Corbett declared, 'what is relevant and what is not. Brother Gratian, your hand is on the Gospels, and so is mine. I am not lying to you. I know precisely what you have done and what you planned, but I want to hear it from your own mouth. Now you can decide either here or before the King in Colchester. I am sure that your superiors in London will not be pleased when the King returns to report what meddling mischief you've been involved in.'

'I cannot and I will not,' Brother Gratian spoke slowly, staring down at his hands, 'speak about the sins of which I shrived Lord Scrope, except to say,' he lifted his head, 'I never absolved what he called his secret sins.' The Dominican shook his head. 'What those were I truly don't know, but yes, I was at Acre thirteen years ago. I joined the Templar order as a novice, a squire. I was never truly happy with my vocation, but God works in mysterious ways. I was sent to Acre.' He stared at Corbett. 'A strange place, Sir Hugh! Its buildings were of an eerie-coloured yellow stone with iron grille-work and windows of coloured glass. That is how I remember it: a yellow haze. Those strange buildings, coated in dust like a phantasm from a nightmare. Acre became the last Christian stronghold, thronged by Templars, Hospitallers, brown-habited monks, Syrian merchants under their silk awnings, beautiful prostitutes with their black slaves thronging the rooms above the wine shops. Galleys clustered in the ports, bringing in more men and supplies. The Saracens swept in, eager to besiege, yet you'd think Acre was a place of rejoicing rather than one of doom. It reeked of every sin, Sir Hugh, like Sodom and Gomorrah, the Cities of the Plain. The nobles still feasted by moonlight on their rooftop terraces. The air smelt of perfume. Whores did business. Jesters and minstrels entertained in the streets. Then it all ended. Death and destruction swooped. The Saracens launched their assault.' Gratian fingered the cord around his waist. 'Oily black smoke curled in as the enemy catapults rained down fire to the rolling sound of their war drums. I'll never forget those drums echoing, an ominous dull beat, drowned now and again by the screech of catapults. The sky turned fiery red. Slowly but surely the walls were breached and weakened. The Saracens drew closer. Waves of white-robed dervishes launched surprise attacks.'

'Brother Gratian,' Corbett interrupted, 'you have seen the wall painting in St Alphege's – the one done by the Free Brethren?'

'Of course,' the Dominican retorted. 'That's not the fall of Babylon; it describes the fall of Acre. The attackers are the Saracens, the defenders depicted as Scrope's retainers. Lord Scrope recognised that immediately.'

'What did he say?'

'Nothing, except to quietly curse and vow vengeance.'

'Was that the reason he attacked the Free Brethren?'

'Of course. He saw them as a real threat.'

'Does the wall painting contain a cryptic message?'

'No, I studied it closely, but saw nothing new there.' Brother Gratian's fingers went to his lips. 'Scrope's men fighting, Scrope himself fleeing, his cousin dead or dying in the infirmary. The reference to Judas could be an insult to Scrope, though I saw no betrayal, whilst the soaring cross is undoubtedly an allusion to the Sanguis Christi.'

'But did Lord Scrope see anything extra?'

'I have told you, Lord Scrope had secret sins. If he did notice anything, he never told me.'

'But how did the Free Brethren know about Acre?'

'Sir Hugh, the story of the siege is well known, particularly in Mistleham.'

'But why were the Free Brethren so eager to depict it? What concerns did it have for them?'

'Perhaps it was just a way of taunting Scrope.'

'Was there any connection between the Free Brethren and those who fought at Acre?'

'You must remember,' the Dominican leaned forward, voice hoarse, 'a company from Mistleham went to Acre with Lord Scrope; none of them, except Claypole, returned, and that includes Father Thomas' brother. Of course people were curious, angry and resentful. Perhaps the Free Brethren took the idea from them, but what that painting secretly contains and why they did it is beyond me.'

'Lord Scrope,' Ranulf broke in harshly, 'also attacked

the Free Brethren because they were arming. Did you see any evidence for that?'

The Dominican coloured and glanced away.

'Brother, please?'

'Look,' he whispered, 'I've served as a soldier. I can recognise a whetstone used for sharpening blades. I did see that on the tombstone outside the deserted church. I was alarmed. The Free Brethren acted as if they did not believe in violence or weapons, so I informed Lord Scrope. It only increased his suspicions.'

'And the crypt in the Church of the Damned?'

'Lord Scrope searched it but found nothing.'

'And the thief Le Riche?' Corbett asked. 'You heard his confession?'

'Of sorts, Sir Hugh. I truly don't understand what happened; that was a matter for Scrope and Claypole. When I did visit Le Riche in the guildhall dungeon, he was witless.'

'What do you mean?'

'He could hardly sit up; he was drunk, intoxicated from wine or an opiate.'

'What did he confess?'

'Nothing, he just slurred his words, moaning about how he'd been betrayed but how things might still turn well.' The Dominican shrugged. 'How could I shrive such a man? He was not worthy of absolution. I left and the next morning he was hanged.'

'And the allegations against the Free Brethren?'

'Oh,' the Dominican rubbed his bony face, 'there was some truth in them. They were lecherous and promiscuous, but, God forgive me, I did my share in fanning the flame of suspicion and rumour against them. They were certainly heretics, Sir Hugh. They did not accept the teaching of our Church on important matters.'

'But not worthy of sudden brutal death?'

'No, that was the work of Scrope and Claypole. They sowed a crop of lies and allegations. They turned Mistleham against the Free Brethren, then Scrope harvested what was sown; he destroyed them early one winter morning.'

'And the warnings about the Mills of the Temple; they were your work?'

Gratian pulled a face. 'Of course,' he whispered.

'A task given to you by your old friends and comrades at the Temple?'

'Acre,' Gratian replied. 'Let me explain.'

Corbett nodded in agreement.

'The Saracens took Acre, forcing the defenders from the walls on to the streets. Those who could, fled immediately to the port. The Templars, myself included, fell back to their donjon overlooking the sea. In our retreat we were joined by others, including the company from Mistleham under Lord Scrope.

A bloody affray, Sir Hugh, ferocious hand-to-hand fighting, but at last we locked ourselves inside and the Saracens laid siege.' Gratian wiped the sheen of sweat from his forehead. 'I will keep it brief. There was a secret tunnel from the donjon leading out to the port. The tunnel itself was safe but the port was being overrun by the Saracens. The Templar commander asked for volunteers to explore the tunnel, discover what was happening in the port, secure a boat and return for everyone else. Of course there was debate. We had injured, weakened men. During our retreat, Lord Scrope's cousin Gaston de Bearn was seriously wounded and lodged with the rest in the small infirmary. Our situation was truly desperate. Scrope volunteered, as did Claypole. I'd seen what a ruthless fighter Scrope was. I reasoned it would be safer to stay with him than in the donjon. We were set to leave early one afternoon. Just as we did, the Saracens launched their final assault. We were left to our own devices. Lord Scrope led us down hollow-stoned galleries. He told us to wait outside the infirmary whilst he visited Gaston. He stayed some time. When he returned, he was griefstricken, carrying Gaston's ring. He announced that his cousin was dead, there was nothing more we could do.'

'Do you think he may have killed Gaston?' Ranulf asked.

'Perhaps,' Gratian murmured. 'The thought did occur to me: a mercy cut. Gaston was too badly injured to be carried away, and if he fell into the hands of the Saracens . . .' Gratian visibly shuddered. 'At the time we were all sweat-soaked and terrified, except for Scrope. He was formidable: cold, fierce with his sword, trusting only in himself. He said we should also save the Temple treasury. I objected, but Claypole was adamant that we follow Scrope's orders. I then reasoned that this had all been planned. Moreover, if Scrope wanted to do something, Claypole, his shadow, never disagreed. Yes,' the Dominican smiled thinly, 'even then I noticed the physical similarities between the two. Claypole and his lord: wherever Scrope went, Claypole always followed. God forgive me,' he whispered. 'Scrope intended to loot the treasury, find a way out and never return.' The Dominican drew a deep breath. 'Now the treasury lay near the entrance to the secret tunnel guarded by one Temple serjeant. He objected, said he had his orders to allow no one in. It happened so swiftly.' Gratian licked his lips. 'Scrope killed him, a swift thrust to the throat. He swept aside my objections, dismissing the serjeant as a fool, asking why should the Saracens secure such precious goods? He took the keys and plundered the treasury, anything that could be carried away. God be my witness,' Gratian held up a hand, 'I never took anything. Scrope and Claypole, however, filled their sacks. We then hurried into the tunnel, a long, hollow passageway leading underground down to the port. By the time we reached it, parts of the harbour had been seized. Scrope killed two Saracen scouts and screamed at us to follow him along the beach. I will never forget that shoreline: corpses bobbed in the waves alongside rafts and bundles of possessions. We found a longboat that had come adrift from one of the ships. We clambered in, and Scrope insisted that we leave. He ignored my plea to return, saying the Templar donjon wouldn't survive the most recent attack. In a sense,' Gratian breathed in deeply, 'he was correct. We rowed out to sea and were picked up by a Venetian galley. The Templar stronghold fell in that last assault; everyone inside was put to the sword.'

He paused. 'We eventually returned to England and went our separate ways. I had no real vocation for the Templars, so I journeyed to Blackfriars and entered the Dominicans. Scrope continued to flourish,' he added bitterly, 'like the cedars of Lebanon. About eighteen months ago, he wrote me a friendly letter. He also asked my superiors if I could be released to be his confessor and spiritual director.' Gratian laughed sourly. 'Scrope was a powerful lord, rich and influential; of course, my superiors agreed.'

'And you?' Corbett asked.

'I was curious. I wanted to find out what had happened. When I arrived, Scrope often talked about our flight, of his regrets, how he'd made mistakes. He also made reference to certain secrets but never discussed them. I wondered if he felt guilty because of the treasury and his flight from Acre.' The Dominican quickly crossed himself. 'No, I suspect it was something else, like the murder of his cousin. In the main he rendered himself pleasant to me. He acted the great manor lord, the faithful son of the Church. I was lulled into the part he wanted me to play. I soon became aware of his world: his adoring, faithful sister, the unstinting loyalty of Claypole, and the cold indifference that existed between Scrope and his wife. Father Thomas was cordial enough, but he too had a deep distrust of his manor lord. Only recently,' Gratian sighed, 'did I realise Scrope's true reason for inviting me.'

'Which was?'

'He wanted to keep an eye on me. He wanted to discover if I knew anything about what had really happened at Acre, if I'd seen or heard something untoward.'

'Had you?'

'No.' Gratian spread his hands. 'True, the killing of that serjeant was murder. I was implicated, and his death always weighed heavily on me. On one occasion

I spoke to Scrope about it. I never did again; his fury knew no bounds.'

'And the Templars?'

'They too had suspicions about what had happened at Acre, but no proof. What they really wanted was the return of their treasure, particularly the Sanguis Christi. When they learnt about my appointment as Scrope's confessor, messengers came to me. The Templars invoked old times; they hinted at what might have happened. They asked for my help. I remembered that serjeant, my own guilt, so as an act of reparation I agreed. It was the least I could do. I sent Scrope those messages about the Mills of the Temple grinding exceedingly slow, but he still refused to concede. Eventually the Templars sent envoys to Mistleham; they disguised themselves as beggars, and lodged in a garret at the Honeycomb. Every so often I would meet them to distribute the Mary loaves. They would pass messages to me and I to them. Now, the plan was that when Lord Scrope gave me the Sanguis Christi, I would journey to London and the Templars would stage a mock ambush, an assault on the road, steal the Sanguis Christi and flee. I would act the innocent injured party. But then, of course, you arrived and Lord Scrope was murdered. The Templars were furious. My lord,' he blinked, 'I did not know about that confrontation with you on the trackway till afterwards. I objected. I knew you would become suspicious.' Brother Gratian cleared his throat. 'I was frightened, wary of the Templars, that's why I wish to be gone . . .'

'And be taken back to London by us,' Ranulf intervened, 'protected against the Templars?'

Brother Gratian nodded in agreement.

Corbett leaned back in his chair and stared at the Dominican. He'd made a mistake about this man. Brother Gratian looked like an inquisitor, a hard, ruthless man, keen to protect the Church and its teaching, but like everyone else, he carried his own bag of past sins and guilt. Nevertheless, had he spoken the truth or simply conceded what he was obliged to?

'Do you know anything,' Corbett asked, 'about Lord Scrope's death?'

The Dominican closed his eyes and shook his head.

'Or anything,' Ranulf interjected, 'that may be of assistance to us?'

'I have told you all I can.' The Dominican rose to his feet. 'Sir Hugh, I can say no more.'

Brother Gratian left, the door closing quietly behind him. Corbett sat for a while staring down at the hilt of his sword.

'Master?' Ranulf queried. 'Has he told us the truth?'

'No,' Corbett declared, 'but I suspect he has told us all he can.'

'Could he be the Sagittarius?' Ranulf asked.

'It's possible.' Corbett conceded. 'It has happened before.' He smiled. 'A man confesses one sin to satisfy the confessor whilst hiding the rest. Gratian is certainly hard-souled, very wary of Lord Scrope. We have also learnt that our Dominican is a born intriguer, as well as a former soldier, experienced in arms, tough and resolute. He would make a worthy opponent.'

'And the wall painting?' Ranulf asked.

'I am not too sure.' Corbett shook his head. 'It might have been a way of taunting Lord Scrope. There is something else, something we've missed, something Lord Scrope recognised as the truth, but what?'

'The deadly nightshade?' Ranulf asked. 'Is that the plant in the painting? Is that why Father Thomas' mysterious visitor gave himself that name?'

'You've spoken the truth, Ranulf.' Corbett rocked himself gently backwards and forwards. 'I suspect Lord Scrope killed Gaston. He fed him a drink, an opiate to lessen the pain of his wounds, to make sure he was dead when the Saracens invaded. Scrope was a soldier; he knew the fight was lost, that is why he plundered the treasury and refused to go back. That could be his secret sin, something that rankled in his soul for years.'

'And Claypole?' Ranulf asked. 'Gratian describes him as Scrope's pet dog, his shadow, but he could have turned.'

'Again correct. Claypole is as ruthless and cruel

as his master. I wouldn't put any sin past him. He'd resort to any villainy, any violence to achieve what he wanted. It leads to a very interesting thesis. Did Claypole become tired of Scrope and turn against his master?'

'He should be questioned, then arrested.' Ranulf got to his feet.

'We certainly have enough to load him with chains, but we will not confront Master Claypole, not yet. Tell the mayor to return home. Let's see what happens. Ranulf, leave me for a while. I wish to think. Oh . . .'

Ranulf turned as he went towards the door.

'Please,' Corbett smiled, 'ask Lady Hawisa if the manor accounts could be brought, particularly those records of receipt and income.'

A short while later Ranulf returned carrying bundles of documents. He stacked these on the table, lit more candles and placed them round. He asked Corbett if he wished to have something to eat or drink, but the clerk just shook his head, pulling across the first ledger. By the time he'd finished, the candles had burnt low and darkness was falling. He pushed the household books away, quietly whispering to himself, then rose to his feet, swinging his cloak around him, and told Chanson, still on guard at the door, to extinguish the candles and remove the accounts.

'What will you do, master?'

'Oh, it's evening time.' Corbett smiled. 'I'll wander the manor.'

For the next two hours Corbett did so, visiting the stables, the buttery, the kitchen, the outhouses, talking to servants, especially those who'd served Lord Scrope for many years. The more he questioned, the more certain he became. By the time he retired that night, having said his prayers and placed his dagger beside him, his suspicions had begun to harden into certainty, but how was he to trap the assassin?

Early the following morning, round the hour of Nones, Physician Ormesby gathered his cloak more firmly about him and glared across the marketplace. He'd received an urgent message from Dame Marguerite to meet him in front of the rood screen in St Alphege's Church, something about the blood registers. He paused at the corner of an alleyway and pulled his beaver hat more firmly down on his head. He just wished the weather would break. He stared across to where the travelling troupe had set up their stage near the church. He would like to have words with the mountebank who was selling potions and philtres. He had met their type many a time before; their so-called cures could kill his patients! He peered up at the mist swirling around the gables and towers of the church. He wondered why Dame Marguerite really needed to see him at such an early hour, but she'd been most insistent; the note had said something about the blood registers, about Claypole's parentage. Ormesby swallowed hard. He wasn't sure, but rumour had it that his own mother had acted as midwife and delivered Claypole. Was it in connection with that? He jumped as a cat scuttled by with a still struggling rat in its jaws. He was almost across the marketplace, half listening to the sounds of stall-holders, when the ominous horn blast rang out like the knell of the Avenging Angel on Doomsday.

The effect in the marketplace, as Physician Ormesby later described it, was as if the Lord of Hell had set up stall there. People ceased what they were doing and ran for the protection of alleyways and porches. Ormesby heard the third blast and realised it came from the church. Drawing his dagger, he hurried across, down the path and through the corpse door, which stood off its latch. He stepped inside. The air was sweet with incense still curling after the Jesus Mass. Father Thomas would not be there. The priest had a strict routine and would have adjourned to his house to break his fast and tend to parish matters. Physician Ormesby heard sobbing, an awful heart-chilling sound. The nave was gloomy; here and there a candle glowed through the juddering shadows. He immediately went to one of the pillars and stared around.

He glimpsed the baptismal font, the image of Christopher on a pillar, the stool in the corner, then he glanced down at the rood screen before the high altar. The glow of candles was stronger there. He saw the body lying just near the entrance to the rood screen, hurried down, then stopped. Dame Marguerite lay sprawled in front of the entrance to the sanctuary, arms extended, face caught in the shock of death, eyes staring blindly. A trickle of blood snaked from the corner of her mouth to stain her white wimple. The arrow shaft had pierced her deep in the left side. A blow to the heart, Physician Ormesby thought; death would have been immediate. The blood was still bubbling around the shaft.

Again that chilling sound of sobbing from behind the rood screen. Ormesby looked up and saw another long shaft embedded in the wood of the screen just near the entrance. Lifting his dagger, he stepped round the corpse and walked into the sanctuary.

Master Benedict crouched there, fingers to his lips, eyes rounded in terror. Other people were now coming into the church. Ormesby ignored these. He knelt down and grasped the chaplain's hand. The man was even more pale-faced than usual, lips quivering.

'We were just standing there,' the chaplain gasped. He let Ormesby help him to his feet. 'We were just standing there talking, waiting for you to come, then

I heard it, the corpse door being opened. I thought it might be Father Thomas. I walked a bit further down, I could see no one, then I heard the hunting horn, three long blasts. I just stood there, and so did Dame Marguerite. She was standing in the entrance to the rood screen. I walked further; the arrow came whirling through the air followed by a chilling scream. I looked over my shoulder. Dame Marguerite lay sprawled on the ground. I hurried back. I could see the shaft had struck deep, here.' He patted his own left side. 'I turned around. I glimpsed a shadow; the Sagittarius was taking aim. I threw myself behind the rood screen. I heard the arrow strike, followed by footsteps.' He paused. 'Footsteps,' he repeated, 'then I heard yours.'

'Oh Lord have mercy on us all!'

Ormesby hastened back through the rood screen. Father Thomas was bending over Dame Marguerite's corpse, sketching the sign of the cross on her forehead. He glanced quickly at the physician.

'I was in the priest house,' he murmured. 'I was doing the accounts. I heard the horn blowing and couldn't believe it. I ran here.' He got to his feet. 'Master Benedict,' he called, 'you are well?'

The chaplain came out from behind the rood screen. He went to Dame Marguerite's corpse and sank to his knees, face in his hands, sobbing like a child.

Ormesby walked down the church, telling the curious to stay by the font, then glanced around, looking for the coffin door. He walked across into the dark transept and tugged at the latch. The door was open. He strode back up the nave; the door to God's Acre through the sacristy was also unlocked.

'I will get the holy oils,' Father Thomas declared. 'I will anoint her, do what I can.'

'What is happening here?'

Claypole, robe flapping about him, came striding up the nave, the heels of his boots clipping on the paving stones. He paused, stared down at Dame Marguerite and whispered something under his breath. Ormesby couldn't determine if it was a prayer or a curse.

'We must send for Corbett,' Ormesby urged. 'You,' he pointed at Claypole, 'dispatch one of your servants. Everybody must stay back, leave everything as it is until Corbett arrives.'

The clerk was breaking his fast in the buttery when Claypole's messenger arrived. Corbett wiped his hands and told Chanson to saddle their horses before hastening off to his own chamber to slip on boots, strap on his war belt and grab his coat and gloves. He met Ranulf in the gallery outside.

'You do not seem surprised, Sir Hugh?'

'No, I'm not.' Corbett clicked his tongue. 'Everything is breaking down, Ranulf. Soon we'll have the truth, but first let's see what mischief brews.'

The marketplace was thronged and they had to fight their way through to St Alphege's. Corbett told Chanson to stay with their horses while he and Ranulf went through the corpse door. A small party was waiting for them before the rood screen. Corbett carefully inspected Dame Marguerite's corpse. The arrow had thrust deep; the blood on her face was now congealed, but her eyes still stared sightlessly with terror. He asked Father Thomas to fetch a small altar cloth and gently covered the abbess' face. He inspected the arrow in the rood screen, then walked back down the church, Ranulf going before him to clear those townspeople thronging in to view the gruesome sight. Corbett inspected the coffin and corpse doors as well as that leading to the sacristy. Ormesby had described how he was almost across the market square when he heard the three horn blasts and hurried into the church to find Dame Marguerite dead and Master Benedict hiding behind the rood screen. The chaplain, now more composed, was still white-faced, his eyes red-rimmed. He haltingly explained how Dame Marguerite had insisted on leaving the safety and security of St Frideswide because she needed to speak to Ormesby most urgently.

'On what matter?' Corbett asked.

'Sir Hugh, I don't know, but,' he lowered his voice, glancing over his shoulder to where Claypole stood with other town dignitaries, 'something about the blood register, about Claypole's claims.'

'And what would that have to do with you, Master Ormesby?'

The physician closed his eyes, took a breath, then opened them again.

'We all know,' he took Corbett by the arm, leading him away, well out of earshot of Claypole and the rest, 'that Lord Scrope was Claypole's natural father; whether he and Alice de Tuddenham were blessed in holy wedlock is a matter of debate. Alice later died in childbirth. Now, I only say this as a supposition, Sir Hugh, but rumour has it that my mother, a midwife in Mistleham, delivered the child. She may have heard or seen something, then told me before she died, or so people think. I don't know! Perhaps that's why Dame Marguerite wanted to see me.'

Corbett thanked him and returned to the chaplain, who, once again, in halting tones, described how he and Dame Marguerite had arrived just before Nones, the time stipulated in her letter to Physician Ormesby. Corbett asked the physician to produce this letter, which he did. Corbett read it quickly. The note was carefully written but it begged Ormesby, 'for the most important reason', to meet Dame Marguerite at the hour of Nones before the rood screen in St Alphege's. He glanced up at the chaplain.

'But why here?' he asked. 'Why didn't she invite Physician Ormesby to St Frideswide in the safety and security of her convent?'

'Because she said this church held a secret,' Master Benedict replied. 'That's what she told me when I begged her to stay. She said she wouldn't put it in the letter, but this church,' he gestured round, 'held the key to all the secrets of Mistleham: the death of her brother, the Sagittarius, and above all, Master Claypole's claims. More than that she wouldn't say. We came in here, we were talking in front of the rood screen, the church was empty. The Jesus Mass had been celebrated. I heard the corpse door open. I thought it was Father Thomas and I walked down, then came the three swift blasts of the hunting horn. I couldn't see clearly. I panicked, then a shadow emerged. I heard the whistle of the arrow as it cut the air, followed by Dame Marguerite's scream. I hurried back and glanced round. The archer had drawn nearer, hooded, cowled and cloaked, only a shadow, but the longbow he carried gleamed in the light. I just ran! I hid behind the rood screen. I heard the arrow strike the wood. I thought he would draw closer but I suppose it was Dame Marguerite he wished to kill. I heard no more until Physician Ormesby arrived.'

Corbett thanked him, walked past the corpse, under the rood screen and up the steps leading to the high altar. He stared at the crucifix, closed his eyes and quoted verses from the Veni Creator Spiritus: 'Light Immortal, Light Divine, visit thou these hearts of thine . . .' He opened his eyes. It was time he primed the trap. He was wasting his time here. He had to return to Mistleham, to explore one further possibility. He turned round and walked back to join the rest.

'Tonight,' he declared, 'I must ask you all to join me at Mistleham Manor. We will assemble in the hall not to feast but to decide on certain matters. I urge you all on your allegiance to the Crown to be there. Fail to do so and you will be put to the horn, proclaimed as an outlaw. Physician Ormesby, that includes you.' Corbett gestured at Dame Marguerite's corpse; the white cloth covering her face was now stained with blood. 'Father Thomas, I would be grateful if you would see that the lady's body be honourably removed. Physician Ormesby, the arrow must be taken out, the body given some sort of semblance before it is taken to St Frideswide.' He thanked them, beckoned to Ranulf and left.

14

We, wishing to have a hasty remedy to this business, have assigned you to enquire on oath . . .

Letter of Edward I, 6 June 1303

The journey back to Mistleham was silent. Corbett refused to be drawn by Ranulf's questions.

'You never asked them, master, where they all were.' Ranulf couldn't curb his curiosity. 'Father Thomas, Claypole and the rest.'

'It doesn't matter where they all were,' Corbett replied enigmatically. 'What matters, Ranulf, is what we are going to do now.' He pulled at his reins and gently stroked his horse's neck. 'Physician Ormesby is keen-witted. Do you remember what he told us? How these mysteries can be solved by discovering what really happened at Acre thirteen years ago and on the Island of Swans the night Lord Scrope was killed. Well,' he urged his horse on, 'we've studied Acre and discovered all we can about what truly happened there; now it's time to return to the Island of Swans. Once back at Mistleham, get Pennywort. Tell him I need the services of his boat, and you, Ranulf, fetch a long pole. I am going to ask Pennywort to row you round the lake. Someone crossed the lake that night. They didn't use the boat, there's no bridge and, to quote Brother Gratian, outside the Gospels, no one walks on water, but someone crossed and I intend to find how they did it!'

The brutal murder of Dame Marguerite had disturbed the manor. When Corbett and Ranulf returned, they found servants gathered in small groups whispering amongst each other. Lady Hawisa came down, face all shocked at the news. Corbett took her hands and kissed her fingers gently.

'My lady, Dame Marguerite is gone to God. I must discover her killer and that of your husband, and the sooner the better. Think of time as sand running through an hour glass; only a few grains remain. I must act and do so swiftly.'

He told Ranulf to keep on his cloak, cowl and gloves and seek out Pennywort. The boatman arrived all agog, wondering what was expected of him. Corbett asked him to row them across to the Island of Swans, told him to secure the boat, and all three went up the steps. Corbett produced the key, broke the seals, unlocked the reclusorium and went inside. It was freezing cold and rather bleak, the air stale. Corbett told Pennywort and Ranulf to stay just within the doorway as he walked slowly around.

'There are six windows here,' he said. 'Two look out towards the back of the reclusorium, the others provide a view on either side of the Island of Swans. Very well.' He went down the steps and, much to Ranulf and Pennywort's astonishment, began to walk around the reclusorium. It was now about noon, bitterly cold, the clouds beginning to break; rooks and crows floated above them, black-feathered wings displayed, their strident cries mocking Corbett as he slipped and slithered on the ice. He kept looking across at the lake, and when he reached the rear of the hermitage, he pointed across to a group of willows on the far side and the narrow path that snaked between the trees.

'I wonder!' he exclaimed, but he didn't bother to explain to his companions. Instead he returned to the jetty and instructed Pennywort to row Ranulf into the centre of the lake and proceed slowly in the direction of those willows. Ranulf was to stand in the stern with the long pole he'd taken from the stables and test the depth of the water as they went. Pennywort immediately dismissed that as a waste of time.

'Have you ever tested the depth?' Corbett teased.

'Yes, but not for the entire lake.'

'Of course not.' Corbett smiled.

'What are we looking for?' Ranulf asked.

'The same as when I scrutinised the receipts and rents of this manor,' Corbett replied. 'We'll know the truth when we see it. Now, sirs . . .'

Pennywort, muttering under his breath, clambered into the boat. Ranulf, carrying his pole, climbed in behind; cloaked and cowled, he looked like the Angel of Death standing in the stern. Pennywort rowed out, then turned in the direction Corbett had instructed. At Corbett's shouted order, Ranulf let the pole down; eventually he had to sit, as most of it disappeared beneath the surface. Corbett walked with them along the bank. Sometimes vegetation and undergrowth sprouting on the edge hid the boat from view, so he called out and Ranulf shouted back that there had been no change. They rounded the island, approaching the rear of the reclusorium. Corbett glimpsed the tops of the willows on the far bank and tried to control his excitement. He was almost level with the trees when he heard Ranulf and Pennywort's loud exclamation. He hurriedly pushed through the bushes to the edge of the lake. Pennywort was trying to keep the flat-bottomed boat stationary as Ranulf jabbed his pole at something beneath the water.

'What is it?' Corbett called, even though he anticipated the answer.

'About a foot or more beneath the boat,' Ranulf exclaimed, 'there's a hard, ridged surface. It's broad, master, about two feet across, like a ledge or shelf.'

'The remains of a bridge, perhaps?' Pennywort called out. 'I never knew. Lord Scrope refused to allow any barge or boat to circle the lake.'

Corbett just stared across at the narrow path between the willows. He called Pennywort to bring his boat closer and row him across; Pennywort tried to, but though the lake grew shallower towards the edge, it was still too deep to wade through, Corbett decided he'd walk back to the jetty and meet them there. When he arrived, Pennywort was waiting, full of surprise at their find. After he'd taken Corbett back to the other side, he quickly moored his boat and followed the royal clerks round the edge of the lake to the clump of willows. Once amongst these, hacking at the trail of undergrowth with his sword, Corbett pointed back.

'If someone entered the manor grounds stealthily at night,' he explained, 'they could lurk here unnoticed by the guards sheltering around their fire under the trees some distance away. Remember, there were no dogs. Both had been killed to prepare for that night of blood. Pennywort, would you have seen anything here?'

The boatman shrugged. 'We'd never even think to look,' he murmured.

'Of course not. Here in this clump of trees the killer prepared. He had a staff.' He pointed to the pole. 'Cut a third off.'

Ranulf, with Pennywort's help, did so. Corbett grasped the staff, then advanced to the edge of the lake.

'Master . . .' Ranulf warned.

Corbett walked on, using the pole to test the water. He felt it hit rock and carefully walked on to the broad ledge beneath. The water rose to about a foot, almost touching the rim of his boots. He edged forward carefully in a straight line. Icy water splashed his legs, but the ledge was quite broad and gritty, whilst the flow of the lake, fed by some underground stream, was not strong.

'It's very similar,' he called back, 'to a ford: shallow water over sure footing!' He found the pole invaluable. Like a blind man with a stick, he would push it forward and then follow. He felt slightly nervous when he reached the centre, but the underwater ridge stretched before him, broad enough to take any slip to the left or right. Moreover, as he approached the far side, the ledge began to rise slightly. The water grew shallower, then he was across, boots crunching on the icy undergrowth along the island edge. He turned and smiled triumphantly, lifting his hands towards his companions, then began the journey back. On one occasion he nearly slipped as the staff wedged in a crack on the ledge, but he reached the far bank safely.

'Nothing!' he exclaimed. 'Some cold water on my legs, but it wasn't too dangerous.'

'But at night?' Ranulf asked.

Corbett held up the staff. 'Shielded by the trees, the killer could have used a shuttered lantern. More importantly,' he pointed to one of the willows,' he may have brought a rope.'

'Of course,' Pennywort breathed, 'A covered lantern to mark the place he left. He'd tie one end of the rope securely around a tree, the other end about his waist.'

'Precisely!' Corbett clapped Pennywort on the shoulder. 'Then he used the staff to find his foothold and move carefully across, as I did. The dark would make no difference; as long as the pole hit hard rock, he was safe. If he slipped or even fell, the rope would secure him. He could haul himself back on to the ledge and carry on. Once on the other side, he'd secure the rope to use on his return. That is how our killer crossed to the Island of Swans.'

'But the reclusorium?' Pennywort stammered. 'How did the killer force an entry? Everything was secure. I had to smash the shutters.'

'Hush.' Corbett opened his purse and pressed a silver piece into the man's hand. 'For now, silence, Pennywort! This is King's business.'

The boatman beamed down at the piece of silver. 'I never knew,' he murmured, 'about the ford.'

'Very few did,' Corbett replied. 'I suspect that many years ago masonry and cement were poured in to support a bridge that was eventually destroyed or fell down, but its rocky foundations are as sure as those of a cathedral, a mass of hardened concrete known only to a few, forgotten over the years. Lord Scrope didn't forget when he built his reclusorium. He insisted that the only way across the lake was by boat, a fact everybody accepted as the truth and that, strangely enough, proved to be his own undoing . . .'

Darkness had fallen when Corbett gathered his guests around the high table on the dais in Mistleham Manor. Lady Hawisa, despite Corbett's request, insisted on serving a light collation for all those invited. The dais gleamed in the light of a long row of candelabra, the fire in the great hearth had been built up, and braziers glowed from the corners of the hall. Corbett's guests arrived together: Claypole, Master Benedict, Ormesby, Father Thomas and Brother Gratian, all graciously welcomed by Lady Hawisa. Corbett had prepared himself well. He'd spoken briefly to Ranulf and Chanson, then drawn up documents; the chancery bag resting against the leg of his chair contained all the letters and warrants he needed. Ranulf had also come prepared, his war belt lying on the floor beside a small arbalest, though Corbett predicted there would be little violence.

The meal began. Corbett allowed Father Thomas to say grace and the servants brought in the wine, bowls of hot broth and platters of cold meat and fresh bread. Lady Hawisa, still garbed in widow's weeds, tried to make conversation, but the atmosphere was tense; those who'd come knew that Corbett had reached his conclusions. They sat like men under sentence waiting for a judge to declare his verdict. Corbett decided to be swift. The first goblet of wine had been drunk when he abruptly rose and walked around behind Claypole's chair. The whisper of conversation died as Corbett put his hand on the mayor's tense shoulder.

'Master Henry Claypole, Mayor of Mistleham, I, Sir Hugh Corbett, Keeper of the King's Secret Seal and Royal Commissioner in these parts, do appeal you of treason, robbery and murder. Treason in that the outlaw John Le Riche deliberately came here to sell you the King's treasure looted from the crypt at Westminster. No . . .' Corbett forced the mayor to remain seated. Ranulf stood up and walked down the other side of the table, the primed arbalest pointing directly at Claypole. The rest of the guests gazed in astonishment.

'I did not—'

'You did!' Corbett leaned down and whispered loudly, 'Such mummery, Master Claypole! Le Riche was experienced, but he was tricked and betrayed by you and Lord Scrope. Where is the rest of the treasure you bought, eh? In your house? I'll produce the necessary warrants and search it from garret to cellar. You are also accused of robbery, because you and Lord Scrope feloniously took the said treasure and hid it. Murder, because you are the Sagittarius. You are a skilled bowman, Master Claypole; both you and Lord Scrope were involved in that too. You rented tenements from your manor lord above the marketplace. You used these as a hiding place as well as your concealment to loose arrows at both the unsuspecting and those you and Lord Scrope wished to rid yourselves of. Murder also because you turned against your master; you wanted the Sanguis Christi as well as the other treasure, not to mention the blood registers. You, Lord Scrope's son, legitimate or not, were privy to many secrets, including that secret ford across the lake.' Corbett lifted his hand at the excited murmur around him. 'Not now,' he declared. 'Perhaps in a day or so, when Master

Claypole goes on trial for his life.' He tightened his grip on Claypole's shoulder until the mayor winced. 'You used that ford the night you murdered Scrope.'

'This is ridiculous!' Claypole screeched. 'I can prove—'

'What?' Corbett intervened. 'That you were busy in the guildhall this morning when Dame Marguerite arrived?'

'As I was in the marketplace when Jackanapes was killed.'

'Your accomplice Lord Scrope was not,' Corbett taunted. 'I mean when Jackanapes was killed. There were two Sagittarius, two bowmen; I shall prove that. As for this morning, I shall also demonstrate, Master Claypole, that you have St Alphege's under constant scrutiny. After all, that is the place from where the blood registers were allegedly stolen. You also watched Dame Marguerite, who fiercely resented your claims. When she arrived unexpectedly at St Alphege's earlier today, you decided to finish the game once and for all. I shall explain the details later. After all, Master Claypole, you are the mayor, you can move around. It is easy to leave a bow with a quiver of arrows in the shadows, slip through one door, notch an arrow, loose and flee again. Ah yes, I have much to say about you and so much to judge. Chanson,' Corbett called down the hall, 'arrest Master

Claypole and take him to the cellars below. Ranulf will go with you. Lady Hawisa . . .'

The lady of the manor, shocked and surprised, could only nod in agreement.

'This is unjust . . .' Claypole tried to gabble his innocence, but the look in his eyes betrayed a deep fear.

'Unjust? No it is not,' Corbett soothed. 'I do not want you to flee or try and rouse the townspeople. Moreover, I need to collect further evidence.'

Claypole tried to struggle, but Ranulf drew his dagger and pricked the side of the mayor's neck. Claypole's resistance collapsed; weeping and cursing, he was bundled from the hall. Corbett retook his seat and lifted the chancery bag on to the table. Ormesby and Father Thomas particularly were full of questions, but Corbett refused to answer them.

'Claypole may not be the sole assassin,' he murmured. 'There is still work to be done.' He pointed at the Dominican. 'Brother Gratian, you knew Claypole long before you came here. Consequently I want you to stay here tonight and visit him. Reason with him, advise him to confess all and throw himself on the King's mercy.'

'I can only do what I can.'

'Good.' Corbett smiled at the Dominican. 'Father

Thomas,' he turned to the parish priest, 'you received my letter this afternoon and did what I asked?'

'I did, Sir Hugh, I—'

'Good,' Corbett murmured, raising his hand for silence as Ranulf came back into the hall. 'Please, Father, talk to Ranulf after this meeting.' He stared down at the chancery bag, then opened it.

'Master Benedict, I have a most important task for you. Dame Marguerite asked me to recommend you to the King; as a mark of respect to her memory, I have done so.' Corbett drew a number of scrolls, tied and sealed, and pushed these across the table. 'At first light tomorrow, I want you to leave here and ride swiftly to the King, who is now residing at Colchester. Seek out Lord Drokensford, give him these letters of recommendation – and they are powerful ones – then hand over these other letters, urgent requests that Lord Drokensford send me a list of items looted from the treasury at Westminster. Such a list will convict Claypole not only of robbery but, as I shall prove, of cold-blooded murder.'

'Are you sure?' Master Benedict smiled. 'I mean, Dame Marguerite lies dead at St Frideswide.'

'Yes, yes, you can return for the funeral,' Corbett declared, 'but this is urgent. Brother Gratian must stay here, as must Father Thomas. I need Ranulf and Chanson for other tasks. I am concerned, wary of

Claypole's associates. The letters will also ask Lord Drokensford to send the Sheriff of Essex and his comitatus here along with the shire muster rolls which will demonstrate that Claypole and his accomplices—'

'Accomplices?' Physician Ormesby couldn't contain himself. 'Sir Hugh, what accomplices?'

'Please bear with me,' Corbett replied. 'I need vital information to prove that Claypole and his accomplices were master bowmen.'

'You said I should lodge here for the night?' Master Benedict queried, 'but I need to collect certain items from St Frideswide. Pay my respects to Dame Marguerite's corpse.'

'Of course.' Corbett turned to Chanson. 'You will accompany Master Benedict back to St Frideswide. He will leave at first light.' He pushed across another document, unsealed and loose. 'This is a warrant that will allow you safe passage anywhere in the kingdom. You are not to delay or be delayed. However, you, Chanson, must return here. I need you to search Claypole's house and other tenements.' Corbett was determined not to be kept or questioned any further. He abruptly rose and bowed towards Lady Hawisa. 'My apologies for what is happening, but these matters are pressing. Master Claypole lies at the root of all the wickedness here. My lady, gentlemen, I bid you good night.'

The company broke up. Master Benedict, clutching his documents, beamed at Corbett and followed Chanson out of the hall. Ranulf had a few whispered words with Father Thomas, who murmured his reply. Ranulf smiled, turned and gestured at Corbett.

Master Benedict Le Sanglier, former chaplain to Dame Marguerite, late Abbess of St Frideswide, rode into the village of Mordern just as daylight strengthened. A thick mist still shrouded the derelict buildings, deepening Mordern's ghostly aspect. The chaplain dismounted, stared round and hobbled his horse, the best the convent stables could provide. He patted the heavy panniers slung either side of the saddle, threw his cloak about his shoulders and walked into the cemetery, looking for the headstone displaying the carving of the Annunciation. When he reached it, he stared down and felt a stab of unease. The grave had been disturbed. A twig snapped somewhere behind him. He whirled around even as the arrow whipped the air above him. He watched in horror as the bowman emerged from the mist, head and face hidden by a cowl. The longbow he held was taut, the arrow notched ready for flight. Master Benedict's throat went dry.

'God save you, sir.' His voice came in a rasp.

'And God save you too, Master Benedict.'

The chaplain turned. Corbett walked towards him, accompanied by Chanson armed with a primed arbalest. Master Benedict blinked. Chanson had made his hasty farewells at St Frideswide and galloped away as if more concerned about events at Mistleham, yet now he was here.

'Please,' Corbett spread his hands, 'your belt with its dagger, sir.'

Master Benedict unbuckled this and let it fall to the ground.

'Ranulf, Chanson,' Corbett called out, 'take our guest to the church.'

Master Benedict glanced back at Ranulf, who'd now drawn closer, the longbow still primed with its sharp iron barb and grey goose feathers. Master Benedict tried to relax, his first panic being replaced by a watchful wariness, eager to exploit any mistake, but Corbett was careful. The chaplain was led into the church and forced to sit with his back to a pillar while Chanson deftly tied his wrists with twine then carefully searched him, pulling out the leather pouch beneath the quilted jerkin as well as the thin knife hidden in the top of his boot. Corbett undid the heavy pouch and shook out the precious items. Jewels, rings and the Sanguis Christi, a beautiful heavy gold cross embedded with five glowing rubies. Its beauty drew exclamations of surprise from

Chanson and Ranulf, who'd also brought in the chaplain's heavy panniers, which contained documents and a second hoard of precious items and keepsakes.

'Enough to hang you!' Corbett murmured.

'Last night,' the chaplain asked, 'that was all mummery?'

'Yes and no.' Corbett squatted before him. Ranulf stood behind, bow at the ready, more arrows lying at his feet. 'Yes, Master Claypole has a great deal to answer for regarding John Le Riche. He undoubtedly formed an alliance to buy treasure stolen from the King. He and Lord Scrope betrayed Le Riche, drugged him then hanged him. For the rest . . .' Corbett shrugged. 'Brother Gratian has to stay until I tell him to go. Physician Ormesby will tend to Lady Hawisa. Father Thomas? Well, he has fulfilled his task. He searched his church both in and out. He found the stave of the small horn bow you used to kill your former accomplice Dame Marguerite.'

Master Benedict just laughed and turned away.

'I will come to that by and by,' Corbett continued. 'Ranulf here talked about the fox, how it steals into the hen coop and causes bloody mayhem, which arouses the farmer, but sooner or later the fox has to leave and confront the danger. You're my fox; I wanted you to do that. I gave you all the letters you needed, including one guaranteeing safe passage, be it on the highways or in a harbour. Desperate to go, you rose to the bait, you had to. Time was passing. The farmer and his dogs were closing in. You grasped the opportunity: *carpe diem* – seize the day. You had to retrieve your plunder from its hiding place at St Frideswide and, of course, you had to come here to collect the rest. You could not resist that, especially as everybody else was busy elsewhere. True?'

Master Benedict just stared back.

'You had no intention,' Corbett continued, 'of going to Colchester. Oh no, you'd leave here and travel swiftly to one of the eastern ports and take ship to foreign parts. It would take weeks, if not months, to discover which harbour you used; even then you might have left under a false name. Rumours would abound. Poor Benedict Le Sanglier,' Corbett made a face, 'who disappeared, probably ambushed and killed on some lonely Essex trackway in the depth of winter. In truth you would be elsewhere, using the treasure you'd stolen to smooth the path before you. Naturally it was a risk. If you'd been alerted or alarmed unduly, you would have got rid of that secret satchel and continued the pretence of being the ever-so-diffident and rather weak chaplain.' Corbett rose to his feet. 'You're certainly no gentle priest. You're wicked, twice as fit for hell as the man you murdered on the Island of Swans.'

Corbett walked away as Chanson brought in dry bracken and kindling. He placed these near the prisoner and doused them with a little oil. The flames soon caught hold. Chanson then moved back to the door, sliding down with his back to the wall, the arbalest still primed on the floor beside him. Ranulf leaned against the crumbling pillar, staring at the killer. Ranulf shivered. He was not remembering Scrope's murdered corpse but poor Jackanapes and those other innocents slain by this murderer. He wondered if Corbett's musing on death and justice was having its effect on him. Were all the hapless victims of this assassin clustering here to seek vengeance, retribution?

Corbett picked up a wineskin and returned to the fire, which separated him from the prisoner. He offered Le Sanglier a drink, but the chaplain shook his head. Corbett didn't like the cold arrogance in the prisoner's eyes: a man who did not care, who still trusted in himself. What would be his last defence? Corbett glimpsed the cross on the chain around Le Sanglier's neck. That was it! Was the prisoner, despite all his wicked deeds a genuine priest who would gabble the first line of Psalm 50, claim he was a cleric, plead benefit of clergy and so escape the rigour of the law? Would this killer, his hands drenched in blood, appear before some Church court only to receive mild punishment?

'I am a priest.' The chaplain seemed to read Corbett's thoughts. Already, despite being in this bleak haunted nave, the freezing cold seeping everywhere, the bonds tight around his wrists and the weapons primed for his destruction, Master Benedict Le Sanglier was eager to assert himself. 'Very well, Master Corbett,' his deliberate insult was accompanied by a smile. 'I made a mistake. For the time being you have trapped me. I was impetuous, eager to be gone. My task was finished, so—'

'Your task,' Corbett retorted, 'was the death of Oliver Scrope.' He stretched his hands out to the fire. 'Now, Master Benedict, for the time being I am like a master in the schools. I am going to construct an argument based more on conjecture than evidence. Nonetheless, as I move towards my conclusion, the proof will emerge. So, to continue the similarity, you, Master Benedict, are like a master mason, the genius behind the house of murder you so carefully constructed. It began in Acre in 1291. We have all heard the accepted story, but I believe there is one important difference: Gaston de Bearn, Scrope's cousin, did not die there. I truly believe this. Somehow he survived Scrope's betrayal, his attempt to murder him and eventually escaped back to France.'

'If he did,' the chaplain sneered, 'why didn't he return to England?'

'To confront Lord Scrope?' Corbett shook his head. 'A powerful manor lord, a hero, a Crusader much favoured by the King? To be accused by a foreigner, and with what proof? No,' Corbett clicked his tongue, 'that would be too dangerous, completely without profit.' He paused. 'Indeed, from the very little I know about Gaston de Bearn, I suspect he would not stoop to that. I think he was a noble soul, a man who inspired others, be it you and the Free Brethren, Dame Marguerite, who loved him, possibly even Lord Scrope, who was deeply haunted by what he'd done.'

Master Benedict's face changed; just for a brief while the arrogance was replaced by honest recognition.

'Gaston escaped,' Corbett continued, 'and some deep relationship developed between him, you and the Free Brethren. Eventually you and the Free Brethren came to England to wreak vengeance on Lord Scrope. Why? I suggest because of Gaston. First, the Free Brethren took great pains to remind Scrope of his evil deeds; hence the painting in St Alphege's as well as their scrolled design of hell with Scrope at its heart. Oh yes,' Corbett added, 'we have seen what was buried with Le Riche, the treasure and the drawings. Both drawings also contain strange symbols. I suggest they are Arabic. I found the same in the painting at St Alphege's, those geometric designs much loved by Muslim artists. Whoever was responsible for those drawings and that painting had lived in Outremer and had some knowledge of Arabic design. Second, the Free Brethren were armed, they were planning to attack, kill or kidnap Lord Scrope. Third, you were party to that. You used Dame Marguerite's wealth to buy them weapons. You also supplied them with information about the reclusorium on the Island of Swans and the secret ford across. No, no . . .' Corbett raised a hand. 'I will explain in a while. Fourth, the painting in St Alphege's contains the design of herbs or plants, in truth nightshade, the potion Lord Scrope probably used in his attempt to poison Gaston in Acre infirmary so many years ago. You adopted that same name when you visited Father Thomas to threaten Scrope with death unless he publicly confessed his sins on the steps of the market cross in Mistleham. Fifth, in one of our conversations you made a hideous mistake. You talked of the survivors at Acre being slaughtered in the dragon courtyard. How did you know such a fact, the name of a Templar courtyard in a small donjon in Outremer? Does that also explain the dragon above the castle in the painting at the parish church?'

'And Dame Marguerite was party to all this?' Master Benedict scoffed. 'Are you saying she was my accomplice? Scrope's adoring sister?'

15

Ad audiendum et terminandum – to hear and finish the business.
Letter of Edward I, 19 November 1303

'Listen,' Corbett made himself more comfortable, 'and listen well. You and the Free Brethren of the Holy Spirit were close to Gaston de Bearn, how and why I still don't know. You are undoubtedly a French priest whilst they were a wandering band of souls who lived for the day until Gaston told you and their leaders a hideous story. How he'd been a Crusader abandoned at Acre by his close friend and kinsman, and worse, nearly murdered by him. I suggest he told you the truth close to his death, in the vespers of his life. You and the Free Brethren swore vengeance. You, a priest, educated, with some patronage, secured letters of accreditation for yourself and them to travel to England. You came first to spy, to learn, to plan. Like all the malignant killers I've known, you can shape your face, your actions, your very soul better than any actor. You arrived at St Frideswide, the gentle priest looking for employment. Dame Marguerite of course entertained you. She read your letters, but you'd also brought something else: proof, be it letters or items, of what truly happened at Acre.'

'And Dame Marguerite simply accepted that?'

'At first there'd be protests, doubts, but I am sure that in that pannier you have a letter from Gaston, a ring perhaps, some keepsake? More importantly, you loved Gaston, you'd lived with him, he was significant in your life as he had been in Dame Marguerite's. You described him closely, both body and soul. It would not take long to convince Dame Marguerite.'

'She was an abbess . . .'

'No, Master Benedict, first and foremost she was Gaston's ardent lover. She obliquely referred to dreams of the past. He was the great passion of her youth. She and Gaston would have kept this hidden from Scrope, but a flame burns as strong secretly as it does clearly in the light of day. I talked to old servants at the manor; they did not deny that. I suggest the pair of them plighted their troth, swore eternal vows before Gaston left with Scrope for Outremer. Dame Marguerite waited for news. Eventually it came: her brother was coming home, but her beloved Gaston, the heart of her life, was dead.' Master Benedict was now attentive, eyes watchful.

'Dame Marguerite could give herself to no one else so she took the solemn vows of a Benedictine nun, assumed the veil and entered St Frideswide. Scrope, entertaining the only guilt he ever suffered, patronised and favoured his sister and she eventually became abbess. Dame Marguerite, however, never forgot Gaston. She wore the ring Gaston gave her as his pledge. I thought the design on it was a deer; in fact it was a stag, the same emblazoned on Gaston's coat of arms as well as on the memorials to him in St Alphege's, the manor chapel and St Frideswide. Indeed, these were Marguerite's tribute to the great love of her life. I doubt if Scrope had anything to do with that. He preferred to forget Gaston, but he had to play the part and indulge his adoring sister. Dame Marguerite had chantry masses sung for Gaston; her community often prayed for his soul. Then you arrived with news that cracked all the foundations of her world.' Corbett paused. He threw more kindling into the flames and stared around. Ranulf still leaned against the pillar, staring malevolently at Master Benedict. Chanson sat open-mouthed by the door, marvelling at the story his master was telling.

'I can only imagine the darkness that engulfed Dame Marguerite's soul,' Corbett declared. 'The lies, the tragedy, the loss of her beloved, the evil deeds of her brother, the waste of her own life, the living of a lie!'

'The serpent truly entered Eden!' Ranulf called out.

'Yes, that's what it was. You were the serpent, Master Benedict. Publicly you were the pious chaplain; privately you wound yourself around Dame Marguerite's soul. Did you seduce her? Did she try and take from you what she had lost? I think that you kindled her murderous fury against her evil brother whilst smilingly inviting her to participate in his destruction.'

Master Benedict gazed back, cold-eyed.

'All was ready,' Corbett continued. 'Messages were sent to the Free Brethren and they duly landed at Dover and journeyed into Essex. Dame Marguerite, at your insistence still playing the faithful sister, the pious abbess, persuaded her brother that the Free Brethren were no danger, so they were allowed to shelter here in Mordern. Secretly, however, you plotted: weapons were bought and practised upon; a plan of the reclusorium was produced, the secret ford described.'

'Secret ford?' Master Benedict jibed.

'Yes the secret ford across the lake to the Island of Swans known to Scrope, Gaston and Dame Marguerite when they played there as children. I mentioned it last night. Dame Marguerite told you about it, she must have done; that is how you, the killer, crossed.

After all, you often visited the manor, Master Benedict. You would become accustomed to crossing over, especially during those spring and summer days, well hidden by that clump of willows behind the reclusorium. You'd also steal out to meet the Free Brethren, and, of course, they were entertained at St Frideswide, where you all could plot to your hearts' content. Except for Jackanapes, fey-witted he might have been, but he could still have noticed something amiss.'

'Yet it was Dame Marguerite who told you that he came here . . .'

'Of course she did, providing valuable information to sustain both your roles as innocents in this matter. You were offering us Jackanapes as a valuable witness, but not for long. He would die before I ever questioned him.'

'Are you alleging I was the Sagittarius?' Master Benedict declared. 'Remember that evening in Mistleham: Dame Marguerite and I were with you when the Sagittarius blew his horn.'

'Yes, that was strange,' Corbett conceded. 'As it is that you mention it now. That evening the horn was blown, but no attack was launched. Why? I suspect that earlier that day, before you attended the banquet, you secretly visited Jackanapes the fool, and bribed him with good silver to blow that horn late at night. You then met him afterwards to pay and collect the horn. After all, a horn is easy to carry and easy to hide; many people have them. On that particular evening you just wished to confuse; you did the same when we journeyed here to clear the dead. It was so easy to slip away into the ruins or the trees and blow three swift blasts, again for the same effect: to confuse, to make me wonder if the Sagittarius really was someone distinct from all those I had met in Mistleham.'

'I was also in the marketplace when Jackanapes was killed.'

'Nonsense! You were there because you knew that was where he lived, and for all I know, you invited him to meet you there for payment. Jackanapes was certainly marked down for death. First because of the horn, and second because he'd been out to Mordern and St Frideswide and may have, in his own antic way, seen or heard something untoward. Now, around the market square in Mistleham stand houses with row upon row of tenements. Most of them are owned by Lord Scrope; some of the rents have been granted to Claypole, even more to St Frideswide's. Garrets and attics, shabby little rooms, stairwells and chambers no bigger than a box, shadowy, narrow places; easy to conceal a bow and a quiver of arrows, easy for someone like yourself, with keys from Dame Marguerite, to slip like a thief up the stairs, seize the concealed bow, then through some arrow slit, hole or window take aim and unleash death. Lady Hawisa's men, led by Pennywort, will make a sweep of such hiding holes. I wager they'll find bows and arrows hidden away. That's what you did when you killed Jackanapes: hastened up a flight of stairs to let murder take wing. Two shafts for Jackanapes – you had to be sure he was dead, his gabbling mouth silenced for ever – then you re-emerged as the pious chaplain.'

'So I am a master bowman as well as a priest?'

'Too true,' Corbett agreed, 'and a very good one! The Sagittarius is a matter to be discussed, but let us return to late last summer. All was secure. You were so assured you made your first mistake. In your confidence you decided to taunt Scrope with that painting. He must have been furious at being given such a brutal, stark reminder of his evil deeds, being portrayed as a Judas. Little wonder he promised to renovate St Alphege's, a small price to pay for removing that painting. You totally underestimated Scrope, an evil, vengeful man. He bided his time, but you, the master mason of murder, made your second mistake. Brother Gratian visited you here. He'd served as a soldier and he noticed how one of the funeral crosses had been used as a whetstone to sharpen blades. Finally John Le Riche, the robber, with his ill-gotten gains, arrived from Westminster. Like any outlaw he sought refuge in Mordern Forest, and the Free Brethren took him under their wing. In many ways your associates were not children of this world; they cared little for wealth. They may also have been curious about Le Riche's secret relationship with Master Claypole and indeed Lord Scrope. Anyway, Le Riche left most of his booty here in trust before he journeyed into Mistleham to do business with Claypole and Scrope. Of course that precious pair duped him. They arrested Le Riche, drugged him, tried him and hanged him out of hand. Again the Free Brethren showed compassion as well as over-confidence. They cut down Le Riche's corpse and buried him and his treasure here under a certain headstone, scrawling the memorial on the sacristy wall of this church. How does it go? "Rich, shall richer be, Where God kissed Mary in Galilee."'

'I certainly agree with your judgement on Scrope,' Master Benedict murmured.

'You still underestimated him,' Corbett declared sharply. 'The painting, the weapons, and, I suspect, he discovered that not only had Le Riche sheltered in Mordern, but most of his booty still lay hidden here. Enough was enough. The Free Brethren were a real danger. Scrope was very frightened. How had they discovered his sin? His Judas-like conduct? Had someone survived the fall of Acre, someone who knew everything? Or was it Gratian or even Claypole? Whatever, they had to be silenced. Scrope became busy sowing rumours, allegations against the Free Brethren, and then he struck. He acted the manor lord defending his own, the faithful son of the Church attacking heretics. The Free Brethren were swiftly massacred. Scrope did not find the treasure, nor had he the wit to understand the scrawl on the sacristy wall. He killed them all, then left their corpses to rot. Why? Well, first he discovered that the Free Brethren were not the angelic beings they'd pretended to be. He must have been delighted to find those weapons and the drawings of Mistleham Manor to justify his actions, but he was also suspicious: he wanted to see if the Free Brethren had any secret sympathisers amongst the community in Mistleham. Anyone who might come out here to bury the corpses.' Corbett paused. Master Benedict's face had grown paler. He was staring dully into the flames as the memories returned.

'You,' Corbett continued, 'like everyone else, were deeply shocked at Scrope's ferocious and ruthless attack. You certainly had not planned for that. You never thought a manor lord would attack in the first light of dawn, putting everyone to the sword. You were not there to advise your comrades that Scrope had decided on all their deaths. He had no choice:

that painting, not to mention Le Riche. Our robber not only hid his plunder here, he may also have told the Free Brethren all sorts of tales about a secret pact to sell stolen royal goods to a mayor and a powerful lord. Little wonder the Free Brethren were so brutally silenced. Nevertheless, you and your accomplice, Dame Marguerite, became genuinely ill with shock, guilty at bringing your colleagues to such a grisly end. Dame Marguerite had learnt of the Templar threats to her brother; now, through you, she began to issue threats on both your accounts about the Mills of God.'

Corbett picked up the wineskin and threw it across. The chaplain clumsily removed the stopper, gulped greedily and handed it back.

'Dame Marguerite also told you about the Sagittarius, who'd appeared years ago threatening her brother. You and she decided the Sagittarius must return. First to deal out terror and justice to the good citizens of Mistleham who'd supported Lord Scrope's attack on the Free Brethren, and second to plan for Scrope's own death. You chose your victims for execution, innocents in Mistleham. You used Dame Marguerite as your constant disguise, as you did when Wilfred and Eadburga were slaughtered. You were not guarding the door at St Alphege's; you slipped away to commit horrid murder. Time, however, was passing. To a certain extent you and Dame Marguerite had lost control over events. The massacre, the hanging of Le Riche, and now the King's men were coming to Mistleham. You plotted furiously. First you, Master Benedict, visited Father Thomas, calling yourself Nightshade. You issued a veiled warning, an ultimatum to Lord Scrope. Of course he recognised the truth behind your message: his evil day had caught up with him. You knew he would not repent. Already you were devising his death. A constant visitor to the manor, residing there with Dame Marguerite, you could hide away bows and arrows. One night you went hunting Scrope's mastiffs; they also had been involved in the attack on Mordern. More importantly, they were guard dogs. Did you first mix an opiate with their meat?'

Master Benedict just smiled.

'Then you grasped the bow and arrows Dame Marguerite had smuggled in for you and slipped out into the darkness like the hunter you are. Two arrows for each hound, one to wound and slow your quarry, the second delivering the killing blow.'

'And then we arrived,' Ranulf interrupted, 'but our presence did not deter you.'

'In a way, Master Benedict,' Corbett declared, 'you were pleased at our arrival. The corpses of your comrades were rotting; we ended all that. Nevertheless, you used the occasion to remind Scrope's men that the

Sagittarius was not far. However, the burning of your dead truly disturbed you. You became ill with fury; I witnessed that. You carried out immediate retribution. You discovered that Scrope's henchman Robert de Scott was wallowing in the Honeycomb. Once again you disappeared into that warren of garrets and chambers above Mistleham marketplace to unleash death before turning on Scrope himself.'

Master Benedict bowed his head and smiled softly. Corbett suspected he was simply hiding his confusion.

'Dame Marguerite then came into her own. By now she truly hated her brother, as she did his shadow Claypole. She was determined to harm the mayor. She'd always hated his pretensions; I suspect even before your revelations to her. Whilst her brother was away in Acre, Dame Marguerite was the one who removed the blood registers from St Alphege's – so that if her brother died childless, Master Claypole could make no claim. True?'

'It's possible.' The chaplain kept his head down. 'Dame Marguerite truly hated Claypole, and if she'd lived, she would have dealt with him.'

'But first her brother,' Corbett declared. 'On the day we burnt the dead at Mordern, you returned to the manor to take Gaston's ring, which, God forgive his hypocrisy, Scrope had placed on the head of the crucified Saviour. You did this before slipping out into

Mistleham to wreak bloody havoc in the marketplace. You strode into that chapel only to be surprised by Lady Hawisa. She came in after you full of rage at her husband and, in the silence of that place, confessed how she had often plotted to kill him with nightshade. She left and so did you, taking the ring to Dame Marguerite as well as the information Lady Hawisa had unwittingly provided.'

Corbett paused and listened to the faint sounds from outside. He thought of the list of murderous deeds this man was responsible for and wondered how Master Benedict could be brought to full justice. First, though, the indictment had to be presented.

'Lord Scrope was now truly frightened,' Corbett continued. 'Dame Marguerite was still acting the role of the loving, loyal sister. Secretly, and I admit this is conjecture, she went to see him. She would act all concerned and anxious, bemoaning how no one could be trusted, how the very walls had ears.' Corbett shrugged. 'It would not be too difficult with Scrope haunted and hunted by the past as well as the present. Dame Marguerite would argue that no one could be trusted, not even his wife, who, she told him, also desired to end his life. She offered to bring proof, revelations about the mysterious threats, either herself or through her faithful chaplain. One of you would cross the secret ford and visit him that night in the reclusorium; that was the best place for such a confession to be made, where no one could see or hear.'

'And Lord Scrope would agree to that?'

'Why not? What did he fear from his faithful sister or her creature, the whey-faced chaplain? God knows what Dame Marguerite offered, what she said, but Scrope certainly accepted.'

'But that ford at night?'

'Nonsense, Master Benedict, you know Mistleham Manor well. You've been there for over a year, Dame Marguerite had shown you the place. You may have even practised crossing it. I did once, quite safely. You could do it easily armed with a staff, a rope and a shuttered lantern horn.'

Master Benedict glanced up in surprise. Corbett noted the fear in his eyes, the realisation of how hard the case pressed against him.

'What had you to fear, cold water? The guards were sheltering well away under some trees. Robert de Scott had been dispatched to hell, the guard dogs slain. Dame Marguerite was ready to swear that you were ill all night. No, no – you safely crossed to the rear of the reclusorium and, as agreed, tapped on a shutter. Lord Scrope, lying on his bed, gets up, pulls aside the drapes, opens the shutters and lets you in. What can he, a warrior, fear from a pious, unarmed chaplain carrying a small pannier bag? Scrope sits down in his chair and you, all nervous, stand over him. You fumble with the bag but swiftly grasp the dagger and plunge it into Scrope's heart. In the blink of an eye Scrope was killed because he had been faced with the totally unexpected and had no time to resist, to struggle. You plunged that dagger deep. Scrope tried to grasp the hilt and bloodied his hands. You just stood and watched the life light fade in your enemy's eyes. You then took the keys from round his neck and ransacked his treasury. You later returned the keys, pulled out your dagger and thrust in the one taken from the crypt at Westminster.'

'And the poison?'

'Oh, you may have disturbed the herb plant at the manor, or the nightshade may have been given to you by Dame Marguerite from her stock of powders in the convent infirmary. Anyway, you poured the phial of poison into the jug, then filled that yew cup. A mysterious, mischievous twist that would suggest Lady Hawisa's guilt. You later departed as you came, through the window, pulling over the drapes, closing the shutter and going back across the ford.'

'I could have been noticed.'

'I doubt it. A dark shadow on a black, freezing

night? You were no longer the timid chaplain, but a soldier skilled and ruthless.'

'But those shutters remained unbarred.'

'Dame Marguerite took care of that. She'd arranged to see her brother the following morning in the reclusorium with Father Thomas, a gesture that would reassure her brother about his midnight visitor. She'd promised to go over to discuss certain concerns, but also to secretly consult with him on what to do next. Scrope would see that as logical reassurance that you were what you pretended to be, his loyal, loving sister's emissary. Father Thomas was a cat's paw: the abbess and the parish priest paying a visit to their manor lord. Of course this is mere conjecture, because Dame Marguerite's real intention was to conceal the mystery of her brother's brutal murder. On that morning she crossed by boat. The door was locked, so she directed Pennywort to break the nearest shutter, which he did. He climbs in and sees the horror. He hastily unlocks the door and Dame Marguerite sweeps in. Father Thomas immediately acts the priest, tending to the corpse. Dame Marguerite, pretending to be all flustered, hastens around the reclusorium. She quickly pulls aside the drapes of that window, lowers the bar, and lifts the pegs against the shutters. Remember, the reclusorium was cloaked in darkness; most of the candles had guttered out. Father Thomas is busy.

Pennywort is standing outside by the door. Dame Marguerite can do what she likes and the mystery is complete. The alarm is then noisily raised. People hasten across, trampling any sign, if any remained, of Scrope's secret assassin.'

'And your vengeance has been carried out,' Ranulf declared.

Master Benedict threw the Clerk of the Green Wax a venomous glance. Proof, Corbett quietly concluded, that if Ranulf was not here, this murderous soul would try and seize any opportunity.

'You are not yet finished,' Corbett remarked. 'Dame Marguerite was infatuated with you – yes? Did she have plans, nurse plots? Oh no, not to elope, but to settle down at St Frideswide with her lover chaplain who'd secure preferment in the royal service. Some madcap scheme that certainly did not match your plans? She might prove to be a burden in the future. Why did you need to stay? Yet you couldn't flee and leave her to bear witness. You continued to be *faux et semblant* – false and dissembling. You encouraged her to act all frightened, as if she too was being threatened by the Sagittarius. That was all your work, the arrow, the message. Again you were trying to divert attention.'

'And in St Alphege's?' Master Benedict broke in, all impetuous, like a master wondering if his scholar had really learnt his lesson.

Corbett bit back his anger. 'If Dame Marguerite was truly frightened,' he murmured, 'she would never have left St Frideswide. Yet you could not kill her there; that would be highly suspicious.'

'So?'

'Master Claypole,' Corbett replied. 'Dame Marguerite was venomously hot against him. You persuaded the lady abbess to send that letter to Physician Ormesby. Why? I truly don't know, except to use him against Claypole.'

'But why meet in St Alphege's.' The question was more of a taunt.

'Oh.' Corbett smiled. 'I suspect you and Dame Marguerite were going to entrap Claypole. Your assertion that the parish church held the solution to all the mysteries was a lie. The Sagittarius would launch an attack against both her and you, only to fail. Physician Ormesby would arrive shortly afterwards to find the abbess and her chaplain all distraught and ready to swear that the secret bowman was no less a person than Master Claypole.'

'And Dame Marguerite was confident about this?'

'Of course! Dame Marguerite wasn't frightened of any Sagittarius; she knew who he really was. In fact she should have been most wary. You accompanied her. You took a short horn bow, along with two arrows pushed through your belt, all hidden beneath your cloak. Dame Marguerite never suspected what you really intended. She thought you adored her. Both of you arrived early in the church – the Jesus Mass was finished, Father Thomas had withdrawn, those parishioners who'd attended had left. If there had been any obstacle, you'd have simply changed your plans accordingly. Dame Marguerite would have to leave the church. Perhaps you could encourage her to move amongst the stalls, or, of course, there was always the journey back to St Frideswide. However, the church was empty, the main door locked. You acted very swiftly. You melt into the shadows, notch one arrow, emerge and loose. In a few heartbeats Dame Marguerite is dead. Another shaft is loosed at the rood screen. You unstring the bow and hide the stave in that dark, cavernous church; only then do you blow the horn and hide behind the rood screen as if terrified out of your wits.'

'So swift?' Le Sanglier jibed.

'Ranulf,' Corbett spoke over his shoulder, 'when I start counting, pick up your bow and two arrows from the quiver, and loose as quickly as you can down the church.' He watched Ranulf stand, bow at the ready. 'One, two, three, four . . .' He had only reached five when the second arrow whistled through the air. 'You see,' Corbett rose to his feet, 'no more than a few heartbeats. Once again the Sagittarius had attacked

Lord Scrope's family. After that you were eager to be gone. I was very wary of that. I had no reason in law to detain you, hence the mummery last night.' He stared at the prisoner. 'I had to trap you.'

'So you have.' Master Benedict lifted his bound hands. 'Now take me to London and put me before King's Bench. I will plead benefit of clergy and demand to be returned to my ordinary, the bishop who ordained me. He will try me, and then what, Master Corbett? A few months in some lonely monastery fasting on bread and water?'

'Perhaps not.' Ranulf drew his sword and, ignoring Corbett's hiss of disapproval, squatted down in front of the prisoner. 'Scrope I understand, but those innocents, the others, why them?'

'Why not?' Master Benedict taunted. 'Their kin attacked mine.'

'I tell you this.' Ranulf moved his sword so its tip rested on the ground, his fingers curled around the crosspiece, 'I swear—'

'Ranulf!' Corbett intervened.

'I swear,' Ranulf shouted, 'if you confirm the truth, we shall offer you a way out. I swear!' He turned, eyes pleading, to Corbett. 'I rarely ask, let alone beg.'

'It must be just and fair,' the chaplain murmured. 'By the way, how did you know it was a short horn bow?'

He gestured with his hand at the longbow lying on the ground.

'Father Thomas, at my request, searched his church,' Ranulf whispered. 'He found the bow hidden deep behind the lady altar.'

Master Benedict simply pulled a face.

'I have your word,' he glanced at Corbett, 'as a guarantee. Untie my bonds.'

Before Corbett could object, Ranulf drew his dagger and slit the rope binding the chaplain's wrists. The prisoner did not move; he simply curled the severed rope off, threw it away, rubbed his wrists and squinted up at Corbett.

'It is as you say, or nearly so, a few small changes here or there. Jackanapes was not as stupid as he pretended. He was greatly mischievous. I patronised him and he was easy to use. I told him to blow the horn then leave it hidden in a secret place and be in the market square at dawn the next morning. I had approached him secretly but he may have known it was me. He could chatter like a squirrel on a branch; he had to die. As for the rest,' Le Sanglier shrugged, 'more or less true. I knew about the ford. I practised crossing many times. Those willows at the rear of the reclusorium cannot be seen. Lord Scrope, of course, was lax; he rightly thought if he was attacked it would be at night. He never realised people would plan during the day. As for Dame Marguerite, I was tiring of her.' He smiled. 'What really enticed her into St Alphege's was my plot to loose my arrows. Of course they were supposed to miss, then we'd blame Claypole. Physician Ormesby was to arrive after the attack, be a witness to our terror. I would swear that the mysterious bowman I'd glimpsed was Master Claypole. Our good mayor is constantly in the guildhall or the marketplace outside St Alphege's. It wouldn't be hard and,' he spread his hands, 'who'd dare contradict a lady abbess and her chaplain?'

'So her death was swift?' Corbett walked back to stand over him.

'Like that!' Master Benedict snapped his fingers.

Corbett crouched down. 'But what was the bond between you and Gaston?'

'Ah, you were correct.' The chaplain pointed to the wineskin. Corbett handed it over, and the prisoner drank greedily. 'I'll be brief.' He smiled, smacking his lips. 'I accept your word, what else can I do? I could demand to be put on trial and plead benefit of clergy,' he pointed at Ranulf, 'but I don't think he'll allow me to live.'

'Very perceptive!' Ranulf whispered.

'Gaston?' Corbett intervened.

'You're right,' the chaplain replied. 'Scrope escaped from Acre. When he entered the infirmary, only the sick and the dying were there. A table inside was littered with all kinds of medicines and herbs, including potions and poisons. Some of the Templars preferred to be drugged against their impending death. Scrope took a cup of wine and mixed the poison; Gaston did not know it. Scrope encouraged him to drink, saying that the wine would dull the pain and that God be his witness, he'd come back for him. Gaston was certain that only Scrope had come into the infirmary. Afterwards Scrope fled; of course he never returned. However, he was hardly out of the infirmary when Gaston was violently sick, spewing up both wine and poison. He then fell into a dead swoon. When he awoke, Acre had fallen. The Saracens showed chivalry to those wounded who looked as if they might survive. The others had been taken out and executed with the rest in the dragon courtyard. I saw that.'

'You?'

'Myself and all the other children. Everyone who could had retreated to the Templar stronghold: soldiers, merchants, traders, men, women and children. When the donjon was stormed, all adults, male and female, were summarily executed. The children, myself included, were made to watch one prisoner after another being forced to their knees, heads sliced off, until we stood ankle deep in blood, weeping and wailing. We were only saved because our looks would fetch a high price in the slave markets.'

'But Gaston did not die?'

'No, he didn't. The Saracen officer who found him was honourable. He was also intrigued. He found the wine goblet, smelt the poison and questioned Gaston. He was very surprised at how one Christian could try and murder a fellow Christian who'd fought alongside him. You know soldiers the world over, they all like a good story. Gaston was seen by Arab physicians, his wounds soon healed and he joined us children shackled in the dragon courtyard. The officer did what he could to ensure Gaston was given good food, and I suppose that's when we met our hero.' The chaplain paused. 'I cannot describe the true horror of that courtyard. Gaston became our protector, our friend. He did what he could for us, shared his food, tended the dying, consoled and comforted everyone else.' He took a deep breath. 'Weeks turned into months. Gaston regained his strength. He was powerful; even then I noticed he had the long arms of a born swordsman. He exercised when he could, then seized his opportunity. One afternoon the officer in charge visited him bringing some food; three Mamelukes also appeared. I know they shouldn't drink, that is their religion, but these three had certainly drunk deep of wine. They began abusing some of the young girls.

Gaston sprang to his feet. He called them cowards, cursing and taunting them, saying that they would not dare to confront a warrior such as himself. The Mamelukes rose to the bait. Gaston offered to meet all three together in combat, declaring that all he needed was a sword and a dagger. He said that if he killed them it would be a sign from Allah that he and the children should be allowed to go free.' The chaplain took another drink from the wineskin. 'By now the challenge was known all over the donjon. The courtyard became flooded with men. The officer was reluctant but I think he knew what was going to happen. He wanted to allow Gaston the opportunity, so he agreed. Gaston's chains were taken off. He was given both sword and dagger.' Master Benedict shook his head. 'I tell you, as God lives, Gaston was a warrior, a skilled swordsman. He killed those Mamelukes swiftly, like a cat with vermin. Fast as a dancer! God was certainly with him that day.' He stretched his hands out towards the fire. 'The entire garrison applauded him. The officer kept his word. The following morning we were taken down to the port, Gaston, myself and the other children.'

'How many?' Corbett asked.

'About twenty in all. We were shipped to Cyprus and from Limasol taken to Marseilles. Gaston then took us north to Angers, where he was known to the local bishop. He had the highest opinion of Gaston and allowed him to settle in a derelict chateau, a beautiful place on the edge of a forest near rich fields and well-stocked streams.'

'You settled there?'

'Oh yes. Gaston called us his Company of the Holy Spirit. I think it was more of a jest than anything else. He was the finest, the best man I have ever met. He became our God, our Saviour, our mother and father, elder brother and elder sister, priest and confessor. He treated us with gentleness, loved and guided us. He believed he'd been saved just to do that.'

'And yet you were skilled in arms?'

'Some of us were. I was the eldest. Gaston explained how in this vale of tears we had to defend ourselves; he taught me how to use the sword, the dagger, and above all the longbow, which he'd grown skilled in when in England. He described the bow's history, its use by the Welsh, though he never talked about his own past.'

'And you really are a priest?' Corbett asked.

'Of course! Gaston said I was highly intelligent so I should be educated. I was patronised by the local bishop, sent to a nearby cathedral school then on to Bordeaux and Paris. Gaston had some wealth; the rest he earned or was given. Local nobles, abbeys and monasteries heard about what he'd achieved and were lavish in their generosity.'

'But he never mentioned England?'

'Never. That door remained closed and sealed.'

'And the rest of your group?'

'Some died, but the others grew strong under Gaston's influence. He did not abandon his faith, only its rules and strictures. The Free Brethren were really his creation. They were tolerated, even favoured by the local clergy, given letters of protection from the papal curia at Avignon. They were harmless, one of many such groups wandering the roads of France.'

'But you?'

'Gaston was proud of me, though I often felt I was a stranger to the vocation I was following. Living proof, perhaps,' he grinned, 'that *cacullus non facit monachum* – the cowl doesn't necessarily make the monk.'

'Then Gaston told you the full truth?'

'Yes, he fell ill two summers ago, a malignancy inside him. He called us back to what he called his sanctuary and said he must explain why he'd been in Acre and what had happened. He told us everything.' The chaplain wiped his mouth on the cuff of his jerkin. 'He did not ask for vengeance; that was my idea. Gaston died. I made enquiries. My fury deepened when I discovered how Lord Scrope had grown fat like a hog in its sty, and so our plan was formed.

We would punish Lord Scrope and escape by sea. The rest,' he shrugged, 'is in the main, as you say.'

'Did you intend to kill Lord Scrope?'

'No, not at first. That was the paradox: because of him, Gaston had remained in Acre and saved us. We hotly debated the question. It was the attempt to murder Gaston that was the real sin. We hoped to make Scrope confess, publicly humiliate him, make him acknowledge the evil he'd done, but as you say, we underestimated him. I never,' he whispered, 'thought he would do it, even after we defied him; that too was a hot-headed mistake. You were correct. I became genuinely ill with guilt and anger.' He smiled at Corbett. 'I thank you for giving their corpses some honour. I came out here secretly to collect any bones. I took them to sacred ground at St Frideswide for burial.' He sighed deeply. 'But yes, once the Free Brethren were massacred, I had no choice but to deal out terror.'

'Even to innocents like the ostler's daughter and the marketplace fool?' Ranulf asked.

'Of course.' Master Benedict climbed to his feet. 'Now, I've kept my word; you keep yours. Master Ranulf, you want my death.'

'No, I don't,' Ranulf replied. 'God does! I will give you a chance, better than you gave your victims. I've heard your story, Master Chaplain, but I still believe you enjoyed the killing. I truly believe that.'

Corbett stepped back, wondering what Ranulf intended.

'As I've said,' the chaplain gestured at Ranulf, 'you want my life.' He spread his hands. 'What use pleading benefit of clergy, exile in a monastery? I know your type, Ranulf-atte-Newgate, you'll be waiting for me, if you ever let me live that long.'

'You talked about the hideous things you witnessed,' Ranulf replied softly. 'So have I, Master Benedict. I've seen men and women stabbed in taverns, my friends hanged for stealing a loaf when they were hungry, and as I listened to you, I thought of a game we used to play. It was called "Hawks Swoop". We'd put a club and a hammer on the ground between us. The first to grasp a weapon could smack the other. We'll play "Hawks Swoop" now. Chanson,' Ranulf called across, 'bring the arbalest.'

The groom of the stables did so. Ranulf laid the crossbow between his feet, a wicked-looking barb beside it. He then picked up the longbow and one of the arrows from the quiver. He let the chaplain inspect these, then placed them at his opponent's feet. Corbett stared in horror at what Ranulf intended.

'No one will interfere,' Ranulf warned. 'Priest, you are a master bowman, swift and deadly. If you strike me before I strike you, then you are free to go. Sir Hugh?'

'Ranulf, this is—'

'Sir Hugh?'

Corbett caught the look in Ranulf's eyes and nodded, though his fingers crept to the hilt of his own dagger. Master Benedict was most skilled. He could notch an arrow faster than Ranulf would ever prime that arbalest.

Master Benedict studied Ranulf carefully and nodded. He stood, body slack, arms down, twisting his wrists to ease any cramp.

'When I have recited the Gloria.' Ranulf smiled. 'Fitting for a murderous priest about to meet his God.'

'Say it and have done with it.'

'*Gloria Patri*,' Ranulf intoned harshly, '*et Filii et Spiritus Sancti . . .*'

The chaplain swiftly reached down, seizing both bow and arrow, bringing them up and stepping back. Ranulf, however, ignored the arbalest; instead he pulled the dagger from his belt and sent it hurtling at the chaplain, striking him full and deep in the chest. Master Benedict staggered back, bow and arrow falling from his hands. Ranulf drew his sword, snaking it out to catch his opponent in the belly, then, stepping closer, thrust it deeper. Master Benedict flailed his hands, head falling back, choking on his own blood.

'I said,' Ranulf pressed firmly on his sword, 'I'd

strike you before you struck me, and so I have!' He pulled out the sword.

Master Benedict's eyes fluttered; he gave a deep sigh, and collapsed to his knees then on to his side.

'Trickery,' Corbett murmured.

'Justice!' Ranulf snarled. He squatted before the dead man and plucked out the dagger. 'He was an assassin, a murderer, Sir Hugh. Did you want him to dance away from the hideous crimes he'd committed? Did you want such a man to slink through the shadows of your nightmares? Perhaps return one day to Leighton Manor, stealing in one night to seek vengeance on you and yours? A wounded animal is a dangerous animal. Master Benedict Le Sanglier deserved his fate. I did what was legal and right.'

'Right maybe,' Corbett queried, 'but legal?'

Ranulf stood up, dug beneath his jerkin and drew out a small parchment scroll. He handed this to Corbett.

'Legal,' he declared, 'just, and right!'

As Corbett undid the scroll, his eyes caught the words 'what the bearer of this letter has done he has done for the good of the King and the safety of the realm'.

'Why, Ranulf,' Corbett glanced up, 'you are growing most astute.'

'For the children of this world,' his companion

quoted back, 'are more astute in their dealings with their own kind than the children of the light.'

'Do you consider yourself to be a child of the light, Ranulf?'

'No, Sir Hugh.' Ranulf touched his master gently on the side of his face. 'I simply work for them.'

Author's Note

This novel is a blend of certain themes. My book *The Great Crown Jewels Robbery of 1303* provides a detailed in-depth study of one of the most outrageous robberies in the history of English crime. Richard Pudlicott and his gang did exist. They suborned and seduced the monastic community at Westminster, though in some cases that didn't require much effort! Edward did send his faithful clerk John de Drokensford (on whom Corbett is based) into London to clear up the crisis. Drokensford did an extremely thorough job. By Christmas 1303 he'd lodged most of the gang in the Tower. A great deal of the treasure was retrieved, a special house being built for it, though eventually the Royal Jewels were moved to the Tower, where they are still displayed today. Pudlicott was eventually hanged, being taken down to execution in a wheel-barrow. His body was skinned and traces of it can still be seen on a door at Westminster Abbey.

John Le Riche, alias John Ramage, was born in Westminster and was a servant of the monks; his mother lived near St Giles, Cripplegate. John had a very bad reputation and had been indicted for other crimes. Around the time of the robbery he had been seen coming and going to the abbey. He suddenly had new-found wealth, being able to equip himself like a knight with horses and weapons. He even had the nerve to dress himself up as a soldier to join the King's army in the north. However, discretion is the better part of valour. Ramage returned to Westminster, where he was sheltered by the monks. After the robbery, he boasted that he had enough money to buy a town! He kept some of the stolen treasure at his mother's house before moving it so as to escape the royal searchers. He should have been arrested but fled without trace. My version of his end could well be accurate; outlaws like Le Riche very rarely died in their beds.

The story about Edward I being attacked by assassins in Outremer is reported by a number of chronicles. Some historians dispute whether the incident took place; I believe it did. The Sagittarius, the medieval equivalent of our random sniper, was a common phenomenon, well reported by the London chronicles as well as the Calender of Coroners' Rolls and the various assizes held in the capital during the period. The judicial aspect of Corbett's investigation is a fair reflection of the times. The 'King's men' were greatly feared. They literally wielded the power of life and death. Moreover, if someone proved obdurate, they could be summoned before King's Bench at Westminster Hall, and this could involve a very long and costly stay in London!

The fall of Acre as described in the novel is accurate. The Templars did hold out to the last man, whilst the collapse of Acre brought an end to any hope of success by Western armies in recovering the Holy Land. Three years after the date of this novel, Philip le Bel launched his infamous attack on the Templars and totally destroyed that order.

The Free Brethren of the Holy Spirit are not entirely fictional. Europe was plagued by such wandering groups. Some were harmless enough; others were a real threat to life and security. The chronicles describe them in fairly vivid terms; it is so easy to picture them tramping the roads of France, Spain and even Essex in England!

Paul C. Doherty
December 2007

www.paulcdoherty.com